D0098379

WHITE CAT

ALSO BY
HOLLY BLACK

Tithe

Valiant

Ironside

The Spiderwick Chronicles

The Field Guide

The Seeing Stone

Lucinda's Secret

The Ironwood Tree

The Wrath of Mulgarath

Beyond the Spiderwick Chronicles

The Nixie's Song

A Giant Problem

The Wyrm King

THE CURSE WORKERS

BOOK ONE

WHITE CAT

HOLLY BLACK

Margaret K. McElderry Books

New York London Toronto Sydney

MARGARET K. McELDERRY BOOKS
An imprint of Simon & Schuster Children's Publishing Division
1230 Avenue of the Americas, New York, New York 10020
This book is a work of fiction. Any references to historical
events, real people, or real locales are used fictitiously.
Other names, characters, places, and incidents are products
of the author's imagination, and any resemblance to actual events
or locales or persons, living or dead, is entirely coincidental.
Copyright © 2010 by Holly Black
All rights reserved, including the right of reproduction
in whole or in part in any form.
MARGARET K. McELDERRY BOOKS is a trademark
of Simon & Schuster, Inc.
For information about special discounts for bulk purchases,
please contact Simon & Schuster Special Sales at 1-866-506-1949
or business@simonandschuster.com.
The Simon & Schuster Speakers Bureau can bring authors
to your live event. For more information or to book an event,
contact the Simon & Schuster Speakers Bureau at 1-866-248-3049
or visit our website at www.simonspeakers.com.
The text for this book is set in Cambria.
Manufactured in the United States of America
10 9 8 7 6 5 4 3 2 1
Library of Congress Cataloging-in-Publication Data
Black, Holly.
White cat / Holly Black.—1st ed.
p. cm.—(The curse workers)
Summary: When Cassel Sharpe discovers that his
older brothers have used him to carry out their criminal
schemes and then stolen his memories, he figures out
a way to turn their evil machinations against them.
ISBN 978-1-4169-6396-7 (hardcover)
ISBN 978-1-4424-0597-4 (eBook)
[1. Science fiction. 2. Swindlers and swindling—Fiction.
3. Memory—Fiction. 4. Criminals—Fiction.
5. Brothers—Fiction.] I. Title.
PZ7.B52878Wh 2010
[Fic]—dc22
2009033979

FOR ALL THE FICTIONAL CATS
I'VE KILLED IN OTHER BOOKS.

ACKNOWLEDGMENTS

Several books were really helpful in creating the world of the curse workers. In particular, David R. Maurer's *The Big Con*, Sam Lovell's *How to Cheat at Everything*, Kent Walker and Mark Schone's *Son of a Grifter*, and Karl Taro Greenfeld's *Speed Tribes*.

I am deeply indebted to many people for their insight into this book. I want to thank everyone at Sycamore Hill 2007 for looking at the first few chapters and giving me the confidence to keep going. I am grateful to Justine Larbalestier for talking with me about liars and Scott Westerfeld for his detailed notes. Thanks to Sarah Rees Brennan for helping me with the feeeelings. Thanks to Joe Monti for his enthusiasm and book recommendations. Thanks to Elka Cloke for her medical expertise. Thanks to Kathleen Duey for pushing me to think about the larger world issues. Thanks to Kelly Link for making the beginning far better and also for driving me around in the trunk of her car. Thanks to Ellen Kushner, Delia Sherman, Gavin Grant, Sarah Smith, Cassandra Clare, and Joshua Lewis for looking at very rough drafts. Thanks to Steve Berman for his help working out the details of the magic.

Most of all, I have to thank my agent, Barry Goldblatt, for his encouragement; my editor, Karen Wojtyla, who pushed me to make the book far better than I thought it could be; and my husband, Theo, who not only put up with me during the writing, but also gave me lots of advice about demerits, scams, private school, and how to talk animal shelters out of things.

CHAPTER ONE

I WAKE UP BAREFOOT, standing on cold slate tiles. Looking dizzily down. I suck in a breath of icy air.

Above me are stars. Below me, the bronze statue of Colonel Wallingford makes me realize I'm seeing the quad from the peak of Smythe Hall, my dorm.

I have no memory of climbing the stairs up to the roof. I don't even know *how* to get where I am, which is a problem since I'm going to have to get down, ideally in a way that doesn't involve dying.

Teetering, I will myself to be as still as possible. Not to inhale too sharply. To grip the slate with my toes.

The night is quiet, the kind of hushed middle-of-the-night

quiet that makes every shuffle or nervous panting breath echo. When the black outlines of trees overhead rustle, I jerk in surprise. My foot slides on something slick. Moss.

I try to steady myself, but my legs go out from under me.

I scrabble for something to hold on to as my bare chest slams down on the slate. My palm comes down hard on a sharp bit of copper flashing, but I hardly feel the pain. Kicking out, my foot finds a snow guard, and I press my toes against it, steadying myself. I laugh with relief, even though I am shaking so badly that climbing is out of the question.

Cold makes my fingers numb. The adrenaline rush makes my brain sing.

"Help," I say softly, and feel crazy nervous laughter bubble up my throat. I bite the inside of my cheek to tamp it down.

I can't ask for help. I can't call anyone. If I do, then my carefully maintained pretense that I'm just a regular guy is going to fade forever. Sleepwalking is kid's stuff, weird and embarrassing.

Looking across the roof in the dim light, I try to make out the pattern of snow guards, tiny triangular pieces of clear plastic that keep ice from falling in a sheet, tiny triangular pieces that were never meant to hold my weight. If I can get closer to a window, maybe I can climb down.

I edge my foot out, shifting as slowly as I can and worming toward the nearest snow guard. My stomach scrapes against the slate, some of the tiles chipped and uneven beneath me. I step onto the first guard, then down to another and across to one at the edge of the roof. There, panting, with the windows too far beneath me and with nowhere left to go, I decide I am not willing to die from embarrassment.

I suck in three deep breaths of cold air and yell.

"Hey! Hey! Help!" The night absorbs my voice. I hear the distant swell of engines along the highway, but nothing from the windows below me.

"HEY!" I scream it this time, guttural, as loudly as I can, loud enough that the words scrape my throat raw. *"Help!"*

A light flickers on in one of the rooms and I see the press of palms against a glass pane. A moment later the window slides open. "Hello?" someone calls sleepily from below. For a moment her voice reminds me of another girl. A dead girl.

I hang my head off the side and try to give my most chagrined smile. Like she shouldn't freak out. "Up here," I say. "On the roof."

"Oh, my God," Justine Moore gasps.

Willow Davis comes to the window. "I'm getting the hall master."

I press my cheek against the cold tile and try to convince myself that everything's okay, that it's not a curse, that if I just hang on a little longer, things are going to be fine.

A crowd gathers below me, spilling out of the dorms.

"Jump," some jerk shouts. "Do it!"

"Mr. Sharpe?" Dean Wharton calls. "Come down from there at once, Mr. Sharpe!" His silver hair sticks up like he's been electrocuted, and his robe is inside out and badly tied. The whole school can see his tighty-whities.

I realize abruptly that I'm wearing only boxers. If he looks ridiculous, I look worse.

"Cassel!" Ms. Noyes yells. "Cassel, don't jump! I know things have been hard . . ." She stops there, like she isn't quite sure what to say next. She's probably trying to remember what's so hard. I have good grades. Play well with others.

I look down again. Camera phones flash. Freshmen hang out of windows next door in Strong House, and juniors and seniors stand around on the grass in their pajamas and nightgowns, even though teachers are desperately trying to herd them back inside.

I give my best grin. "Cheese," I say softly.

"Get down, Mr. Sharpe," yells Dean Wharton. "I'm warning you!"

"I'm okay, Ms. Noyes," I call. "I don't know how I got up here. I think I was sleepwalking."

I'd dreamed of a white cat. It leaned over me, inhaling sharply, as if it was going to suck the breath from my lungs, but then it bit out my tongue instead. There was no pain, only a sense of overwhelming, suffocating panic. In the dream my tongue was a wriggling red thing, mouse-size and wet, that the cat carried in her mouth. I wanted it back. I sprang up out of the bed and grabbed for her, but she was too lean and too quick. I chased her. The next thing I knew, I was teetering on a slate roof.

A siren wails in the distance, drawing closer. My cheeks hurt from smiling.

Eventually a fireman climbs a ladder to get me down. They put a blanket around me, but by then my teeth are chattering so hard that I can't answer any of their questions. It's like the cat bit out my tongue after all.

The last time I was in the headmistress's office, my grandfather was there with me to enroll me at the school. I remember watching him empty a crystal dish of peppermints into the pocket of his coat while Dean Wharton talked about what a fine young man I would be turned into. The crystal dish went into the opposite pocket.

Wrapped in a blanket, I sit in the same green leather chair and pick at the gauze covering my palm. A fine young man indeed.

"Sleepwalking?" Dean Wharton says. He's dressed in a brown tweed suit, but his hair is still wild. He stands near a shelf of outdated encyclopedias and strokes a gloved finger over their crumbling leather spines.

I notice there's a new cheap glass dish of mints on the desk. My head is pounding. I wish the mints were aspirin.

"I used to sleepwalk," I say. "I haven't done it in a long time."

Somnambulism isn't all that uncommon in kids, boys especially. I looked it up online after waking in the driveway when I was thirteen, my lips blue with cold, unable to shake the eerie feeling that I'd just returned from somewhere I couldn't quite recall.

Outside the leaded glass windows the rising sun limns the trees with gold. The headmistress, Ms. Northcutt, looks puffy and red-eyed. She's drinking coffee out of a mug with the Wallingford logo on it and gripping it so tightly the leather of her gloves over her knuckles is pulled taut.

"I heard you've been having some problems with your girlfriend," Headmistress Northcutt says.

"No," I say. "Not at all." Audrey broke up with me after the winter holiday, exhausted by my moodiness. It's impossible to have problems with a girlfriend who's no longer mine.

The headmistress clears her throat. "Some students think you are running a betting pool. Are you in some kind of trouble? Owe someone money?"

I look down and try not to smile at the mention of my tiny criminal empire. It's just a little forgery and some bookmaking. I'm not running a single con; I haven't even taken up my brother Philip's suggestion that we could be the school's main supplier for underage booze. I'm pretty sure the headmistress doesn't care about betting, but I'm glad she doesn't know that the most popular odds are on which teachers are hooking up. Northcutt and Wharton are a long shot, but that doesn't stop people laying cash on them. I shake my head.

"Have you experienced mood swings lately?" Dean Wharton asks.

"No," I say.

"What about changes in appetite or sleep patterns?" He sounds like he's reciting the words from a book.

"The problem is my sleep patterns," I say.

"What do you mean?" asks Headmistress Northcutt, suddenly intent.

"Nothing! Just that I was *sleepwalking*, not trying to kill myself. And if I wanted to kill myself, I wouldn't throw myself off a roof. And if I *was* going to throw myself off a roof, I would put on some pants before I did it."

The headmistress takes a sip from her cup. She's relaxed her grip. "Our lawyer advised me that until a doctor can assure us that nothing like this will happen again, we can't allow you to stay in the dorms. You're too much of an insurance liability."

I thought that people would give me a lot of crap, but I never thought there would be any real consequences. I thought I was going to get a scolding. Maybe even a couple of demerits. I'm too stunned to say anything for a long moment. "But I didn't do anything wrong."

Which is stupid, of course. Things don't happen to people because they deserve them. Besides, I've done plenty wrong.

"Your brother Philip is coming to pick you up," Dean Wharton says. He and the headmistress exchange looks, and Wharton's hand goes unconsciously to his neck, where I see the colored cord and the outline of the amulet under his white shirt.

I get it. They're wondering if I've been worked. Cursed. It's not that big a secret that my grandfather was a death worker for the Zacharov family. He's got the blackened stubs where his fingers used to be to prove it. And if they read the paper, they know about my mother. It's not a big leap for Wharton and Northcutt to blame any and all strangeness concerning me on curse work.

"You can't kick me out for sleepwalking," I say, getting to my feet. "That can't be legal. Some kind of discrimination against—" I stop speaking as cold dread settles in my stomach, because for a moment I wonder if I could have been cursed. I try to think back to whether someone brushed me with a hand, but I can't recall anyone touching me who wasn't clearly gloved.

"We haven't come to any determination about your future here at Wallingford yet." The headmistress leafs through some of the papers on her desk. The dean pours himself a coffee.

"I can still be a day student." I don't want to sleep in an empty house or crash with either of my brothers, but I will. I'll do whatever lets me keep my life the way it is.

"Go to your dorm and pack some things. Consider yourself on medical leave."

"Just until I get a doctor's note," I say.

Neither of them replies, and after a few moments of standing awkwardly, I head for the door.

Don't be too sympathetic. Here's the essential truth about me: I killed a girl when I was fourteen. Her name was Lila, she was my best friend, and I loved her. I killed her anyway. There's a lot of the murder that seems like a blur, but my brothers found me standing over her body with blood on my hands and a weird smile tugging at my mouth. What I remember most is the feeling I had looking down at Lila—the giddy glee of having gotten away with something.

No one knows I'm a murderer except my family. And me, of course.

I don't want to be that person, so I spend most of my time at school faking and lying. It takes a lot of effort to pretend you're something you're not. I don't think about what music I like; I think about what music I should like. When I had a girlfriend, I tried to convince her I was the guy she wanted me to be. When I'm in a crowd, I hang back until I can figure out how to make them laugh. Luckily, if there's one thing I'm good at, it's faking and lying.

I told you I'd done plenty wrong.

I pad, still barefoot, still wrapped in the scratchy fireman's blanket, across the sunlit quad and up to my dorm room. Sam Yu, my roommate, is looping a skinny tie around the collar of a wrinkled dress shirt when I walk through the door. He looks up, startled.

"I'm fine," I say wearily. "In case you were going to ask."

Sam's a horror film enthusiast and hard-core science geek who has covered our dorm room with bug-eyed alien masks and gore-spattered posters. His parents want him to go to MIT and from there to some profitable pharmaceuticals gig. He wants to do special effects for movies. Despite the facts that he's built like a bear and is obsessed with fake blood, he has so far failed to stand up to them to the degree that they don't even know there's a disagreement. I like to think we're sort of friends.

We don't hang out with many of the same people, which makes being sort of friends easier.

"I wasn't doing . . . whatever you think I was doing," I tell him. "I don't want to die or anything."

Sam smiles and pulls on his Wallingford gloves. "I was just going to say that it's a good thing you don't sleep commando."

I snort and drop onto my cot. The frame squeaks in protest. On the pillow next to my head rests a new envelope, marked with a code telling me a freshman wants to put fifty dollars on Victoria Quaroni to win the talent show. The odds are astronomical, but the money reminds me that someone's going to have to keep the books and pay out while I'm away.

Sam kicks the base of the footboard lightly. "You sure you're okay?"

I nod. I know I should tell him that I'm going home, that he's about to become one of those lucky guys with a single, but I don't want to disturb my own fragile sense of normalcy. "Just tired."

Sam picks up his backpack. "See you in class, crazyman."

I raise my bandaged hand in farewell, then stop myself. "Hey, wait a sec."

Hand on the doorknob, he turns.

"I was just thinking . . . if I'm gone. Do you think you could let people keep dropping off the money here?" It bothers me to ask, simultaneously putting me in his debt and making the whole kicked-out thing real, but I'm not ready to give up the one thing I've got going for me at Wallingford.

He hesitates.

"Forget it," I say. "Pretend I never—"

He interrupts me. "Do I get a percentage?"

"Twenty-five," I say. "Twenty-five percent. But you're going to have to do more than just collect the money for that."

He nods slowly. "Yeah, okay."

I grin. "You're the most trustworthy guy I know."

"Flattery will get you everywhere," Sam says. "Except, apparently, off a roof."

"Nice," I say with a groan. I push myself off the bed and take a clean pair of itchy black uniform pants out of the dresser.

"So why would you be *gone*? They're not kicking you out, right?"

Pulling on the pants, I turn my face away, but I can't keep the unease out of my voice. "No. I don't know. Let me set you up."

He nods. "Okay. What do I do?"

"I'll give you my notebook on point spreads, tallies, everything, and you just fill in whatever bets you get." I stand, pulling my desk chair over to the closet and hopping up on the seat. "Here." My fingers close on the notebook I taped above the door. I rip it down. Another one from sophomore year is still up there, from when business got big enough I could no longer rely on my pretty-good-but-not-photographic memory.

Sam half-smiles. I can tell he's amazed that he never noticed my hiding spot. "I think I can manage that."

The pages he's flipping through are records of all the bets made since the beginning of our junior year at Wallingford, and the odds on each. Bets on whether the mouse loose in Stanton Hall will be killed by Kevin Brown with his mallet, or by Dr. Milton with his bacon-baited traps, or be caught by Chaiyawat Terweil with his lettuce-filled and totally humane trap. (The odds favor the mallet.) On whether Amanda, Sharone, or Courtney would be cast as the female lead in *Pippin* and whether the lead would be taken down by her understudy. (Courtney got it; they're still in rehearsals.) On how many times a week "nut brownies with no nuts" will be served in the cafeteria.

Real bookies take a percentage, relying on a balanced book to guarantee a profit. Like, if someone puts down five bucks on a fight, they're really putting down four fifty, and the other fifty cents is going to the bookie. The bookie doesn't care who wins; he only cares that the odds work so he can use the money from the losers to pay the winners. I'm not a real bookie. Kids at Wallingford want to bet on silly stuff, stuff that might never come true. They have money to burn. So some of the time I calculate the odds the right way—the real bookie way—and some of the time I calculate the odds my way and just hope I get to pocket everything instead of paying out what I can't afford. You could say that I'm gambling too. You'd be right.

"Remember," I say, "cash only. No credit cards; no watches."

He rolls his eyes. "Are you seriously telling me someone thinks you have a credit card machine up in here?"

"No," I say. "They want you to take their card and buy something that costs what they owe. Don't do it; it looks like you stole their card, and believe me, that's what they'll tell their parents."

Sam hesitates. "Yeah," he says finally.

"Okay," I say. "There's a new envelope on the desk. Don't forget to mark down everything." I know I'm nagging, but I can't tell him that I need the money I make. It's not easy to go to a school like this without money. I'm the only seventeen-year-old at Wallingford without a car.

I motion to him to hand me the book.

Just as I'm taping it into place, someone raps loudly on the door, causing me to nearly topple over. Before I can say anything, it opens, and our hall master walks in. He looks at me like he's half-expecting to find me threading a noose.

I hop down from the chair. "I was just—"

"Thanks for getting down my bag," Sam says.

"Samuel Yu," says Mr. Valerio. "I'm fairly sure that breakfast is over and classes have started."

"I *bet* you're right," Sam says, with a smirk in my direction.

I could con Sam if I wanted to. I'd do it just this way, asking for his help, offering him a little profit at the same time. Take him for a chunk of his parents' cash. I could con Sam, but I won't.

Really, I won't.

As the door clicks shut behind Sam, Valerio turns to me. "Your brother can't come until tomorrow morning, so you're going to have to attend classes with the rest of the students. We're still discussing where you'll be spending the night."

"You can always tie me to the bedposts," I say, but Valerio doesn't find that very funny.

My mother explained the basics of the con around the same time she explained about curse work. For her the curse was how she got what she wanted and the con was how she got away with it. I can't make people love or hate instantly, like she can, turn their bodies against them like Philip can, or take their luck away like my other brother, Barron, but you don't need to be a worker to be a con artist.

For me the curse is a crutch, but the con is everything.

It was my mother who taught me that if you're going to screw someone over—with magic and wit, or wit alone—you have to know the mark better than he knows himself.

The first thing you have to do is gain his confidence. Charm him. Just be sure he thinks he's smarter than you are. Then you—or, ideally, your partner—suggest the score.

Let your mark get something right up front the first time. In the business that's called the "convincer." When he knows he's already got money in his pocket and can walk away, that's when he relaxes his guard.

The second go is when you introduce bigger stakes. The big score. This is the part my mother never has to worry about. As an emotion worker, she can make anyone trust her. But she still needs to go through the steps, so that later, when they think back on it, they don't figure out she worked them.

After that there's only the blow-off and the getaway.

Being a con artist means thinking that you're smarter than everyone else and that you've thought of everything. That you can get away with anything. That you can con anyone.

I wish I could say that I don't think about the con when I deal with people, but the difference between me and my mother is that I don't con myself.

CHAPTER TWO

I ONLY HAVE ENOUGH time to pull on my uniform and run to French class; breakfast is long over. Wallingford television crackles to life as I dump my books onto my desk. Sadie Flores announces from the screen that during activities period the Latin club will be having a bake sale to support their building a small outdoor grotto, and that the rugby team will meet inside the gymnasium. I manage to stumble through my classes until I actually fall asleep during history. I wake abruptly with drool wetting the sleeve of my shirt and Mr. Lewis asking, "What year was the ban put into effect, Mr. Sharpe?"

"Nineteen twenty-nine," I mumble. "Nine years after Prohibition started. Right before the stock market crashed."

"Very good," he says unhappily. "And can you tell me why the ban hasn't been repealed like prohibition?"

I wipe my mouth. My headache hasn't gotten any better. "Uh, because the black market supplies people with curse work anyway?"

A couple of people laugh, but Mr. Lewis isn't one of them. He points toward the board, where a jumble of chalk reasons are written. Something about economic initiatives and a trade agreement with the European Union. "Apparently you can do lots of things very skillfully while asleep, Mr. Sharpe, but attending my class does not seem to be one of them."

He gets the bigger laugh. I stay awake for the rest of the period, although several times I have to jab myself with a pen to do it.

I go back to my dorm and sleep through the period when I should be getting help from teachers in classes where I'm struggling, through track practice, and through the debate team meeting. Waking up halfway through dinner, I feel the rhythm of my normal life receding, and I have no idea how to get it back.

Wallingford Preparatory is a lot like how I pictured it when my brother Barron brought home the brochure. The lawns are less green and the buildings are smaller, but the library is impressive enough and everyone wears jackets to dinner. Kids come to Wallingford for two very different reasons. Either private school is their ticket to a fancy university, or they got kicked out of public school and are using their parents' money to avoid the school for juvenile delinquents that's their only other option.

Wallingford isn't exactly Choate or Deerfield Academy, but it was willing to take me, even with my ties to the Zacharovs. Barron thought the school would give me structure. No messy house. No chaos. I've done well too. Here, my inability to do curse work is actually an advantage— the first time that it's been good for anything. And yet I see in myself a disturbing tendency to seek out all the trouble this new life should be missing. Like running the betting pool when I need money. I can't seem to stop working the angles.

The dining hall is wood-paneled with a high, arched ceiling that makes our noise echo. The walls are hung with paintings of important heads-of-school and, of course, Wallingford himself. Colonel Wallingford, the founder of Wallingford Preparatory, killed by curse work a year before the ban went into effect, sneers down at me from his gold frame.

My shoes clack on the worn marble tiles, and I frown as the voices around me merge into a single buzzing that rings in my ears. Walking through to the kitchen, my hands feel damp, sweat soaking the cotton of my gloves as I push open the door.

I look around automatically to see if Audrey's here. She's not, but I shouldn't have looked. I've got to ignore her just enough that she doesn't think I care, but not too much. Too much will give me away as well.

Especially today, when I'm so disoriented.

"You're late," one of the food service ladies says without looking up from wiping the counter. She looks past retirement age—at least as old as my grandfather—and a few of her permed curls have tumbled out the side of her plastic cap. "Dinner's over."

"Yeah." And then I mumble, "Sorry."

"The food's put away." She looks up at me. She holds up her plastic-covered hands. "It's going to be cold."

"I like cold food." I give her my best sheepish half smile.

She shakes her head. "I like boys with a good appetite. All of you look so skinny, and in the magazines they talk about you starving yourselves like girls."

"Not me," I say, and my stomach growls, which makes her laugh.

"Go outside and I'll bring you a plate. Take a few cookies off the tray here too." Now that she's decided I'm a poor child in need of feeding, she seems happy to fuss.

Unlike in most school cafeterias, the food at Wallingford is good. The cookies are dark with molasses and spicy with ginger. The spaghetti, when she brings it, is lukewarm, but I can taste chorizo in the red sauce. As I sop up some of it with bread, Daneca Wasserman comes over to the table.

"Can I sit down?" she asks.

I glance up at the clock. "Study hall's going to start soon." Her tangle of brown curls looks unbrushed, pulled back with a sandalwood headband. I drop my gaze to the hemp bag at her hip, studded with buttons that read POWERED BY TOFU, DOWN ON PROP 2, and WORKER RIGHTS.

"You weren't at debate club," she says.

"Yeah." I feel bad about avoiding Daneca or giving her rude half answers, but I've been doing it since I started at Wallingford. Even though she's one of Sam's friends and living with him makes avoiding Daneca more difficult.

"My mother wants to talk with you. She says that what you did was a cry for help."

"It was," I say. "That's why I was yelling 'Heeeelp!' I don't really go in for subtlety."

She makes an impatient noise. Daneca's family are cofounders of HEX, the advocacy group that wants to make working legal again—basically so laws against more serious works can be better enforced. I've seen her mother on television, filmed sitting in the office of her brick house in Princeton, a blooming garden visible through the window behind her. Mrs. Wasserman talked about how, despite the laws, no one wanted to be without a luck worker at a wedding or a baptism, and that those kinds of works were beneficial. She talked about how it benefited crime families to prevent workers from finding ways to use their talents legally. She admitted to being a worker herself. It was an impressive speech. A dangerous speech.

"Mom deals with worker families all the time," Daneca says. "The issues worker kids face."

"I know that, Daneca. Look, I didn't want to join your junior HEX club last year, and I don't want to mess with that kind of stuff now. I'm not a worker, and I don't care if you are. Find someone else to recruit or save or whatever it is you are trying to do. And I don't want to meet your mother."

She hesitates. "I'm not a worker. I'm not. Just because I want to—"

"Whatever. I said I don't care."

"You don't care that workers are being rounded up and shot in South Korea? And here in the U.S. they're being forced into what's basically indentured servitude for crime families? You don't care about any of it?"

"No, I don't care."

Across the hall Valerio is headed toward me. That's enough to make Daneca decide she doesn't want to risk a demerit for not being where she's supposed to be. Hand on her bag, she walks off with a single glance back at me. The combination of disappointment and contempt in that last look hurts.

I put a big chunk of sauce-soaked bread in my mouth and stand.

"Congratulations. You're going to be sleeping in your room tonight, Mr. Sharpe."

I nod, chewing. Maybe if I make it through tonight, they'll consider letting me stay.

"But I want you to know that I have Dean Wharton's dog and she's going to be sleeping in the hallway. That dog is going to bark like hell if you go on one of your midnight strolls. I better not see you out of your room, not even to go to the bathroom. Do you understand?"

I swallow. "Yes, sir."

"Better get back and start on your homework."

"Right," I say. "Absolutely. Thank you, sir."

I seldom walk back from the dining hall alone. Above

the trees, their leaves the pale green of new buds, bats weave through the still-bright sky. The air is heavy with the smell of crushed grass, threaded through with smoke. Somewhere someone's burning the wet, half-decomposed foliage of winter.

Sam sits at his desk, earbuds in, huge back to the door and head down as he doodles in the pages of his physics textbook. He barely looks up when I flop down on the bed. We have about three hours of homework a night, and our evening study period is only two hours, so if you want to spend the break at half-past-nine not freaking out, you have to cram. I'm not sure that the picture of the wide-eyed zombie girl biting out the brains of senior douchebag James Page is part of Sam's homework, but if it is, his physics teacher is awesome.

I pull out books from my backpack and start on trig problems, but as my pencil scrapes across the page of my notebook, I realize I don't really remember class well enough to solve anything. Pushing those books toward my pillow, I decide to read the chapter we were assigned in mythology. It's some more messed-up Olympian family stuff, starring Zeus. His pregnant girlfriend, Semele, gets tricked by his wife, Hera, into demanding to see Zeus in all his godly glory. Despite knowing this is going to kill Semele, he shows her the goods. A few minutes later he's cutting baby Dionysus out of burned-up Semele's womb and *sewing him into his own leg.* No wonder Dionysus drank all the time. I just get to the part where Dionysus is being raised as a girl (to keep him hidden from Hera, of course), when Kyle bangs against the door frame.

"What?" Sam says, pulling off one of his buds and turning in his chair.

"Phone for you," Kyle says, looking in my direction.

I guess before everyone had a cell phone, the only way students could call home was to save up their quarters and feed them into the ancient pay phone at the end of every dorm hall. Despite the occasional midnight crank call, Wallingford has left those old phones where they were. People occasionally still use them; mostly parents calling someone whose cell battery died or who wasn't returning messages. Or my mother, calling from jail.

I pick up the familiar heavy black receiver. "Hello?"

"I am very disappointed in you," Mom says. "That school is making you soft in the head. What were you doing up on a roof?" Theoretically Mom shouldn't be able to call another pay phone from the pay phone in prison, but she found a way around that. First she gets my sister-in-law to accept the charges, then Maura can three-way call me, or anyone else Mom needs. Lawyers. Philip. Barron.

Of course, Mom could three-way call my cell phone, but she's sure that all cell phone conversations are being listened to by some shady peeping-Tom branch of the government, so she tries to avoid using them.

"I'm okay," I say. "Thanks for checking in on me." Her voice reminds me that Philip's coming to pick me up in the morning. I have a brief fantasy of him never bothering to show up and the whole thing blowing over.

"Checking up on you? I'm your mother! I should be there! It is so unfair that I have to be cooped up like this while you're gallivanting around on rooftops, getting into the kind of trouble you never would have if you had a stable family—a mother at home. That's what I told the judge. I told him that if he put me away, this would happen. Well, not this specifically, but no one can say I didn't warn him."

Mom likes to talk. She likes to talk so much that you can mmm-hmm along with her and have a whole conversation in which you don't say a word. Especially now, when she's far enough away that even if she's pissed off she can't put her hand to your bare skin and make you sob with remorse.

Emotion work is powerful stuff.

"Listen," she says. "You are going home with Philip. You'll be among our kind of people, at least. Safe."

Our kind of people. Workers. Only I'm not one. The only nonworker in my whole family. I cup my hand over the receiver. "Am I in some kind of danger?"

"Of course not. Don't be ridiculous. You know I got the nicest letter from that count. He wants to take me on a cruise with him when I get out of here. What do you think of that? You should come along. I'll tell him you're my assistant."

I smile. Sure she can be scary and manipulative, but she loves me. "Okay, Mom."

"Really? Oh, that'll be great, honey. You know this whole thing is so unfair. I can't believe they would take me away from my babies when you need me the most. I've spoken to my lawyers, and they are going to get this whole thing straightened out. I told them you need me. But if you could write a letter, that would help."

I know I won't. "I have to go, Mom. It's study period. I'm not supposed to be on the phone."

"Oh, let me talk to that hall master of yours. What's his name. Valerie?"

"Valerio."

"You just get him for me. I'll explain everything. I'm sure he's a nice man."

"I've really got to go. I've got homework."

I hear her laugh, and then a sound that I know is her lighting a cigarette. I hear the deep inhalation, the slight crackle of burning paper. "Why? You're done with that place."

"If I don't do my homework, I will be."

"Sweetheart, you know what your problem is? You take everything too seriously. It's because you're the baby of the family—" I can imagine her getting into that line of theorizing, stabbing the air for emphasis, standing against the painted cinder block wall of the jail.

"Bye, Mom."

"You stay with your brothers," she says softly. "Stay safe."

"Bye, Mom," I say again, and hang up. My chest feels tight.

I stand in the hallway a few moments longer, until the break starts and everyone files down to the common lounge on the first floor.

Rahul Pathak and Jeremy Fletcher-Fiske, the other two junior-year soccer players in the house, wave me over to the striped couch they've settled on. I wave back, take a hot chocolate packet, and mix it into a large cup of coffee. I think technically the coffee is supposed to be for staff, but we all drink it and no one says anything.

When I sit down, Jeremy makes a face. "You got the heebeegeebies?"

"Yeah, from your mother," I say, without any real heat. HBG is the abbreviation for some long medical term that means "worker," hence "the heebeegeebies."

"Oh, come on," he says. "Seriously, I have a proposition for you. I need you to hook me up with somebody who can work my girlfriend and make her really hot for me. At prom. We can pay."

"I don't know anyone like that."

"Sure you do," Jeremy says, looking at me steadily, like I'm so far beneath him he can't figure out why he has to even try to persuade me. I should be delighted to help. That's what I'm for. "She's going to take off her charms and everything. She wants to do it."

I wonder how much he'd pay for it. Not enough to keep me out of trouble. "Sorry. I can't help you."

Rahul takes an envelope out of the inside pocket of his jacket and pushes it in my direction.

"Look, I said I can't do it," I say again. "I can't, okay?"

"No, no," he says. "I saw the mouse. I am completely sure it was heading toward one of those glue traps. Dead before tomorrow." He mimes his hand slashing across his throat with a grin. "Fifty dollars on glue."

Jeremy frowns, like he's not sure he's ready to give up

trying me, but he's not sure how to get the conversation back to where he wants it either.

I shove the envelope into my pocket, forcing myself to relax. "Hope not," I say quickly, reminding myself that after I get back to the room, I'm going to make Sam note down the amount and for what. It'll be good practice. "That mouse is good for business."

"Yeah, because you just want to keep taking our money," says Rahul, but he smiles when he says it.

I shrug my shoulders. There's no good answer.

"I bet it chews off one of its feet and gets away," Jeremy says. "That thing is a survivor."

"So *bet*, Jeremy," Rahul says. "Put up."

"I don't have it on me," says Jeremy, turning the front pockets of his pants inside out with an exaggerated gesture.

Rahul laughs. "I'll cover you."

The mocha burns my throat. I'm hating everything about this conversation. "If you need to collect, Sam's going to be taking care of things for me."

They stop their negotiation and look across the room at Sam. He's sitting at the table in front of a pile of graph paper, painting a lead figurine. Next to him Jill Pearson-White rolls strange-sided dice and pumps her fist into the air.

"You trust him with our money?" Rahul asks.

"I trust him," I say. "And you trust me."

"You sure we can still trust you? That was some serious *One Flew Over the Cuckoo's Nest*–type behavior last night." Jeremy's new girlfriend is in drama club, and it shows in his movie references. "And now you're going away for a while?"

Even with the coffee running in my veins and the long nap this afternoon, I'm tired. And I'm sick of explaining about the sleepwalking. No one believes me anyway. "That's personal," I say, and then tap the part of the envelope sticking out of my pocket. "This is professional."

That night, lying in the dark and looking up at the ceiling, I'm not sure the sugar and caffeine I've gulped will be enough. There is no way they'll ever let me back into Wallingford if I sleepwalk again, so I don't want to risk dozing off. I can hear the dog outside the door, its toenails clicking across the wood planks of the hallway before it settles into a new spot with a soft thud.

I keep thinking about Philip. I keep thinking about how, unlike Barron, he hasn't looked me in the eyes since I was fourteen. He never even lets me play with his son. Now I am going to have to stay in a house with him until I can figure my way back to school.

"Hey," Sam says from the other bed. "You're creeping me out, staring at the ceiling like that. You look dead. Unblinking."

"I'm blinking." I keep my voice low. "I don't want to fall asleep."

He rustles his covers, turning onto his side. "How come? You afraid you're going to—"

"Yeah," I say.

"Oh." I'm glad I can't see his expression in the darkness.

"What if you did something so terrible that you didn't want to face anyone who knew about it?" My voice is so soft that I'm not even sure he can hear me. I don't know what made me say it. I never talk about stuff like that, and certainly not with Sam.

"You *did* try to kill yourself?"

I guess I should have seen that coming, but I didn't. "No," I say. "Honest."

I imagine him weighing possible responses, and I wish I could take back the question. "Okay. This terrible thing. Why did I do it?" he asks finally.

"You don't know," I say.

"That doesn't make sense. How can I not know?" The way we're talking reminds me of one of Sam's games. *You reach a crossroads and there's a small twisty path going toward the mountains. The wide path seems to run in the direction of town. Which way do you go?* Like I'm a character he's trying to play and he doesn't like the rules.

"You just don't. That's the worst part. It's not something you want to believe you'd ever do. But you did." I don't like the rules either.

Sam leans back against the pillows. "I guess I'd start with that. There must be a reason. If you don't figure out why, you'll probably do it again."

I stare up into the darkness and wish that I wasn't so tired. "It's hard to be a good person," I say. "Because I already know I'm not."

"Sometimes," Sam says, "I can't tell when you're lying."

"I never lie," I lie.

* * *

After not sleeping all night, I'm pretty dazed in the morning. When Valerio bangs on the door, I answer, fresh from a cold shower that jolted me awake enough to put on some clothes. He looks relieved to find me alive and in my room. Next to Valerio stands my brother Philip. His expensive mirrored sunglasses are pushed up onto his slicked-back hair, and a gold watch flashes on his wrist. Philip's tanned skin makes his teeth look whiter when he smiles.

"Mr. Sharpe, the board of trustees talked to the school's legal team, and they want me to communicate to you that if you want to come back to school, you need to be evaluated by a physician, and that physician must be able to assure the school that nothing like the incident that took place the night before last will happen again. Do you understand me?"

I open my mouth to say that I do, but my brother's gloved hand on my arm stops me.

"You ready?" Philip asks lightly, still smiling.

I shake my head, gesturing around me at the lack of any bags, the scattered schoolbooks, the unmade bed. Yeah, sure, Philip has finally shown up, but it would be nice if he'd asked me if I'm all right. I almost fell off a roof. Clearly something is wrong with me.

"Need some help?" Philip offers, and I wonder if Valerio notices the edge in his voice. In the Sharpe family the worst thing you can do is be vulnerable in front of a mark. And everyone who isn't us is a mark.

"I'm good," I say, grabbing a canvas bag out of the closet.

Philip turns to Valerio. "I really appreciate you looking after my brother."

This so surprises the hall master that, for a moment, he doesn't seem to know what to say. I guess that few people consider calling the local volunteer firemen to drag a kid off a roof as great care. "We were all shocked when—"

"The important thing," Philip interrupts smoothly, "is that he's okay."

I roll my eyes as I shove stuff into the bag—dirty clothes, iPod, books, homework stuff, my little glass cat, a flash drive I keep all my reports on—and try to ignore their conversation. I'm just going to be gone a couple of days. I don't need much.

On the way out to the car, Philip turns to me. "How could you be so stupid?

I shrug, stung in spite of myself. "I thought I grew out of it."

Philip pulls out his key fob and presses the remote to unlock his Mercedes. I slide into the passenger side, brushing coffee cups off the seat and onto the floor mat, where crumpled printouts from MapQuest soak up any spilled liquid.

"I hope you mean sleepwalking," Philip says, "since you obviously didn't grow out of stupid."

CHAPTER THREE

I PUSH BRUSSELS SPROUTS around my plate and listen to my nephew scream from his high chair until Maura, Philip's wife, gives him some frozen plastic thing to bite. The skin around Maura's eyes is dark as a bruise. At twenty-one, she looks old.

"I put some blankets on the pullout couch in the office," she says. Behind her are grease-spattered cabinets and paper-strewn laminate countertops. I want to tell her that she doesn't need to worry about me on top of everything else.

"Thanks," I say instead, because the blankets are already in the office and I don't want to rock the boat of Philip's hospitality by seeming ungrateful. I don't, for instance, want to point out that the kitchen is too warm, almost suffocating. It reminds me of the holidays, when the oven has been on all day. And that makes me think about our father sitting at the dinner table, smoking long, thin cigarillos that yellowed his fingertips, while the turkey cooked. Sometimes, on bad days, when I really miss him, I'll buy cigarillos and burn them in an ashtray.

Right now, though, all I miss is Wallingford and the person I could pretend to be when I was there.

"Grandad is coming tomorrow," Philip says. "He wants you to go over to the old house and help him clean it out. He says he wants it all fixed up for Mom, when she gets out."

"I don't think that's what *she* wants," I say. "She doesn't like people messing with her stuff."

He sighs. "Tell that to him."

"I don't want to go," I say. Philip means the house we grew up in—a big old place stuffed with the many things our parents accumulated. No garage sale was left unplundered as they grifted their way across the country each summer, while we kids stayed down in the Pine Barrens with Grandad. By the time dad died, the junk was so piled up that there were tunnels instead of rooms.

"Then don't," Philip says, and for a moment I actually think he's going to look me in the eye, but he addresses my collar instead. "Mom can take care of herself. She always has. I doubt she's even going back to that dump when she finishes her sentence."

Mom and Philip have been on the outs since the trial, when he reluctantly bullied witnesses to help her defense team. Philip's a physical worker—a body worker—who can break a leg with the brush of his pinkie. I don't think he forgave Mom for being convicted despite him.

Plus the blowback made him pretty sick.

I sigh. Unsaid is where I'm supposed to go if not with Grandad. I very much doubt Philip is planning on letting me stay. "You can tell Grandad I'm only his manservant till I get back in school. And that'll take me a week, at most."

"Tell him yourself," Philip says.

Maura folds her arms across her chest. It's so strange to see her bare hands that I'm embarrassed. Mom hated gloves at home; she said that families were supposed to trust one another. I guess Philip believes that too. Or something.

It's different when the hands belong to someone I'm not related to, even if she is my sister-in-law. I try and force my gaze to her collarbone.

"Don't let him bully you into staying at that creepy place," Maura tells me.

"We used to live there!" Philip gets up and takes a beer from the fridge. "Anyway, I'm not the one telling him to go." He pops the top, takes a long swig, and unbuttons the neck of his white dress shirt. I see the necklace of keloids, where his maker cut across his throat to symbolize the death of Philip's previous life, and then packed the wound with ash until it scarred in a long, swollen line. It looks like a flesh-colored worm coiled above his collarbone. All laborers, minor crime bosses, have them. Just like a rose over the heart showed you were one of the Russian *bratva*, or like a *yakuza* inserts pearls under the skin of his penis for every year in jail. Philip got his scars three years back; now all he has to do to see people flinch is loosen his collar.

I don't flinch.

The big six worker families came into power all down the East Coast in the thirties and have remained that way ever since. Nonomura. Goldbloom. Volpe. Rice. Brennan. Zacharov. They control everything, from the cheap and probably fake charms dangling near lighters on convenience store counters, to tarot card readers at malls who offer little curses for twenty extra dollars, to assault and murder done for those who can afford it and know who to pay. And my brother's one of the people you pay, just like my Grandad was.

Maura looks away from him, gazing dreamily out the windows at the mostly dead stretch of grass outside the apartment. "Do you hear the music? Outside."

"Cassel wants to stay at the old house," says Philip with a quick, quelling look in my direction. "And there's no music, Maura. No music, okay?"

Maura hums a little as she starts collecting the plates.

"Are you okay?" I ask her.

"She's fine," says Philip. "She's tired. She gets tired."

"I'm going to go do my homework," I say, and when neither of them stops me, I go upstairs to Philip's office in the loft. The couch is made up with new sheets, and the blankets she promised are piled on one end, so freshly washed that I smell the laundry detergent. Sitting in the leather chair in front of the desk, I spin around and switch on the computer.

The screen flickers to life, revealing a background screen littered with folders. I open a browser window and check my email. Audrey sent me a message.

I click so fast that it opens twice.

"Worried about u," it reads. That's it. She didn't even sign her name.

I met Audrey the beginning of freshman year. She usually sat on the cement wall of the parking lot at lunch, drinking coffee and reading old Tanith Lee paperbacks. One time it was *Don't Bite the Sun*. I'd read it too; Lila had loaned it to me. I told her I liked *Sabella* better.

"That's because you're a romantic," she said. "Guys are romantic—no, really. Girls are pragmatic."

"That's not true," I told her, but sometimes, after we started dating, I wondered if she was right.

It takes me twenty minutes to write back to her: "Home for wk. Looking forward to lotsa daytime tv." I hope that it conveys the right amount of nonchalance; it certainly took long enough to fake.

Finally, I hit send and groan, feeling stupid all over again.

Most of the rest of my email that isn't spam are links to the video of me clinging to the Smythe roof that someone already uploaded to YouTube, and a few messages from teachers, giving me the week's assignments. I take the latter as a sign that all is not lost in terms of getting back into Wallingford, despite the former. I still have last night's homework to finish too, but before I start, I want to figure out how I'm going to convince the school to forget all about the incident on the roof. After a little bit of Googling, I find two sleep specialists within an hour's drive. I print out both addresses and save both logos as jpgs on my flash drive. It's a start. I take it for granted that no doctor is going to put his reputation on the line to guarantee I won't sleepwalk again, but I can find a way around that.

I am feeling pretty cocky, so I decide to tackle weaseling out of Grandad's cleaning plan. I call Barron's cell. He answers on the second ring, sounding out of breath.

"You busy?" I ask.

"Not too busy for my brother who almost took a nose-dive. So, what happened?"

"I had a weird dream and started sleepwalking again. It was nothing, but now I'm stuck at Philip's mercy until the school realizes that I'm not going to kill myself." I sigh. Barron and I were on the outs when we were kids, but now he's practically the only person in my family I can really talk to.

"Philip pissing you off?" Barron says.

"Let's put it this way: If I stay here long enough, I *am* going to kill myself."

"The important thing is that you're okay," Barron says, which is satisfying, if patronizing.

"Can I come stay with you?" I ask. Barron's at Princeton, studying pre-law, which is pretty funny because he is a compulsive liar. He's the kind of liar who totally forgets what he told you the last time, but he believes every single lie with such conviction that sometimes he can convince you of it. I don't think he'll last half a minute in court before he'll make up something outrageous about his client.

"I'd have to ask my roommate," he says. "She's dating this ambassador, and he's always sending a car to take her to New York. She might not want more stress."

Yeah, like that. "Well, if she's not there a lot, maybe she won't mind. Otherwise, maybe I can do some couch surfing." I lay it on thick. "There's always the bus stop."

"Why can't you stay with Philip?"

"He's farming me out to Grandad to clean the old house. He hasn't said so, but I don't think he wants me here."

"Don't be paranoid," Barron says. "Philip wants you there. Of course he does."

Philip would have wanted Barron.

When I was about seven, I used to follow a thirteen-year-old Philip around the house, pretending we were superheroes. He was the main hero and I was his sidekick, the Robin to his Batman. I kept pretending to be in trouble so he could come and save me. When I was in the old sandbox, it was a giant hourglass that would smother me. I was in the leaky baby pool being chased by sharks. I would call and call for him, but it was always Barron who finally came.

He was already Philip's real sidekick at ten, good for taking care of things that Philip was too busy for. Like me. I spent most of my childhood jealous of Barron. I wanted to be him, and I resented that he got to be him first.

That was before I realized I was never going to be him.

"Maybe I could just come for a few days," I say.

"Sure, sure," he says, but it's not a commitment. It's stalling. "So, tell me what this crazy dream you had was. What made you go up on the roof?"

I snort. "A cat stole my tongue and I wanted to get it back."

He laughs. "Your brain is a dark place. Next time, just let the tongue go, kid."

I hate being called a kid, but I don't want to argue.

We say good-bye and I plug my phone into its charger and plug that into the wall. I email my completed assignments.

I've started opening random folders on Philip's computer when Maura comes to the door. There are lots of pictures of naked girls lying on their backs, pulling off long velvet gloves. Girls touching bare breasts with shockingly bare hands. I close the obviously misfiled etching of a guy in crazy-looking pantaloons wearing a giant diamond pendant. As scandalous stuff goes, it's all pretty tame.

"Here." She holds out a cup of what smells like mint tea. Her eyes don't quite focus on mine, and two pills rest in her palm. "Philip said to give you these."

"What are they?"

"They'll help you rest."

I take the pills and swig the tea.

"What's going on with you two?" she asks. "He's so odd when you're here."

"Nothing," I say, because I like Maura. I don't want to tell her that Philip probably doesn't want me alone in the house with her or his son because of Lila. Philip saw my face, saw the blood, got rid of the body. If I was him, I wouldn't want me here either.

*   *   *

I wake in the middle of the night with a raging need to piss. My head feels fuzzy, and at first I barely notice the voices downstairs as I stagger down the carpeted hall. I pee, then reach to flush. I stop with my hand on the lever.

"What are you doing here?" Philip is asking.

"Came up as soon as I heard." Grandad's voice is unmistakable. He lives in a little town called Carney, in the Pine Barrens, and he's picked up the trace of an accent there— or he's let some vestige of an old accent creep back in. Carney is like a graveyard where everyone already owns their plots and has built houses on top of them. Practically no one in town isn't a worker, and very few of the workers there are younger than sixty; it's where they go to die.

"We're taking good care of him." For a moment I'm thrown, trying to figure out if I'm hearing right. Barron's downstairs. I can't figure why he didn't tell me he was coming. Mom used to say that he and Philip hid things because I was the youngest, but I knew it was because they were workers and I wasn't. Even Grandad wasn't coming upstairs to add me to their little conference.

I might be a member of the family, but I am always going to be an outsider.

Murdering someone didn't help, although, from a certain perspective, you'd think it might have. At least it proved I was capable of being a criminal.

"Kid needs someone to keep an eye on him," Grandad says. "Something to keep his hands busy."

"He needs a rest," Barron says. "Besides, we don't even know what happened. What if someone was after him?

What if Zacharov found out what happened to Lila? He's still looking for his daughter."

The thought makes my blood turn to ice.

Someone snorts. I figure it is Philip, but then Grandad says, "And he's supposed to be safe with you two clowns?"

"Yeah," Philip says. "We've kept him safe this long."

I draw near to the stairs, squatting down on the balcony over the living room. They must be in the kitchen, since I can hear them very clearly. I'm ready to go down there and tell them just how clearly I can hear them. I'm going to force them to involve me.

"Maybe you don't have time to worry about your brother, considering how much you should be worrying about that wife of yours. Think I can't tell? And *you* shouldn't be working her."

That stops me, foot on the first carpeted step. Working her?

"Leave Maura out of this," Philip says. "You never liked her."

"Fine," Grandad says. "None of my concern how you run your house. You'll see soon enough. I just think you've got your hands full."

"He doesn't want to go with you," Philip says. I'm surprised—either Philip really hates Grandad telling him what to do or Barron convinced him to let me stay after all.

"What if Cassel was up on that roof 'cause he wanted to jump? Think of what he's been through," Grandad says.

"He's not like that," says Barron. "He's kept his nose clean at that school. Kid needs a rest, is all."

The door of the master bedroom opens and Maura steps out into the hall. Her flannel nightgown rides up on one hip. I can see the corner of her underwear.

She blinks but doesn't seem surprised to see me on the balcony. "I thought I heard voices. Is someone here?"

I shrug, my heart beating hard. It takes me a moment to realize I haven't been caught doing much of anything. "I heard voices too."

She looks too thin. Her collarbones seem like knives threatening to slice through her skin. "The music's so loud tonight. I'm afraid I won't be able to hear the baby."

"Don't worry," I say softly. "He must be sleeping like—well, like a baby." I smile, even though I know the joke's lame. She makes me nervous. She looks like a stranger in the dark.

She sits down beside me on the carpet, straightening her nightgown and dangling her legs between the balusters of the stairs. I can count the knobs of her spine. "I'm going to leave him, you know. Philip."

I wonder what he's done to her. I'm pretty sure she doesn't know she's been worked, but if it's a love curse, maybe it's wearing off. They do, although it can take six or even eight months. I wonder if I can ask her if she's visited my mom in prison. Mom has to wear gloves, but she could easily have picked out a few threads to let skin brush skin while saying good-bye. "I didn't know," I say.

"Soon. It's a secret. You'll keep my secret, right?"

I nod quickly.

"How come you aren't down there? With the others?"

I shrug. "Kid brothers always get left out, right?" They're still talking downstairs. I can't quite hear the words, but I'm afraid to stop talking, for fear she might hear what they're saying about her.

"You're not a good liar. Philip's good, but not you."

"Hey," I say, honestly offended. "I am an excellent liar. I am the finest liar in the history of liars."

"Liar," she says, a slow smile spreading across her face. "Why did your parents call you Cassel?"

I'm defeated and amused. "Mom loved extravagant names. Dad insisted that his first son be named after him—Philip—but after that, she got to name Barron and me whatever fanciful thing she wanted. If she'd had her way, Philip would have been Jasper."

She rolls her eyes. "Come on. Are you sure they aren't from her family? Traditional names?"

"Who knows? It's all a mystery. Dad was blond and I bet he found the name Sharpe in a Cracker Jack box of fake IDs. As for Mom's side of the family, Gramps says that his father—her grandfather—was a maharaja of India. He sold tonics from Calcutta to the Midwest. Makes some sense that we could be Indian. His last name, Singer, could be derived from Singh. But that's just one of his stories."

"Your grandfather told me that someone in your family was descended from a runaway slave," she says. I wonder what she thought when she married Philip. People are always coming up to me on trains and talking to me in different languages, like it's obvious I'll understand them. It bothers me that I never will.

"Yeah," I say. "I like the maharaja story better. And don't even get me started on the one where we're Iroquois. Or Italian. And not just Italian, but *descended from Julius Caesar.*"

That makes her laugh loudly enough that I wonder if they hear her downstairs, but the rhythm of their voices doesn't change. "Was he a worker?" she asks, low again. "Philip doesn't like to talk about it."

"Great-Grandad Singer?" I ask. "I don't know." With the blackened finger stubs on his left hand, I'm pretty sure she knows that my grandfather's a death worker. Every kind of curse gives off some kind of blowback, but death curses kill a part of you. If you're lucky, it rots some of your fingers. If not, maybe it rots your lungs or heart. Every curse works the worker, my grandfather says.

"Did you always know you couldn't do it? Could your mother tell?"

I shake my head. "No. When we were little, she was afraid we would work someone by accident. She figured it would come on eventually, so she didn't encourage us." I think about Mom's quick appraisal of a mark and the host of shady skills she did encourage us to learn. It makes me almost miss her. "I used to pretend that I was, though. A worker. One time I thought I turned an ant into a stick until Barron told me he'd switched them to mess with me."

"Transformation, huh?" Maura's smile is distant.

"What's the point of pretending to be anything less than the most talented practitioner of the very rarest curses?" I ask.

She shrugs. "I used to think I could make people fall down. Every time my sister skinned her knee, I was sure it was me. I cried when I realized it wasn't."

Maura glances toward her son's room. "Philip doesn't want us to test the baby, but I'm afraid. What if our child hurts someone by accident? What if he's one of those kids born with crippling blowback? At least if he tested positive, we'd know."

"Just keep him gloved," I say, knowing Philip will never agree to the test. "Until he's old enough to try a small working." In health class our teacher used to say that if someone came toward you on the street with bare hands, consider those hands to be as potentially deadly as unsheathed blades.

"All kids develop differently—no one can know when he'd be ready," Maura says. "The little baby gloves are so cute, though."

Downstairs, Grandad's warning Barron about something. His voice swells, and I catch the words "In my day we were feared. Now we're just afraid."

I yawn and turn to Maura. They can spend all night debating what they want to do with me, but that isn't going to stop me from scamming myself back into school. "Do you really hear music? What does it sound like?"

Her smile turns radiant, although her gaze stays on the carpet. "Like angels shrieking my name."

The hair stands up all along my arms.

CHAPTER FOUR

IN MY PARENTS' HOUSE, nothing was ever thrown away. Clothes piled up, formed drifts that grew into mountains Philip, Barron, and I would climb and leap from. The heaps of garments filled the hallway and chased my parents out of their own bedroom, so that they eventually slept in the room that was once Dad's office. Empty bags and boxes filled in the gaps in the clutter, boxes that once held rings and sneakers and clothes. A trumpet that my mother wanted to make into a lamp rested atop a stack of tattered magazines filled with articles Dad planned to read, near the heads and feet and arms of dolls Mom promised she would stitch together for a kid from Carney, all beside an endless heap of replacement buttons, some still in their individual glassine bags. A coffeemaker rested on a tower of plates, propped up on one end to keep coffee from flooding the counters.

It's strange to see it all, just the way it was when my parents lived here. I pick up a nickel off the countertop and flip it along my knuckles, just like Dad taught me.

"This place is a pigsty," Grandad says, walking out of the dining room, clipping a suspender onto his pants.

After spending months living in the orderly dorms of Wallingford, where they give you a Saturday detention if your room doesn't pass semi-regular inspections, I feel the old conflicting sense of familiarity and disgust. I breath in the moldy, stale smell, with something sour in it that might be old sweat. Philip drops my bag onto the cracked linoleum floor.

"What's the chance of me borrowing the car?" I ask Grandad.

"Tomorrow," he says. "If we get enough done. You make a doctor's appointment?"

"Yeah," I lie, "that's why I need the car." What I need is to have enough time alone that I can put my plan to get back into Wallingford into effect. That does involve a doctor, but not one who's expecting me.

Philip takes off his sunglasses. "Your appointment is when?"

"Tomorrow," I say impulsively, shifting my gaze to Philip and elaborating. "At two. With Dr. Churchill, sleep specialist. In Princeton. That okay with you?" The best lies have as much truth in them as possible, so I tell them exactly where I'm planning on going. Just not why.

"Maura sent over some stuff," Philip says. "Lemme bring it in before I forget." Neither of them suggests coming with me to the completely fabricated appointment, which fills me with profound and undeserved relief.

Someone could cut through the mess in our house and look at it like one might look at rings on a tree or layers of sediment. They'd find the black-and-white hairs of a dog we had when I was six, the acid-washed jeans my mother once wore, the seven blood-soaked pillowcases from the time I skinned my knee. All our family secrets rest in endless piles.

Sometimes the house just seemed filthy, but sometimes it seemed magical. Mom could reach into some nook or bag or closet and pull out anything she needed. She pulled out a diamond necklace to wear to a New Year's party along with citrine rings with gems as big as thumbnails. She pulled out the entire run of Narnia books when I was feverish and tired of all the books scattered beside my bed. And she pulled out a set of hand-carved black and white chess pieces when I finished reading Lewis.

"There's cats out there," my grandfather says, looking out the window as he washes a coffee cup in the sink. "In the barn."

Philip sets down a bag of groceries carefully. His expression is strange.

"Feral," says Grandad, using a fork to pry an ancient piece of toast out of the old toaster, and tossing it into the trash bag he hooked over the basement doorknob.

I walk over to where he's standing and peer out the

window. I can see them, tiny liquid shapes. A tabby jumps atop a rusted can of paint, while a white cat sits in a patch of long weeds, just the end of its tail twitching. "You think they've been living here long?"

My grandfather shakes his head.

"I bet they were pets. They look like pets."

Grandad grunts.

"Maybe I should bring them some food," I say.

"Put it in a trap," says Philip. "Better catch them before they breed out of control."

After Philip leaves, I put out food anyway—a can of tuna they won't come near while I'm standing there, but fight over when I stand at the bottom of the driveway. I count five cats—the white one, two tabbies that I have a hard time telling apart, a fluffy black cat with a spot of white under its chin, and a runty butterscotch one.

Me and Grandad spend the rest of the morning grimly cleaning the kitchen, switching out our regular gloves for rubber. We throw out a pile of rusty forks, a sieve, and some pans. We pull up some linoleum and discover a nest of roaches that scatter so quickly that, despite stomping after them, most get away. I call Sam after lunch, but Johan answers his cell. Sam, apparently, is busy testing to see if the seniors control "the airspace above senior grass." This experiment takes the form of holding one foot slightly above the restricted ground until someone tries to punch him in the head. I say I'll call back.

"Who you phoning?" my grandfather asks, wiping his face with his T-shirt.

"No one."

"Good thing," he says, "since we got so much work to do."

I straddle one of the kitchen chairs and rest my chin on the back frame. "You think there's something wrong with me, or what?"

"Here's what I think: I'm cleaning out this house. I'm not young, so you're supposed to help. You don't want to be some kind of useless pretty boy."

I laugh. "I might be young, but I wasn't born yesterday. That's no answer."

"If you're so smart, you tell me what's going on." He grins after he says it, like verbal wrangling is his idea of fun. Being with him makes me think of being a kid, running around his yard in Carney, safe and free for the summer. He didn't need us to help him chat up a mark or shove some stolen item down our pants. He made us mow the lawn instead.

I decide I'll try a different tactic to show him I'm paying attention. "What's going on? I don't know what's wrong with me, but there's definitely something wrong with Maura."

He stops grinning. "What do you mean?"

"Did you see her? She looks terrible. And she thinks she's hearing music. And I heard you say that Philip was working her."

Grandad shakes his head and dumps his sweaty shirt on the table. "He's not—"

"Oh, come on," I say. "I saw her. Do you know what she said to me?"

He opens his mouth, but there's a banging before he can speak, and we both turn. Audrey's face is framed in the dirty glass of the back door. She frowns, as though sure she's in the wrong place, but then she twists the knob and pushes the door hard enough to unstick it.

"How did you find me?" I ask, shock making me as cold-sounding as I ever hoped to be.

"All our addresses are printed in the student directory," she says, shaking her head like I'm a total idiot.

"Right," I say, because I *am* a total idiot. "Sorry. Come in. Thanks for—"

"Did they kick you out?" She puts one blue-gloved hand on her hip. She's talking to me, but she's staring at the piles of papers and ashtrays, mannequin hands and tea strainers that litter the countertops.

"For now," I say, willing my voice not to crack. I thought I was familiar with the sick feeling of missing someone, of missing Audrey, but right now I realize how much more I'll miss her if I can't see her every day in class or sitting on the grass in the quad. All of a sudden I don't care about the proper amount of ignoring. "Come into the living room."

"I'm his grandfather." Grandad holds out his left hand. The rubber glove hangs limply where his fingers are missing. I'm just glad she can't see the stumps. Nothing but death-magic rotted flesh.

Audrey blanches, holding her gloved hand against her stomach as though she's just realized what he is.

"Sorry," I say. "Gramps, this is Audrey. Audrey, my grandfather."

"A pretty girl like you can call me Desi," he says, slicking back his hair and grinning like he's a rascal daring to be reprimanded.

He's still grinning as we walk past him into the living room.

I sit down on the ripped cushion of our couch. I wonder what she thinks of the house and if she's going to say anything about it or about my grandfather. When I was a kid and brought friends over, I was defiantly proud of the chaos. I liked that I knew how to jump over the piles and the shattered glass while they stumbled. Now it just seems like an ocean of crazy that I have no way to explain.

She reaches into her shiny black pocketbook and takes out a handful of printouts.

"Here," she says, dumping the papers on my lap and flopping down beside me. Her red hair's slightly damp—as though she's just come from the shower—and cold against my arm.

Lila's hair was blond, soaked red with blood the last time I saw her.

I press my eyes shut hard, press my fingers over them until I see nothing but black. Until I push the images away. When I was Audrey's boyfriend, I thought that by making her like me, by making her think I was like everyone else, I'd become like everyone else.

I think about winning her back, wondering if I could do it. Wondering how long before I screw up and she leaves me again. I'm just not a good enough con man to keep her.

"Some 'sleep aid' pills can cause sleepwalking," Audrey

says, pointing to the papers. "Unofficially. I brought some articles from the library. Some guy was even driving in his sleep. I was thinking you could just say—"

"That I was medicating myself for insomnia?" I ask, rolling over and pressing my face against her shoulder, breathing in the smell of her, filtered through sweater fabric.

She doesn't push me away. I consider kissing her right there on the dirty couch, but some instinct of self-preservation stops me. Once someone's hurt you, it's harder to relax around them, harder to think of them as safe to love. But it doesn't stop you from wanting them. Sometimes I actually think it makes the wanting worse.

"It doesn't have to be true. You can just *say* you were taking sleeping pills," she says, like I don't understand lying, which is sort of sweet and sort of humiliating.

It's not a bad plan, really. If I had been smarter and had thought of it myself earlier, I'd probably still be at school. "I already told them I had a history of sleepwalking as a kid."

"Crap," she says. "Too bad. There's this other pill in Australia that's made people binge eat and paint their front doors while asleep." She tilts her head, and I see six tiny protective amulets slide across her collarbone. Luck. Dreams. Emotion. Body. Memory. Death. The seventh one— transformation—is caught on the edge of her sweater.

I imagine crushing her throat in my hands and am relieved to be horrified. I feel guilty when I think of killing girls, but it's the only way I know to test myself, to make sure that whatever terrible thing is inside of me isn't about to get out.

I reach out and unhook the little stone pendant, letting it fall against her neck. Hematite. Probably a fake. There aren't enough transformation workers around for there to be many real amulets. One worker every generation or two. That charm makes me wonder if the rest are fake too. "Thanks. For trying. It was a good idea."

She bites her lip. "Do you think this has something to do with your dad dying?"

I shift abruptly, so that my back's against the armrest. Real smooth. "Do I think what has to do with it? He was in a car accident in the middle of the day."

"Sleepwalking can be triggered by stress. What about your mom being in jail? That's got to be stressful."

My voice rises. "Dad's been dead for almost three years and mom's been locked up practically as long. Don't you think—"

"Don't get mad."

"I'm not mad!" I rub my hand over my face. "Okay, look. I almost fall off a roof, I'm getting kicked out of school, and you think I'm a head case. I've got reasons to be pissed." I take a deep breath and try to give her my most apologetic smile. "But not at you."

"That's right," she says, shoving me. "Not at me."

I catch her gloved hand in mine. "I can handle Northcutt. I'll be back at Wallingford in no time." I hate having her here in the middle of my messy house, already knowing more about me than is comfortable. I feel turned inside out, the raw parts of me exposed.

I don't want her to leave, either.

"Look," she whispers with a glance in the direction of the kitchen. "I don't want to set you off again, but do you think you could have been touched? You know, heebeegeebies?"

Touched. Worked. Cursed. "To sleepwalk?"

"To throw yourself off a roof," she says. "It would have looked like suicide."

"That's a pretty expensive work." I don't want to tell her I've thought about it, that my whole family thought about it so much they even had a secret meeting to discuss the possibility. "Plus, I lived. That makes it less likely."

"You should ask your granddad," she says softly.

If you're so smart, you tell me what's going on.

I nod, barely noticing as she puts the papers back into her purse. Then she hugs me lightly, and I can't help but notice that. My hands rest on the small of her back and I can feel her warm breath against my neck. With her, I could learn to be normal. Every time she touches me, I feel the heady promise of becoming an average guy.

"You better go," I say, before I can do something stupid.

At the door, as she leaves, I turn to look at my grandfather's face. He's twisting a screwdriver into the stove to pop off a crusted burner, without any apparent concern that the entire Zacharov family might be after me. He's worked for them, so it's not like he doesn't know what they're capable of—he knows better than I do.

Maybe that's why he's here.

To protect me.

The thought makes me need to lean against the sink from a combination of horror, guilt, and gratitude.

*　　*　　*

That night, in my old room with the ratty Magritte posters taped to the ceiling and bookshelves stuffed with robots and Hardy Boys novels, I dream of being lost in a rainstorm.

Even though it's a dream, and I'm pretty sure it's a dream, the rain feels cold against my skin and I can barely see with the water in my eyes. I hunch over and run for the only visible light, shading my face with one hand.

I come to the worn door of the barn behind the house. Ducking through the doorway, however, I decide I was mistaken about it being our barn. Instead of the old tools and discarded furniture, there's only a long hallway, lit by torches. As I get closer, I realize that the torches are held by hands too real to be plaster. One hand shifts its grip on a metal shaft, and I leap back from it. Then, stepping closer, I see how the wrist of each has been severed and stuck on the wall. I can see the uneven slice of the flesh.

"Hello," I call, like I did from the roof. This time, no one answers.

I glance back. The barn door is still open, sheets of rain forming puddles on the wooden planks. Because it's a dream, I don't bother to go back and close the door. I just head down the hall. After what seems like a disproportionately long time walking, I come to a shabby door with a handle made from the foot of a stag. The coarse fur tickles my palm as I pull it.

Inside sits a futon from Barron's dorm room and a dresser I'm sure I recall Mom buying off of eBay, intending to paint it apple green for the guest room. I open the drawers and find several pairs of Philip's old jeans. They're dry, and the top pair fits me perfectly when I pull them on. There's a white shirt that was Dad's hanging on the back of the door; I remember the cigarillo burn just below the elbow and the smell of my father's aftershave.

Since I know I'm dreaming, I'm not frightened, just puzzled, when I walk back into the hall and this time find steps going up to a painted white door with a hanging crystal pull. The pull looks like the kind that summons servants in grand houses on PBS shows, but this one is made from glittering parts of an old chandelier. When I pull it, a series of bells rings loudly, echoing through the space. The door opens.

An old picnic table and two lawn chairs rest in the middle of a large gray room. Maybe I'm still in the barn after all, because the spaces between the planks in the walls are wide enough that I can see rain against a storm-bright sky.

The table is draped with some kind of embroidered silk cloth and topped with silver candlesticks, two silver chargers, and gilt-edged plates, the center of each covered by a silver dome. Cut glass goblets stand at each place setting.

Out of the gloom, cats come, tabbies and calicos, marmalade cats and butterscotch cats and cats so black I can barely tell them from their shadows. They creep toward me, hundreds of them, swarming over one another to get close.

I jump up onto one of the chairs, snatching a candle-stick, not sure what sick thing my brain is about to conjure next when a small, veiled creature walks into the room. It's wearing a tiny gown, like the kind that expensive dolls wear. Lila had a whole row of dolls in dresses like that; her mother would yell at her if she touched them. We played with the dolls anyway when her mother wasn't looking. We dragged the princess one through Grandad's backyard pretending she was being held captive by one of my Power Rangers, with a broken Tamagotchi as an interstellar map—until its dress was streaked with grass stains and torn along the hem. This dress is torn too.

The veil slips and falls. Underneath is a cat's face. A cat, standing on two legs, her triangle head tilted to one side, almost like her neck's been broken, her body covered in the dress.

I can't help it, I laugh.

"I need your help," says the tiny figure. Her voice is sad and soft and sounds like Lila's, but with an odd accent that might just be how cats sound when they talk.

"Okay," I say. What else can I say?

"A curse was placed on me," the Lila cat says. "A curse that only you can break."

The other cats watch us, tails flicking, whiskers twitch-ing. Still silent.

"Who cursed you?" I ask, trying to smother my laughter.

"You did," says the white cat.

At that my smile becomes more of a grimace. Lila's

dead and cats shouldn't stand, shouldn't press their paws together in supplication, shouldn't talk.

"Only you can undo the curse," she says, and I try to watch the movement of her mouth, the flash of her fangs, to see how she can speak without lips. "The clues are everywhere. We don't have much time."

This is a dream, I remind myself. A deeply messed-up dream, but a dream just the same. I've even dreamed about a cat before. "Did you bite out my tongue?"

"You seem to have it back," the white cat says, her shadowed eyes unblinking.

I open my mouth to speak, but I feel claws on my back, nails sinking into my skin and I yelp instead.

Yelp and sit up. Wake up.

I hear the steady patter of rain against my window and realize that I'm soaked, blankets wet and clinging. I'm back in my room, in my old bed, and my hands are shaking so hard that I have to press them underneath my body to make them stop.

CHAPTER FIVE

WHEN I STAGGER DOWN
to the kitchen in the morning, I find Grandad boiling coffee
and frying eggs in bacon grease. I have on jeans and a faded
Wallingford T-shirt. I don't miss my itchy gloves or stran-
gling tie; comfort's the consolation prize for getting booted,
I guess, but I don't want to get too used to it.

I found a leaf stuck to my leg while I was getting
dressed, and that was enough to make me remember waking, drenched with rain. I've been sleepwalking again,
but the more I think about the dream, the more confused
I get. Nothing lethal happened, which takes the Zacharov
revenge scenario off the table. So maybe it's just guilt that

makes me dream of Lila. Guilt makes you crazy, right? It festers inside of you.

Like in Poe's "The Tell-tale Heart," which Ms. Noyes made us read out loud, where the narrator hears the heart of his victim beating beneath the floorboards, louder and louder until he confesses, *"I admit the deed! Here, here! It is the beating of his hideous heart!"*

"I need to talk to you," I say, taking out a mug and pouring milk into it first, then adding the coffee. The milk billows up from the bottom, along with flecks of dust I should have probably checked for. "I had a weird dream."

"Let me guess. You got tied up by lady ninjas. With big hooters."

"Uh, no." I take a sip of the coffee and wince. Grandad made it ridiculously strong.

My grandfather shoves a strip of bacon in his mouth with a grin. "Guess it would have been kind of weird if we'd had the same dream."

I roll my eyes. "Well, you'd better not tell me anything else. Don't ruin the surprise in case I have it tonight."

Grandad chuckles, but it turns into a wheeze.

I look out the window. There are no cats on the grass. As I watch Grandad pour ketchup onto his eggs, the red liquid spreading, I think, *There's too much blood, and I don't remember stabbing her, but a wet knife is in my hand and the blood is smeared over the floorboards like a thick glaze.*

"So are you going to tell me about the dream you did

have?" My grandfather sits down at the table, smacking his lips.

"Yeah," I say, blinking as I remember where I am. Mom said those sudden, sickening flashes of the murder would get better over time, but they just got less frequent. Maybe some small decent part of me didn't want to forget.

"You waiting for an engraved invitation?" Grandad asks.

"The dream started with me outside in the rain. I walked out to the barn, and then I woke up in my bed, with mud all over my feet. Sleepwalking again, I guess."

"You guess?" he asks.

"Lila was in my dream." I force the words out. We never talk about Lila or the way the whole family protected me, after. How my mother wept into the fur collar of her sweater and hugged me and told me that even if I had done it, then she was sure that little Zacharov bitch deserved it, and she didn't care what anyone said, I was still her baby. How there was something dark under my fingernails and I couldn't seem to get it out. I tried with my own nails and then with a butter knife, pressing until I started to bleed. Until my blood washed away the other darkness.

So my own conscience is finally doing me in. It's about time.

Grandad raises an eyebrow. "Maybe it would help if you talk about her. Talk about killing her. Get it off your chest. I've done bad things, kid. I'm not going to judge you."

Mom got arrested not long after Lila's murder. Not

because of me, not exactly, but she was off her game. She wanted a big score and she wanted it fast.

"What do you want me to say? I killed her? I know I did, even if I don't remember it. I always wondered if Mom paid someone to make me forget the details. Maybe she thought if I didn't remember how it felt, I wouldn't do it again." There's got to be something dead inside me, because normal people don't stand over the corpse of someone they love and feel nothing but a distant, horrible joy. "Lila was a dream worker, and so I guess the sleepwalking and the nightmares seem ironic. I'm not saying I don't deserve them; I just want to understand why they're happening."

"Maybe you should come down to Carney. See your uncle Armen. He can still do some memory work. Maybe he can help you remember."

"Uncle Armen has Alzheimer's," I say. He's a friend of Grandad's from when they were kids, and not really even my uncle.

Grandad snorts. "Nah. Blowback. But let's see what that fancy doctor thinks first."

I pour more coffee into my cup. A week after Lila died and Barron and Philip hid her body wherever bodies get hidden, I went to a pay phone and called Lila's mother. I'd promised I wouldn't, had listened to my grandfather explain that if anyone found out what I'd done, the whole family would pay. I knew that the Zacharovs were unlikely to forget who had dug the grave and mopped up the blood and failed to turn me in, but I couldn't stop thinking about Lila's mother alone in that house.

Alone and waiting for her daughter to come home.

The ringing seemed too harsh. I felt light-headed. When her mother answered, I hung up. Then I walked around to the back of the convenience store and puked my guts out.

Grandad stands up. "How about you start on the upstairs bathroom? I'm going out for supplies."

"Don't forget the milk," I say.

"*My* memory's fine," he shoots back at me as he reaches for his jacket.

The floor tiles of the bathroom are cracked and torn in places, and there's a cheap white cabinet shoved against one wall. Inside are dozens and dozens of mismatched towels, some full of holes, and amber-colored plastic bottles with a few pills in each. On the shelf beneath that there are jars crusted with dark liquids and tins of powder.

As I clean silken balls full of baby spiders from the corners of the shower and toss out sticky, mostly empty shampoo bottles, I can't stop thinking about Lila.

We were nine when we met. Her parents' marriage was coming apart and she and her mother went to live with her grandmother in the Pine Barrens. She had wooly blond hair, one brown eye and one green one, and all I knew about her was that Grandad said her father was someone important.

Lila was what anybody might expect from a girl who could give you nightmares with a bare-handed touch, from the head of the Zacharov family's daughter. She was spoiled rotten.

At nine she beat me mercilessly at video games, raced

up hills and trees so fast I was always three steps behind her long legs, and bit me when I tried to steal her dolls and hide them. I couldn't tell if she hated me half the time, even when we spent weeks hiding under the branches of a willow tree, drawing civilizations in the dirt and then crushing them like callous gods. But I was used to brothers who were fast and cruel and I worshipped her.

Then her parents divorced. I didn't see her again until we were both thirteen.

Grandad comes back with several shopping bags around the time it starts to rain again, most of them full of Windex, beer, or paper towels. He's also brought back traps.

"For raccoons, but they'll work," he says. "And they're humane—says so on the package—so don't get your panties in a twist. There's no guillotine attachment."

"Nice," I say, lifting them out of the trunk.

He leaves me alone to carry them to the barn. The cats are in there; I can see their eyes gleaming as I set up the first metal cage with its swinging door. I pop the tab on a can of wet food, sliding it inside the trap. Something thumps softly to the ground behind me and I turn.

The white cat stands not three feet from me, pink tongue licking her sharp teeth. In the afternoon light I can see that her ear's torn. Crusts of garnet scabs—fresh—run along the back of her neck.

"Here, kitty kitty," I say, nonsense words coming automatically from my mouth. I open another can. The cat jumps when the lid cracks open, and I realize how tense I've been.

Like she's going to speak. But the cat's just a cat. Just an underfed stray living in a barn and about to be trapped.

I reach out a gloved hand, and she shies back. Smart animal.

"Here, kitty kitty," I say.

The cat approaches me slowly. She sniffs my fingers, and as I hold my breath, she rubs her cheek against my hand; soft fur and twitching whiskers and the edge of her teeth digging into my skin.

I put down the can of cat food, watching as she laps at it. I reach out to stroke her again, but she hisses, back arching and fur lifting. She looks like a snake.

"That's more like it," I say, petting her anyway.

She follows me back to the house. Her shoulder blades jut out of her back, and her white coat's streaked with mud. I let her into the kitchen anyway and give her water in a martini glass.

"You're not bringing that dirty animal in here, are you?" my grandfather says.

"She's a cat, Grandad, not a cockroach."

He regards her skeptically. His T-shirt's covered in dust and he's pouring bourbon into one of those big plastic soft drink cups that come with their own straws. "What do you want with a cat?"

"Nothing. I don't know. She looks hungry."

"You going to let all of them in here?" Grandad asks. "I bet they're all hungry."

I grin. "I promise no more than one at a time."

"This is not why I bought those traps."

"I know," I say. "You bought the traps so we can catch all the cats, drop them off in a field ten miles from here, and take bets on which one comes back first."

He shakes his head. "You better get back to cleaning, smart-ass."

"I have that doctor's appointment with—," I say.

"I remember. Let's see how much you can get done before you have to leave."

Shrugging, I go into the living room with a bunch of flat boxes and packing tape. I build the boxes and drag in the trash can from out back. Then I start going through the piles.

The cat watches me with shining eyes.

Circulars advertising charms and an old fur muff that looks like it has mange go in the trash can. Paperbacks go back onto shelves unless they look like something I want to read or the pages look too crumbly. A basket of leather gloves, some of them stuck together from being too close to a heating vent, goes into the trash as well.

No matter how much I throw away, there's always more. Piles slide into one another and confuse me about where I was clearing last. There are dozens of wadded-up plastic bags, one with a pair of earrings and the receipt still attached, others holding a random swatch of cloth or the crust of a sandwich.

There are screwdrivers, nuts and bolts, my fifth-grade report card, the caboose from a toy train, rolls of PAID stickers, magnets from Ohio, three vases with dried flowers in them and one vase overstuffed with plastic flowers, a cardboard box of broken ornaments, a sticky mess of something dark and melted covering an ancient radio.

As I pick up a dust-covered dehumidifier, a box full of photographs spills across the floor.

They're black-and-white pinups. The woman in them is wearing wrist-length summer gloves, a vintage corset, and nylon panties. Her hair's styled like Bettie Page's and she's kneeling on a couch, smiling at the person taking the pictures, a man whose fingers show up in one of the pictures wearing an expensive-looking wedding ring over his black gloves. I know the woman in the pictures.

Mom looks pretty good.

The first time I realized I had a talent for crime was after Mom took me out—just me—for a cherry slushy. It was a scorching summer day and the leather seat in her car was hot from the sun, burning the backs of my legs just slightly unpleasantly. My mouth had turned bright red when we pulled into a gas station and then around back, like Mom was going to put air in the tires.

"See that house?" she asked me. She was pointing to a ranch-style place with white aluminum siding and black shutters.

"I want you to go through that window in the back by the stairs. Just shimmy on in and grab the manila envelope off the desk."

I must have stared at Mom like I didn't understand her.

"It's a game, Cassel. Do it as fast as you can and I'll time you. Here, give me your drink."

I guess I knew it wasn't a game, but I ran anyway and I boosted myself up on the water spigot and poured through the window with the boneless grace of little kids. The manila envelope was right where Mom'd said it would be. Nearby, piles of paper rested under coffee cups stuffed with pens and rulers and spoons. There was a little glass cat on the desk with what looked like glittering gold inside it. The air-conditioning made the sweat dry on my arms and back as I held the sculpture up to the light. I tucked the cat into my pocket.

When I brought the envelope back to her, she was sucking on my slushy.

"Here," I said.

She smiled. Her mouth was bright red too. "Good work, sweetie." And I realized that the reason she had taken me instead of my brothers was just that I was the smallest, but it didn't bother me, because I also realized that I could be useful. That I didn't need to be a worker to be useful. That I could be good at things, better than they were, even.

That knowledge sang through my veins like adrenaline.

Maybe I was seven. I'm not sure. It was before Lila.

I never told anyone about the cat.

I stack the photographs, with a few more of Grandad and Lila's dad in Atlantic City in front of a bar. They're standing with an older man that I don't know, arms draped over each others' shoulders.

I sweep layers of dust from under the couches and chairs until it billows up and chokes me.

When I flop down to rest, I find a notebook shoved under one of the cushions, filled with Mom's writing. No more racy photos, just boring stuff. "Oil tank removal—buried" is scrawled on one side of the page, while the other side reads, "get carrots, chicken (whole), bleach, matches, motor oil." Two pages later there are some addresses, with one circled. Then a script for calling a car dealership and talking them out of a rental car for a week. There are a few more scripts for different scams, with notes on the side. I read them over, smiling despite myself.

In a couple of hours I'm going to run my own scam, so I better study up.

In our family—maybe in every family—there's this idea that the kids take after someone from another generation. Like Philip is supposed to take after our granddad, my mom's father. Philip's the one who dropped out of high school to join up with the Zacharovs and got his keloid necklace a few years later. He's big on loyalty and stability, even if he pays his rent by busting kneecaps. I picture him in forty years retired to Carney, chasing a new generation of worker kids off his lawn.

The family legend says that Barron is just like Mom, even though he works luck and she works emotion. Mom can make anyone her friend, can strike up a conversation anywhere because she genuinely believes that the con is a game. And all she cares about is winning every single time.

That leaves me to be like my luck worker dad, except

that I'm not. He was the person that held things together. When he was alive, Mom acted normal most of the time. It was only when he was gone that she started chasing around millionaires with her gloves off. The second time a guy woke up at the end of a cruise a hundred grand lighter and head over heels in love, his lawyer called the cops.

She can't help it. She loves the con.

I tell myself I'm not like her, but I have to admit I love it too.

I flip through the notebook, looking for I don't know what—maybe something familiar, maybe just some secret that will make me laugh. As I turn more pages, I find an envelope taped to a divider. Written beside it are the words "Give this to Remember!" I rip it open and find a memory charm, silver, with the word "remember" stamped on it and an uncracked blue stone set off center. It looks old, the silver tarnished black in the grooves and the whole piece heavy in my hand.

Charms to throw off curse work, charms like the ones Audrey has hanging around her neck, are as old as curses themselves. Workers make them by cursing stone—the only material that absorbs a whole curse, including the blowback. Then that stone is primed and will swallow up a curse of the same type. So if a luck worker curses a piece of jade and wears it against her skin, and then someone tries to curse her with bad luck, the jade breaks and she's not affected. You have to get another charm each time you're worked, and you have to have one for each type of magic, but you're safe. Only rock is effective, not silver or gold, leather or wood. Certain people prefer one type to another; there are charms made out of everything from gravel to granite. If what I'm holding is a charm, the blue stone is what powers it.

I wonder if Mom grifted some ancestral heirloom or if it actually belongs to her. It's kind of funny to think of forgetting a memory charm. I tuck it into my pocket.

While cleaning the living room, I find a button-making machine, two plastic bags of bubble wrap, a sword with rust staining the blade, three broken dolls I don't remember anyone owning, an overturned chair that creeped me out as a kid because I swore it looked identical to one I'd seen on television the night before Barron and Philip dragged it home, a hockey stick, and a collection of medals for various different military accomplishments. It's almost noon by the time I finish, and my hands and the cuffs of my pants are black with filth. I throw away stacks of newspapers and catalogs, bills that probably went unpaid for years, plastic bags of hangers and wires, and the hockey stick.

The sword I lean against the wall.

The outside of the house is already piled with garbage bags from the morning's work. There's enough stuff that we're going to have to take a trip to the dump before long. I look over at the neighbors' tidy houses with their manicured lawns and brightly painted doors, and then back at my own. The shutters hang off kilter on either side of a row of front-facing windows, and one of the panes is broken. The paint is so worn that the cedar shingles look gray. The house is rotting from the inside.

I'm in the process of dragging the chair out to the side of the road when Grandad comes downstairs and dangles the keys in front of me.

"Be back in time for dinner," he says.

I take the keys, gripping them hard enough for the teeth to dig into my palm. Leaving the chair where it is, I head out the driveway as if I really have an appointment to be late for.

CHAPTER SIX

THE ADDRESS I GOT OFF the Internet for Dr. Churchill's office is on the corner of Vandeventer Avenue in the center of Princeton. I park next to a fondue restaurant and check myself in the rearview mirror, finger-combing my hair flat in the hopes of making myself look more like a good kid, reliable. Even though I washed my hands three times in the bathroom of a convenience store when I stopped for coffee, I can still feel the oily grit of dirt on my skin. I try not to rub my fingers against my jeans as I walk into the reception area and up to the desk.

The woman answering the phone has dyed red curls and glasses hanging around her neck on a beaded chain. I wonder if she made the chain herself; irrationally I associate crafting with friendliness. She looks like she might be in her fifties from the lines on her face and all the silver at her roots. "Hi," I say. "I have an appointment at two."

She looks at me without smiling and taps the keyboard in front of her. I know there's not going to be anything on her screen about me, but that's okay. It's part of my plan.

"What's your name?" she asks.

"Cassel Sharpe." I try to stick to the truth as much as possible, in case there's a need for elaboration or photo identification. As she clicks around to figure out who made a mistake, I take stock of the office. There's a young woman behind the desk, wearing light purple scrubs, and I think she might be a nurse, since there's only one doctor's name—Dr. Eric Churchill, MD—on the door. The few files on top of the cabinets in the back are in dark green folders, and a note about the holiday hours is taped to the front of the desk. On stationery. I reach for it.

"I don't see anything here, Mr. Sharpe," she says.

"Oh," I say, my hand freezing. I can't rip the tape without her noticing the movement. "Oh." I try to seem worried and hope that she'll take pity on me and do some more fruitless searching or, better yet, go ask someone.

She doesn't seem to notice my fake distress and seems, in fact, more irritated than sympathetic. "Who made the appointment?"

"My mom. Do you think it might be under her name?" The nurse in the scrubs takes out a file and sets it on the counter, close to where I'm standing.

"There's no Sharpe here," the receptionist says, her gaze steady. "Maybe your mother made a mistake?"

I take a deep breath and concentrate on minimizing tells. Liars will touch their faces, obscuring themselves. They'll stiffen up. They'll do any of dozens of nonverbal things—breathe quickly, talk fast, blush—that could give them away. "Her last name's Singer. Could you check?"

As she turns her face toward the screen, I slide the file off the counter and under my coat.

"No. No Singer," she says, with profound annoyance. "Would you like to call your mother, maybe?"

"Yeah, I better," I say contritely. As I turn, I pull the stationery sign off the front of the desk. I have no idea if she sees me. I force myself not to look back, just to keep walking with one arm crossed over my coat to keep the file in place, and the other sliding the sheet of paper into the file, everything perfectly natural.

I hear a door close and a woman—maybe the patient that goes with the file—say, "I don't understand. If I'm cursed, then what good is this amulet? I mean, look at it, it's covered in emeralds; are you telling me it's no better than a dime-store—"

I don't pause to hear the rest. I just walk toward the doors.

"Mr. Sharpe," a male voice says.

The doors are right in front of me. Just a few more steps will take me through them, but I stop. After all, my plan won't work if they remember me, and they'll remember a patient they have to chase down. "Uh, yeah?"

Dr. Churchill is a tan, thin man with thick glasses and close-cropped curling hair as white as eggshells. He pushes his glasses back up onto the bridge of his nose absently. "I don't know what happened to your appointment, but I've got some time right now. Come on back."

"What?" I say, turning toward the receptionist, hand still holding my coat closed. "I thought you said—"

She frowns. "Do you want to see the doctor or not?"

I can't think of anything to do but follow.

A nurse leads me to a room with an examining table covered in crinkly paper. She gives me a clipboard with a form that asks for an address and insurance information. Then she leaves me alone to stare at a chart showing the different stages of sleep and their waveforms. I rip the lining of my coat enough to drop the file inside it. Then I sit on the end of the table and write down facts about myself that are mostly true.

There are several brochures on the counter: "The Four Types of Insomnia," "Symptoms of HBG Assault," "Dangers of Sleep Apnea," and "All About Narcolepsy."

I pick up the one on HBG assault. That's the legal term for what my mother did to that rich guy. Assault. There are bullet points with a list of symptoms, and the caution that the diagnostic differential (whatever that means) on each is pretty broad:

- Vertigo
- Auditory Hallucinations
- Visual Hallucinations

- Headaches
- Fatigue
- Increased Anxiety

I think of Maura's music and wonder just how weird the hallucinations can get.

My phone buzzes and I take it out of my pocket automatically, still staring at the pamphlet. I'm not surprised by any of the information—like, I know I get headaches a lot because my mother gave an emotional working the way other parents give a time-out—but it's still strange to see it printed in black and white.

I flip open my phone and let the pamphlet fall to the floor. *Get over here*, the message reads. *We've got a big problem.* It's the only text message I've ever gotten where everything is spelled right. It's from Sam.

I push the buttons to call him back immediately, but the call goes to voice mail and I realize he must be in class. I check the time on my phone. A half hour more until lunch. I text quickly—*wht did u do?*—which might not be the most sensitive message, but I'm imagining disaster.

I'm imagining him caught with my book, ratting me out. I'm imagining being doomed to sifting through my parents' detritus until Grandad finds some other odd job for me.

The reply comes fast. *Payout.*

I breathe. Someone must have won a bet and, of course, he doesn't have the cash to cover it. *B ovr soon*, I text back as the door opens and the doctor walks in.

Dr. Churchill takes the clipboard and looks at it

instead of at me. "Dolores says there was some kind of mix-up?"

I assume that Dolores is the unfriendly reception desk lady. "Mom told me that I had an appointment with you today." The lie comes out easily; I even sound a little resentful. There's a tipping point with lies, a point where you've said something so many times that it feels truer than the truth.

He looks at me then, and I feel like he sees more than I want him to. I think about the file sitting in my coat, so close that he could reach down and grab it before I could stop him. I hope he doesn't have a stethoscope, because my heart is trying to beat its way out of my chest. "So why'd she make you an appointment with a sleep specialist? What kind of problems are you having?" he asks.

I hesitate. I want to tell him about waking up on the roof, about my sleepwalking and the dreams, but if I do, he might remember me. I know he's not going to write the note I need—no doctor in his right mind would—but I can't risk him writing Wallingford any other kind of letter.

"Let me guess," he says, surprising me, because how could anyone *guess* why a patient came to a sleep clinic? "You're here for the test." I have no idea what he's talking about.

"Right," I say. "The test."

"So, who canceled the appointment? Your father?"

I'm in over my head, with nothing to do but play along. "Probably my father."

He nods like that makes sense, fishing around in a drawer until his gloved hand emerges holding a fistful of electrodes. He begins attaching them to my forehead, their sticky sides pulling at my skin. "Now we're going to measure your gamma waves." He switches on a machine and it jumps to life, needles skittering across paper in the pattern that's mirrored on a screen to my left.

"Gamma waves," I repeat. I'm not even asleep, so I don't see the point in measuring my gamma waves. "Is this going to hurt?"

"Quick and painless." The doctor peers down at the paper. "Any reason why you think you're hyperbathygammic?"

Hyperbathygammic. That long medical term for worker. HBG. Heebeegeebies.

"Wh-what?" I stammer.

His eyes narrow. "I thought—"

I think of the woman I heard in the reception area. She was complaining about getting worked, and she sounded like they'd done a test on her to prove it. But he's not asking me if I think I've been worked. He's asking if I think I'm a *worker*.

This is the new test, the one that they keep talking about on the news, the one that conservative politicians want to make mandatory. Theoretically, compulsory testing will keep HBG kids from breaking the law by accident when using their powers for the first time. Theoretically, the results are supposed to stay private, so there's no harm, right? But no one really thinks those results are going to stay private.

They'll wind up with the government, which loves to draft workers for counterterrorism and other odd jobs. Or—legally or not—those results wind up in the hands of local authorities. If mandatory testing happens, the rest will be hard on its heels. Yeah, I know the slippery slope argument is a logical fallacy, but occasionally a slope feels particularly greased.

Supporters of the proposition have urged nonworkers to go get tested. The idea is simple. Even if workers don't get the test, they'll be the only ones to refuse it. That way, even if compulsory testing doesn't pass, it'll still be easier to figure out who's hyperbathygammic.

I hop off the table, ripping the electrodes off my skin. I might not get along with my family, but being part of some database of nonworkers used like a net to trap Philip and Barron and Grandad is horrible. "I have to go. I'm sorry."

"Sit back down. We'll be done in just a moment," he says, grabbing for the wires. "Mr. Sharpe!"

This time when I head for the doors, I don't stop until I'm through them. Keeping my head down, I ignore the nurse calling after me and the people in the waiting room staring. I ignore everything but my need to be somewhere other than here.

I keep telling myself to breathe as I drive. My foot pushes harder and harder on the gas pedal and my fingers fiddle with the radio just to have some sound to drown out the single thought: *I screwed up.*

I was supposed to be inconspicuous, but I'd become

memorable. Plus, I used my own name. I know where I went wrong: when the doctor said he knew what I was there for. I have this problem. Sometimes I'm too in love with the con; even when it goes wrong, I'd rather let it turn on me than walk. I should have stopped the doctor and corrected him, but I was too curious, too eager to play along and see what he would say next.

I still have the stationery. I can still make the plan happen. With recrimination pounding in my ears louder than the music, I pull into the Target parking lot. The front displays are all pastel baskets with chocolate eggs in them, even though it seems like they'd get stale before Easter. I walk to electronics and pick up a disposable cell phone. My second stop is a copy shop, where I rent computer time. The steady hum of the copiers and the smell of printer ink remind me of school and calm, but when I take the file out of my bag, my heart starts racing all over again.

The other mistake I made. Stealing a file. Because I was memorable enough now that they might think of me when they consider all the ways the file could have gone missing.

All I need is the sleep center's logo—the resolution on the one from the Internet is so bad I can't use it for anything but a fax. I don't need a file. A file could get me in real trouble. But when I saw the folder on that counter, I just grabbed.

And now, letting it fall open on this counter, I feel even more stupid. It's just some woman's name, her health insurance, a bunch of numbers and charts with jagged lines. None of it means anything to me. The only good thing is that Dr. Churchill signed one of the pages; at least I can copy his scrawl.

I flip though a few more pages, until I see a graph labeled "gamma waves" with red circles around the spikes in the jagged line. Gamma waves. A little Googling explains what I'm looking at. Apparently dream work puts someone into a sleep state that's like deep sleep, except with gamma waves. Gamma waves—according to the article—are usually present only during waking or light REM sleep. On the chart, gamma waves are present during the deepest sleep stages, when there's no eye movement and when both sleepwalking and night terrors occur. That's what proves she was sleep worked.

Apparently, according to the same site, gamma waves are the key to determining if you're a worker too. Worker gammas are higher than normal people's, asleep or awake. Much higher.

Hyperbathygammic.

I stare at the screen. This information has always been available to me with only a few clicks of a mouse, and yet I never really thought about it. Sitting here, I try to figure out why I handled the situation in the doctor's office so badly. I wasn't cunning. I panicked. My mother instructed me over and over again not to tell anyone anything about the family—not what I knew and not what I guessed—so it's awful to realize that nothing needs to be said. They could know through your skin.

And yet. And yet there's a pathetic part of me that wants to call the doctor and say, *You almost finished the test.*

Did you get a result? And he'd go, *Cassel, everyone's wrong about you. You're the awesomest worker on Awesome Street. We don't know why you didn't figure it out. Congratulations. Welcome to the life you're supposed to have.*

I have to push those thoughts out of my head. I can't afford to get any more distracted. Sam's waiting for me at Wallingford, and if I want to do more than visit the campus over and over again to sort out his messes, I have to fix a letter.

First I scan in the stationery. Then I find the font that the address is in, use the photo editing program to get rid of the old information, and type in the phone number of my new prepaid cell. I erase all the text about the office's holiday hours and type my own words in their place. "Cassel Sharpe has been my patient for several years. Against the strict orders of this office, he discontinued his medication, which resulted in an episode of somnambulism."

I'm not sure what to type next.

Another quick Google turns up a bit of likely doctorish mumbo jumbo. "The patient indicated a stimulant-dependant sleep disorder that induced bouts of insomnia. He has been prescribed medication and is sleeping through the night with no more incidents. As insomnia is often causal for sleepwalking, I believe there is no medical reason for Cassel to be restricted from classes or to be monitored at night."

I smile at the screen, wishing to grab hold of one of the businessmen getting pie charts printed and show him how smart I am. I feel like bragging. I wonder what else fake Dr. Churchill could convince Wallingford to believe.

"Furthermore," I write, "I have eliminated any outside assault as a cause for the patient's sleepwalking."

No point in them worrying about something that's probably just my crazy self-immolating guilt. No point in my worrying about it either.

I print my letter out on the fake stationery and print myself a fake envelope. Then I lick it and pay my bill at the copy shop. As I drop the letter into the mailbox, I realize that my plan better have a second prong if I'm going to stay unsuspended.

Stop sleepwalking.

I get to Wallingford around four, which means Sam's at play practice. It's easy to slip into the Carter Thompson Memorial Auditorium and sit in one of the seats in the back. The lights are dim there, all of them flooding the stage, where the cast are blocking Pippin murdering his dad.

"Stand closer to one other," Ms. Stavrakis, the drama teacher, says, clearly bored. "And lift that knife high, Pippin. It's got to catch the light so we can see it."

I see Audrey standing next to Greg Harmsford. She's smiling. Even though I can't see her face clearly, memory tells me that the blue sweater she's wearing is the color of her eyes.

"Please try to stay dead," Ms. Stavrakis calls to the kid playing Charles, James Page. "You only have a few moments of lying there before we bring you back to life."

Sam walks out on the stage and clears his throat. "Um, excuse me, but before we do this again, can we at least try out the effect? It looks lame without the blood packet and we need the practice. Uh, and don't you think it would be awesome if Pippin *shot* Charles instead of stabbing him? Then we could use the caps and it would really splatter."

"We're talking about the eighth century here," Ms. Stavrakis says. "No guns."

"But at the beginning of the musical they're in different historical costumes from different time periods," he says. "Doesn't that imply—"

"No guns," says Ms. Stavrakis.

"Okay, how about we use one of the packets? Or I could attach a blood capsule to the end of the retractable blade."

"We have to run through the rest of the scene, Sam. See me before rehearsal tomorrow and we'll talk about this. Okay?"

"Fine," he says, and stalks backstage. I get up and follow him.

I find him standing by a table. Bottles of red liquid rest on it next to scattered condom wrappers. I can hear Audrey's voice somewhere on the other side, yelling something about a party on Saturday night.

"What the hell goes on back here?" I ask him. "Drama club parties hard."

Sam turns around suddenly. I don't think he had any idea I was there. Then he looks down at what's in front of him and laughs nervously.

"They're for the blood," he says, but I can see red creeping up his neck. "You fill them up. They're pretty sturdy, but they pop easy too."

I pick one up. "Whatever you say, man."

"No, look." He takes it from me. "You rig a small explosive charge onto a foam-covered metal plate, and then you cover the charge with the blood pack. It's powered by a battery, so you just have to tape it and thread the trigger down the actor's body to somewhere out of sight. Like, with gaffer tape. If it's for a video or something, seeing wires doesn't matter so much. You can just edit them out. But onstage it's got to look neat."

"Right," I say. "It's a shame they won't let you do it."

"They're not big on my prosthetics either. I wanted to give James a beard. I mean, has Ms. Stavrakis even seen paintings of Charlemagne? Totally bearded." He looks at me for a long moment. "Are you okay?"

"Sure. Of course. So who won what?"

"Oh, yeah, sorry." He goes back to putting his equipment away. "Two teachers were spotted hooking up—practically no one bet on it, but three people did. Your payout is, like, six hundred bucks." He corrects himself. "Our payout."

"I guess the house doesn't always win." I miscalculated my odds in a big way, but I don't want him to know how big a hit I'm going to take. I rely on people making bad bets. "Who?"

He grins. "Ramirez and Carter."

I shake my head. Music teacher and the freshman English teacher. Both married to other people. "Evidence? You better not be handing out any winnings without—"

He flips open his laptop and shows me the picture. Ms. Carter's got her hand on the back of Ms. Ramirez's neck and her mouth on the front of it.

"Doctored?" I ask hopefully.

He shakes his head. "You know, people have been acting really weird since I took over your operation. Asking my friends about me."

"People don't like to think of their bookies as having friends. Makes them nervous."

"I'm not going to give up my friends."

"Of course you're not," I say automatically. "I'll go get the cash. Look," I say, and sigh. "I'm sorry if I seem like a hard-ass or whatever, asking you for evidence." My skin itches with discomfort. I've been acting like Sam's a fellow criminal.

"You aren't being weird," he says, looking puzzled. "No weirder than usual, anyway. You seem fine, man."

I guess he's used to suspicious people with crappy tempers. Or maybe I've never seemed as normal as I thought. Trudging down the path to the library, I keep my head down. I'm pretty sure that if Northcutt or any of her lackeys see me, they'll consider my roaming around campus a violation of my "medical leave." I manage to avoid looking anyone in the eye or walking into anyone on the way to the library.

Lainhart Library is the ugliest building on campus, constructed with a musician's donated funds in the eighties, when apparently people thought that a round building tilted at a weird angle was just the thing to update all the grand old brick edifices surrounding it. But as ugly as it is on the outside, the inside is couch-filled and comfortable. Bookshelves fan out from a central parlor with lots of seating and a massive globe that seniors try to steal year after year (a popular bet).

The librarian waves from behind her big oak desk. She's just out of library school and has cat's-eye glasses in every color of the rainbow. Several losers put down money on hooking up with her themselves. I felt bad when I told them the odds I'd assigned.

"Good to have you back, Cassel," she says.

"Good to be back, Ms. Fiske." Once spotted, I figure the best I can manage is not being conspicuous. Hopefully by the time she figures out I'm not back for real, I will be.

My working money—a total of three thousand dollars—is hidden between the pages of a big leather-bound onomasticon. I've kept it there for the last two years without incident. No one ever touches it but me. My only fear is that the book will be culled, since no one ever uses an onomasticon, but I think Wallingford keeps it because it looks expensive and obscure enough to reassure visiting parents that their kids are learning genius-type stuff.

I open the book and slide out six hundred dollars, poke around for a couple of minutes acting like I'm considering reading some Renaissance poetry, and then slink back to the dorm, where Sam's supposed to meet me. As I step off the stairs and into the hall, Valerio walks out of his room. I dodge to the side, into the bathroom, and then close myself in a stall. Leaning against the wall while waiting for my heart to start beating normally, I try to remind myself that so long as no one sees you doing something embarrassing, there's no reason to be humiliated. Valerio doesn't follow. I text Sam.

He walks into the bathroom moments later, laughing. "What a clandestine spot for a meeting."

I push open the stall door. "Laugh it up." There's no rancor in my voice, though. Just relief.

"The coast is clear," he says. "The eagle has flown the coop. The cow stands alone."

I can't help smiling as I dig out the money from my pocket. "You are a master of deception."

"Hey," he says. "Can you teach me to calculate odds? Like, if there was something I wanted to take bets on? And what's the deal with the point spreads on the games? How do you figure those? You aren't doing it the way they say online."

"It's complicated," I say, stalling. What I mean is: It's fixed.

He leans against the sink. "We Asians are all math geniuses."

"Okay, genius. Maybe another time, though?"

"Sure," he says, and I wonder if he's already planning to cut me loose from my own business. I figure I can probably screw him somehow if he does, but the thought of having to plan it just makes me tired.

Sam counts the money carefully. I watch him in the mirror. "You know what I wish?" he asks when he's done.

"What?"

"That someone would convert my bed into a robot that would fight other bed robots to the death for me."

That startles a laugh out of me. "That would be pretty awesome."

A slow, shy smile spreads across his mouth. "And we could take bets on them. And be filthy rich."

I lean my head against the frame of the stall, looking at the tile wall and the pattern of yellowed cracks there, and grin. "I take back anything I might have implied to the contrary. Sam, you *are* a genius."

I'm not good at having friends. I mean, I can make myself useful to people. I can fit in. I get invited to parties and I can sit at any table I want in the cafeteria.

But actually trusting someone when they have nothing to gain from me just doesn't make sense.

All friendships are negotiations of power.

Like, okay, Philip has this best friend, Anton. Anton is Lila's cousin; he came down to Carney with her in the summers. Anton and Philip spent three heat-soaked months drinking whatever liquor they could get out of the locals and working on their cars.

Anton's mother is Zacharov's sister Eva, making him Zacharov's closest living male relative. Anton made sure that Philip knew that if Philip wanted to work for the family, that meant he was going to be working for Anton. Their friendship was—and is—based on Philip's acknowledgment that Anton's in charge and Philip's ready to follow his lead.

Anton didn't like me because my friendship with Lila seemed to come without acknowledgment of his status.

One time, when we were thirteen, he walked into Lila's grandmother's kitchen. Lila and I were wrestling over some dumb thing, banging into the cabinets and laughing. He pulled me off her and knocked me to the floor.

"Apologize, you little pervert," he said.

It was true that all the pushing and shoving was mostly an excuse to touch Lila, but I'd rather get kicked around than admit it.

"Stop it!" she screamed at Anton, grabbing for his gloved hands.

"Your father sent me down here to keep an eye on you," he said. "He wouldn't want you spending all your time with this deviant. He's not even one of us."

"You don't tell me what to do," Lila told him. "Ever."

He looked back down at me. "How about I tell *you* what to do, Cassel? Get down on your knees. That's how you're supposed to act in front of a laborer princess."

"Don't listen to him," Lila said stiffly. "Stand up."

I was starting to rise when he kicked me in my shoulder. I fell back onto my knees.

"Stop it!" she yelled.

"Good," he said. "Now why don't you kiss her foot? You know you want to."

"I said leave him alone, Anton," said Lila. "Why do you have to be such a jerk?"

"Kiss her foot," he said, "and I'll let you up." He was nineteen and huge. My shoulder hurt and my cheeks were already burning. I leaned forward and pressed my mouth to the top of Lila's sandaled foot. We'd been swimming earlier that day; her skin tasted like salt.

She jerked her leg back. Anton laughed.

"You think you're in charge already," she said, her voice trembling. "You think Dad's going to make you his heir, but I'm his daughter. Me. I'm his heir. And when I am the head of the Zacharov family, I won't forget this."

I stood up slowly and walked back to Grandad's house.

She wouldn't talk to me for weeks after, probably because I'd done what Anton told me instead of what she'd said. And Philip went on like nothing had happened. Like he'd already chosen who he cared more about, already chosen power over me.

I can't trust the people I care about not to hurt me. And I'm not sure I can trust myself not to hurt them, either.

Friendships suck.

I look at the clock on my phone on my way to the car and figure that I better head home if I want my grandfather not to notice how long I've been gone. But I have one more stop to make. On my way out to the car, I call Maura. She's the final ingredient in my plan: someone to answer the prepaid phone if it rings.

"Hello?" she says softly. I hear the baby crying in the background.

"Hey," I say, and let out my breath. I was worried Philip would answer. "It's Cassel. You busy?"

"Just trying to clean some peaches off the wall. You looking for your brother? He's—"

"No," I say, maybe a little too fast. "I have to ask for a favor. From you. It would really help me out."

"Okay," she says.

"All you have to do is answer a cell phone I'm going to give you and pretend that you're the receptionist at a sleep center. I'll write down exactly what you have to say."

"Let me guess. I have to say that you can go back to school."

"Nothing like that. Just confirm the office sent over a letter and that the doctor is with a patient but he'll call them back. Then call me and I'll handle the rest. I don't think it will even come to that. They might want to verify the office really sent out the letter, but that's probably it."

"Aren't you too young to be living a life of crime?"

I smile. "Then you'll do it?"

"Sure. Bring over the phone. Philip isn't going to be back for an hour. I'm assuming that you don't want him to know about this."

I grin. She sounds so normal that it's hard to recall a sunken-eyed Maura perched at the top of the stairs, talking about angels. "Maura, you are a goddess. I will carve your likeness in mashed potatoes so all can worship you like I do. When you leave Philip, will you marry me?"

She laughs. "You better not let Philip hear you say that."

"Yeah," I say. "Are you still? I mean, does he know?"

"Know about what?"

"Oh," I say awkwardly. "The other night. You were talking about leaving—but, hey, I guess you guys worked things out. That's great."

"I never said that," Maura says, her voice flat. "Why would I say that when Philip and I are so happy?"

"I don't know. I probably misunderstood. I gotta go. I'll be over with the phone." I hang up, my hands slippery with sweat. I have no idea what just happened. Maybe she doesn't want to say anything over the phone, in case people are listening. Or maybe someone's there—someone she couldn't talk in front of.

I think of Grandad saying Philip was working her, and I wonder if *I* misunderstood. Maybe she really doesn't remember what she said, because he hired someone to take those memories from her. Maybe she doesn't remember lots of things.

Maura opens the door when I ring the bell, but only partway. She doesn't invite me in either. Unease roils in my stomach.

I look at her eyes, trying to read *something* from them, but she just looks blank, drained. "Thanks again for doing this." I hold out the phone, wrapped in a slip of paper with directions on it.

"It's fine." Her leather gloves brush mine as she picks up the cell, and I realize she's about to close the door. I stick my foot in the gap to stop her.

"Wait," I say. "Hold on a second."

She frowns.

"Do you remember the music?" I ask her.

She lets the door fall open, staring at me. "You hear it too? It started just this morning and it's so beautiful. Don't you think it's beautiful?"

"I've never heard anything like it," I say warily. She honestly doesn't remember. I can think of only one person who'd benefit from her forgetting to leave her husband.

I dig around in my pocket and take out the memory charm. *Give this to remember.* It looks like an heirloom, something that might be passed on to a favored daughter-in-law to welcome her to the family. "My mother wanted you to have this," I lie.

She shrinks back, and I remember that not everyone likes my mother. "Philip doesn't like me to wear charms," she says. "He says a worker's wife shouldn't look afraid."

"You can hide it," I say quickly, but the door's already closing.

"Take care of yourself," Maura says through the sliver of space that remains. "Good-bye, Cassel."

I stand on the steps for a few moments with the charm still in my hand, trying to think. Trying to remember.

Memory is slippery. It bends to our understanding of the world, twists to accommodate our prejudices. It is unreliable. Witnesses seldom remember the same things. They identify the wrong people. They give us the details of events that never happened. Memory is slippery, but my memories suddenly feel slipperier.

After Lila's parents divorced, she got dragged around Europe for a while, then spent several summers in New York with her father. I only knew where she was because her grandmother told my grandmother, so I was surprised to walk into the kitchen one day and see Lila there, sitting on the counter and talking to Barron like she'd never been gone.

"Hey," she said, cracking her gum. She'd cut her hair chin length and dyed it bright pink. That and thick eyeliner made her look older than thirteen. Older than me.

"Scram," said Barron. "We're talking business."

My throat felt tight, like swallowing might hurt. "Whatever." I picked up my Heinlein book and an apple and went back to the basement.

I sat staring at the television for a while as an anime guy with a very large sword hacked up a satisfying amount of monsters. I thought about how much I didn't care that Lila was back. After a while she came down the stairs and flopped onto the worn leather couch next to me. Her thumbs were stuck through holes in her mouse gray sweater, and I noticed a Band-Aid along the curve of her cheek.

"What do you want?" I asked.

"To see you. What do you think?" She gestured to my book. "Is that good?"

"If you like hot cloned assassins. And who doesn't?"

"Only crazy people," she said, and I couldn't help smiling. She told me a little about Paris, about the diamond her father had bid on and won at Sotheby's, which was supposed to have belonged to Rasputin and given him eternal life. About the way she'd had her breakfast on a balcony, drinking milky cups of coffee and eating bread slathered with sweet butter. She didn't sound like she'd missed south Jersey very much, and I couldn't blame her.

"So, what did Barron want?" I asked her.

"Nothing." She bit her lip as she pulled all that pink hair into a sleek, tight ponytail.

"Secret worker stuff," I said, waving my hands around to show how impressed I was. "Ooooh. Don't tell me. I might run to the cops."

She studied the warped yarn around her thumb. "He says it's simple. Just a couple of hours. And he promised me eternal devotion."

"That spends well," I said.

Worker stuff. I still don't know where they went or what she did, but when she got back, her hair was messed up and her lipstick was gone. We didn't talk about that, but we did watch a lot of black-and-white caper movies in the basement, and she let me smoke some of the unfiltered Gitanes she'd picked up in Paris.

Poisonous jealousy thrummed through my veins. I wanted to kill Barron.

I guess I settled for Lila.

CHAPTER SEVEN

I GET BACK TO THE OLD house in time for dinner, which turns out to be goulash of some kind, thick with noodles and dotted with slivers of carrot and pearl onions. I eat three plates and wash it all down with black coffee as the cat winds around my ankles. I hand her down all the beef I can nonchalantly pick out.

"How'd the doctor's visit go?" Grandad is drinking coffee too, and his hand shakes a little as he brings the cup to his lips. I wonder what else is in the cup.

"Fine," I say slowly. I don't want to tell him about the test or about Maura and her missing memories, but that leaves me with very little to say. "They hooked me up to a machine and wanted me to try and sleep."

"Right there in the office?"

That did sound pretty unlikely, but there's no backing down now. "I managed to doze a little. They were just trying to get some basic results. A baseline, he said."

"Hu-uh," Grandad says, and gets up to clear the dishes. "That must be why you were so late."

I pick up my plate and walk to the sink, saying nothing.

Later that night, when I'm covered with dust but most of the upstairs is clean, we watch *Band of the Banned*. On it, curse workers who belong to a secret FBI team use their powers to stop other workers, mostly drug dealers and serial killers.

"You want to know how to tell if someone's a worker?" Grandad asks with a grunt. He's saved the chair I hate and is sitting in it, his face lit with blue from the screen. The hero of the show, MacEldern, has just kicked down a door while an emotion worker makes the bad guys weep with remorse and begin a rambling confession. It's pretty lame, but Grandad won't let me change the station.

I look at the blackened stumps of my grandfather's fingers. "How?"

"He's the only one gonna deny he's got powers. Everyone else thinks they got something. They got some story about the one time they wished for a bad thing to happen to someone and it did, or wished for some moron to love them and got loved. Like every goddamn coincidence in the world is a working."

"Maybe they do have a little power," I say. "Maybe everyone does."

Grandad snorts. "Don't go believing that crap. You might not be a worker, but you come from a proud worker family. You're too smart to sound like—wasshisname—who said that if kids took enough LSD, they'd unlock their powers."

One in a thousand people is a worker, and of all of them, 60 percent are luck workers. People just want to game the odds. Grandad should understand that.

"Timothy Leary," I say.

"Yeah, well, see how that turned out. All those kids trying to give each other the touch, winding up half out of their heads, imagining they'd worked and been worked, imagining they were dying from blowback, clawing each other apart. The sixties and seventies were stupid decades, full of misinformation and crazy rock stars trying to be prophets, pretending to be workers. You know how many workers were hired just to do the work Fabulous Freddie said he did alone?"

There's no point in trying to distract Grandad from his rants once he's gotten started. He loves them way too much to bother realizing I've heard them about a million times before. The best I can hope for is to push him toward some new rant. "You ever get hired by one of them? You would have been, what, twenty-, thirtysomething back then?"

"I did what old man Zacharov said, didn't I? No freelancing. Know some people who did, though." He laughs. "Like a guy who toured with Black Hole Band. Physical worker. Really good. Someone pissed off the band, that someone'd be in traction."

"I would have thought emotion work would be more popular." Despite myself I'm drawn in. Usually when he delivers this speech, I feel like he's giving it to the rest of the family and I'm just overhearing it. This time we're alone. And I think of all the stuff I've seen photos of on the Internet or on VH1 specials from back then. Performers with goat heads, mermaids who danced in tanks until they drowned because the transformer hadn't known what she was doing when she'd cursed them, people remade like cartoons with big heads and huge eyes. All turning out to be the work of a single transformation worker who died of an overdose in her hotel room, surrounded by worked animals that stood on two legs and spoke gibberish.

There aren't any transformation workers for bands to hire to do any of that today, even if it was legal. There might be one in China, but no one's heard about him for a long time.

"Well, no one can work a crowd. Too many people. There was this one kid who tried. He figured what the heck; he'd ride out the blowback. He'd let a whole crowd of people touch him, one after another, and make them feel euphoric. Like he was a drug."

"So the blowback would be euphoric too, right? Where's the harm in that?"

The white cat jumps onto the couch next to me and starts shredding the cushions with her claws.

"See, that's the problem with kids—that's how you all think. Like you're immortal. Like all the stupid things you're doing, no one ever thought of before. He went crazy. Sure, drooling, grinning, happy crazy, but crazy all the same. He's the son of one of the bigwigs in the Brennan family, so at least they can afford to take care of him."

Grandad goes off again on his rant about the dumbness of kids in general and worker kids in specific. I reach over to pet the cat and it quiets under my hand, not purring, just going still as stone.

Before I go to bed that night, I root through the medicine cabinet. I take two sleeping pills and fall asleep with the cat at my elbow.

I don't dream.

Someone's shaking me. "Hey, sleepyhead, get up."

Grandad hands me a cup of too strong coffee, but this morning I'm grateful for it. My head feels like it's packed with sand.

I reach for my pants and pull them on. My hands automatically tuck in the pockets, but halfway through the gesture I realize something's missing. The amulet. Mom's amulet. The one I tried to give Maura.

Remember.

I go down on my knees and crawl under the bed. Dust, paperback novels I haven't seen in years, and twenty-three cents.

"What are you looking for?" Grandad asks me.

"Nothing," I say.

*   *   *

When we were little, Mom would stand Philip and Barron and me next to each other and tell us that family was everything, that we were the only people we could really rely on. Then she would touch our shoulders with her bare hands, each in turn, and we would be suffused with love for one another, suffocated by love.

"Promise your brothers that you will love one another forever and ever and that you will do whatever you have to to protect one another. You will never hurt one another. You will never steal from one another. Family is the most important thing. There is no one who will love you like your family."

We would hug and cry and promise.

Emotion work fades over months and months, until a year later you feel silly about the stuff you did and said when you were worked, but you don't forget what it was like to be glutted with those emotions.

Those were the only times I've ever felt safe.

Still holding the coffee, I walk outside to clear my head. One foot in front of the other. The air is cold and clean, and I suck in lungfuls like a drowning man.

Things fall out of pockets, I tell myself, and figure that before I melt down completely, I should check the car. If it's there, wedged down in the seat or glittering on one of the floor mats, I am going to feel pretty stupid. I hope I get to feel stupid.

Impulsively I flip open my cell. There are a couple of missed calls from my mother—she must hate not being able to call me on a landline—but I ignore them and call Barron. I need someone to answer questions, someone I can trust not to protect me. The call goes right to voice mail. I stand there, hitting redial again and again, listening to the ringing. I don't know who else to phone. Finally it occurs to me that there might be a way to call his dorm room directly.

I phone the main number for Princeton. They can't seem to find his room, but I remember his roommate's name.

A girl picks up, her voice throaty and soft, like the phone woke her.

"Oh, hey," I say. "I'm looking for my brother Barron?"

"Barron doesn't go to school here anymore," she says.

"What?"

"He dropped out a couple of months into the year." She sounds impatient, no longer sleepy. "You're his brother? He left a bunch of his stuff, you know."

"He's forgetful." Barron *has* always been forgetful, but right now forgetting seems ominous. "I can pick up whatever he left."

"I already mailed it." She stops speaking abruptly, and I wonder what went on between the two of them. I can't imagine Barron dropping out of school because of a girl, but I can't imagine Barron dropping out of Princeton for any reason. "I got tired of him promising to come get it and never showing up. He never even gave me money for the postage."

My mind races. "The address you mailed all that stuff too—do you still have it?"

"Yeah. You sure you're his brother?"

"It's my fault I don't know where he is," I lie quickly.

"After dad died I was a real brat. We had a fight at the funeral and I wouldn't take any of his calls." I'm amazed when my voice hitches in the right place automatically.

"Oh," she says.

"Look, I just want to tell him how sorry I am," I say, further embroidering my tale. I don't know if I sound sorry. What I feel is a cold sort of dread.

I hear the rustling of papers along the line. "Do you have a pen?"

I write the address on my hand, thank her, and hang up as I walk back to the house. There I find my grandfather stacking up dozens of holiday cards he's pulling out from behind a dresser. Glitter dusts his gloves. It's odd how empty the rooms look stripped of junk. My footsteps echo.

"Hey," I say. "I need the car again."

"We still got the bedroom upstairs to do," he says. "Besides the porch and the parlor. And even the rooms that are done we got to box up."

I lift the phone and wave it slightly, like it's to blame. "The doctor needs me to go back for some more tests." Lie until even you believe it—that's the real secret of lying. The only way to have absolutely no tells.

Too bad I'm not quite there yet.

"I thought it might be something like that," he says with a deep sigh. I wait for him to call me out, to say that he's already talked to the doctor or that it's been clear to him from the start that I'm full of it. He doesn't say any of those things; he reaches into the pocket of his jacket and tosses me the keys.

My amulet isn't on the floor of Grandad's Buick or

stuck in the crease of the driver's seat, although I do find a crumpled-up take-out bag. I stop for gas and buy more coffee and three chocolate bars. While I wait for the guy to come back with my change, I program Barron's new address into the GPS on my phone. The place is in Trenton, on a street I've never been.

I don't have much more to go on than a hunch that all the weird things—my sleepwalking, Maura's contradictory memories, Barron's dropping out of school without telling anyone, even the missing amulet—are related.

But as my foot presses on the gas and the car speeds faster, I feel like for the first time in a long while I'm heading in the right direction.

Lila had her fourteenth birthday party at some big hotel of her father's in the city. It was the kind of thing where lots of workers got together, passed around envelopes that only theoretically had to do with the party, and talked about things that were better not overheard by the likes of me. Lila pulled me into her hotel room an hour before it was supposed to start. She had on a ton of glittery black makeup and an oversize shirt with a cartoon cat face on it. Her hair wasn't pink anymore; it was white blond and spiky.

"I hate this," she said, sitting down on the bed. Her hands were bare. "I hate parties."

"Maybe you could drown yourself in a bucket of champagne," I said amiably.

She ignored me. "Let's pierce each other's ears. I want to pierce your ears."

Her ears were already hung with tiny pearls. I bet if I scratched them against my teeth, they'd turn out to be real. She touched an earring self-consciously, like she could hear my thoughts. "I got these done with an ear gun when I was seven," she said. "My mom told me that she would give me ice cream if I didn't cry, but I cried anyway."

"And you want more holes because you think pain will distract you from all the annoying celebrating? Or because stabbing me will make you feel better?"

"Something like that." She smiled enigmatically, went into the bathroom, and came out with a wad of cotton balls and a safety pin. After setting them down on top of the minibar, she pulled out one of the tiny bottles of vodka. "Go get ice from the machine."

"Don't you have friends—I mean, not that we're not friends, but—"

"It's complicated," she said. "Jennifer hates me because of something Lorraine and Margot told her. They're always making up stuff. I don't want to talk about them. I want ice."

"You are kind of a bully," I said.

"I have to be able to order people around someday," she said, her gaze steady. "Like Dad does. Besides, you already knew I was a bully. You know me."

"What makes you think I even want my ears pierced?"

"Girls think pierced ears are hot. Besides, *I* know *you*, too. You like to be bullied."

"Maybe I did when I was nine," I said, but I took the bucket into the hall and brought it back full of ice.

She walked over to the dresser, hopped up, and pushed

a pile of CDs, underwear, and folded-up notes onto the floor.

"Come here," she said, her voice hushed, dramatic. "First you light the match, and then you run the pin through the flame. See?" Lila struck the match and twirled the pin in its fire. Her eyes shone. "It goes black and iridescent. Now it's sterile."

I pushed up the shaggy black mop of my hair and tilted my head like a willing sacrifice. The press of the ice made me shiver. Her legs were slightly apart and I had to stand between her knees to get close enough.

"Hold still," she said, her fingers cold on my skin. I watched melting ice running down her wrist to drip off her elbow. We both waited, quietly, as though this was a ceremonial rite. After a minute or so she dropped the cube and pressed the pin against my ear, slowly stabbing through.

"Ow!" I pulled away at the last moment.

She laughed. "Cassel! The pin's sticking half out of your ear."

"It *hurt*," I said, half in astonishment. But it wasn't that. It was too much sensation—the feel of her thighs holding me in place mixing with the sharp pain.

"You can hurt me worse if you want," she said, and pushed the pin through with a sudden, savage thrust. I sucked in my breath.

She slid off the dresser to fetch new ice for her own ear from the bucket. Her eyes were glittering. "Do mine up high. You're going to have to really press to get through the cartilage."

I ran a safety pin above a match and lined it up above the ear holes she already had. Lila bit her lip, but she didn't cry out, even though I saw her eyes water. She just dug her fingers into the corduroy striping of my pants as I pressed. The metal pin bent a little, and I wondered if I was going to be able to get it all the way through, when it suddenly went with an audible pop. She made a strangled sound, and I carefully closed the safety pin so that it hung like a fancy formal earring at the very top of her ear.

Then she dipped the cotton swabs in vodka to wipe away the blood and poured us a gagging shot apiece. Her hands were shaking.

"Happy birthday," I said.

I heard steps outside the door, but Lila didn't seem to notice them. Instead she leaned in. Her tongue was as hot as a match on my ear, and it made my body jerk in surprise. I was still trying to convince myself that it had really happened when she stuck out her tongue and showed me my own blood.

That was when the door opened and Lila's mother walked in. She cleared her throat, but Lila didn't step back. "What's going on in here? Why aren't you ready for your party?"

"I'll be fashionably late," Lila said, a smile threatening at the corners of her mouth.

"Have you been drinking?" Mrs. Zacharov looked at me like I was a stranger. "Get out."

I walked past Lila's mother and out the door.

The party was in full swing when I got there, full of

people I didn't know. I felt out of place as I stalked to my seat, and my ear throbbed like a second heart. Overcompensating, I tried to be funny in front of Lila's friends and wound up being so obnoxious that some boy she went to school with threw a punch at me in the men's room. I pushed him, and he gashed his head on one of the sinks.

The next day Barron told me he had asked Lila out. They'd started dating around the time I was being escorted from the hotel.

According to my GPS, Barron's new place is a row house on a street with cracked sidewalks and a few boarded-up apartment buildings. One of his front windows is missing most of its glass and is partially covered with duct tape. I open the screen door and knock on the cheap hollow-core door beyond. Paint flakes off on my hands.

I knock, wait, and knock again. There's no answer and no motorcycle parked nearby either. I don't see any lights on through the newspaper taped up in place of blinds.

There's a basic lock and a dead bolt on the door. Easy to get around. My driver's license slid through the gap unlocks the first. The dead bolt is trickier, but I get a wire from the trunk of the car, thread it through the keyhole, and rake it over the pins until they all stick at the right height. Luckily Barron hasn't upgraded to anything fancy. I turn the knob, pick up my license, and walk into the kitchen.

For a moment, looking at the laminate countertops, I think I've broken into the wrong house. Covering the white cabinets are sticky notes: "Notebook will tell you what you forgot," "Keys on hook," "Pay bills in cash," "You are Barron Sharpe," "Phone in jacket." A carton of milk sits open on the counter, its curdled contents gray with cigarette ash. Butts float on the surface. There's a pile of bills—mostly student loans—all of them unopened.

"You are Barron Sharpe" doesn't leave a lot of room for doubt.

His laptop and a pile of manila folders cover the card table in the center of the kitchen. I slump down on one of the chairs and glance over the files—legal briefs from my mother's appeal. He's made notes in ketchup red marker, and it finally occurs to me that this could be the reason he dropped out of school. He must be managing the case. That makes some sense, but not enough.

There's a composition notebook sitting under one of the folders, marked February to April. I flip it open, expecting to see more notes on the case, but it looks a lot like a diary. At the top of each page is a date, and beneath it is an obsessively detailed list of what Barron ate, who he talked to, how he was feeling—and then at the bottom, a bulleted list of things to be sure to remember. Today started:

March 19

Breakfast: Protein shake
Ran 1 mile
Upon waking, experienced slight lethargy and
soreness in muscles.

Wore: light green buttoned shirt, black cargo
pants, black shoes (Prada)

Mom continues to complain about the other inmates, how
much she's suffering without us, and her fear that, basically,
we're out of her control. She needs to realize that we're
grown up, but I don't know if she's ready for that. As we get
closer and closer to the trial, I worry more about what life's
going to be like when she comes home.

She says that she's enticed some millionaire and is pinning
a lot of her hopes on him. I have sent her clippings about
him. I'm worried about her getting herself in trouble again
and I honestly can't believe that this man has no idea who
she is—or that if he doesn't, that he's going to remain
ignorant. When she does get out of jail, she is going to have
to be more circumspect, something I'm sure she's not going
to be willing to do.

I can't remember faces from high school. I ran into
someone on the street who said he knew me. I told him
that I was Barron's twin and that I went to another school.
I must study the yearbook.

Philip is as tedious as ever. He acts as though he is
resolved to do what is necessary, but he isn't. It's not just
weakness but a continual romantic need to believe himself
manipulated against his will instead of admitting he wants
power and privilege. He sickens me more each day, but
Anton trusts him in a way that Anton will never really trust
me. But Anton believes I can deliver, and I doubt he can say
that about Philip.

Maybe the money we get will be enough to control Mom for a while. By the time this is over, Anton'll owe us everything.

The notes for today stop there, but glancing back over the past few weeks, I can see that he recorded random details, conversations, and feelings as though he expected to forget them. I open the laptop gingerly, not sure what other weirdness I'm going to discover, but it's set to sleep, with the page showing my YouTube debut.

The raw footage was taken with a cell phone, so the quality is grainy and I don't look like much more than a pale, shirtless blob, but I wince when I look like I'm losing my balance. I hear someone yell "jump" in the background, and the angle swings toward the crowd. In that moment I see her. A white shape near the scrubby bushes. The cat, licking her paw. The cat I was chasing in my dream. I stare at the video and stare at her, trying to make some sense of how a cat from my dream—a cat that looks a lot like the cat that has been sleeping at the foot of my bed—could have really been there that night.

I take the notebook off the table and flip to the day the video was uploaded.

March 15th

Breakfast: Egg whites
Ran 1 mile
Upon waking, felt fine. Clipped nose hair.

Wore: dark blue jeans (Monarchy), coat, blue
dress shirt (HUGO)

Logged into C's email and found video. Clearly shows L.
but no clues as to where she is now. C is at the old house,
but G there and keeping an eye on everything. P says he's
going to take care of it. This is all his fault.

Beware the ides of March. Some joke. I found her collar,
but no clue as to how she got out of it. P must have not
clipped it on correctly. I have to find a way to use this to
wedge P and A further apart.

I have to control the situation.

"Control" is underlined twice, the second line so heavy that
it ripped through the page.

I stare at the entry until the words blur in front of
me. C is Cassel—the video must have been of me up on
the roof. P must be Philip. A could be Anton, since Barron
mentioned him before. I blink at G for a moment and then
realize it's for our grandfather. But L? I immediately think
of Lila, even though it makes no sense.

I grab the laptop and play the video of me again,
frame by frame. We barely see any of the crowd; the
camera pans over people too fast to catch anything but
blurs. The only faces I can pick out belong to students.
No Lila. No dead girls. No one that doesn't belong. No
one wearing a collar.

The only thing in that video that could be wearing a collar is the cat.

Only you can undo the curse.

The thought is so absurd that it actually makes me grin.

I walk toward the bathroom to splash water on my face, but as I pass a door, the strong smell of ammonia stops me. It opens into a room, empty except for a metal cage that sits near the window. The hinged wire door is open. The newspaper stuffed into the cage and the wooden floor around it is stained with what, given the sharp smell and the yellowing, is probably cat piss. Thick crusted layers of it, like something was kept locked up for a long time and not cleaned up after.

I hold my breath and lean closer. Caught in a wire joint are a few short white hairs. I back out of the room.

Barron's losing his memories. So's Maura, and maybe me too. I don't remember the details of Lila's murder. I don't remember how I got onto the roof. I don't remember what happened to my memory charm.

Let's say someone is taking those memories. I don't think that's too much of a stretch.

Let's also say someone gave me that dream, the one where the cat was begging for help. If I were cursed to have it, that would mean someone had to touch me, hand to skin. The cat—the one that slept on my bed, the one near my dorm room in the video—did touch me.

So maybe the cat gave me the dream.

Of course, that's ridiculous. Cats are animals. They can no more perform curse work than they can perform a sonata or compose a villanelle.

Unless the cat was really a girl. A girl who was a dream worker. Lila.

Which would mean something far different—not just that some memories of murdering her were stolen from me. It would mean she's not dead.

CHAPTER EIGHT

IN BARRON'S BATHROOM the beige tile walls look too familiar, but like I'm seeing them from the wrong angle.

It's crazy, the idea of Lila being a cat. The idea that Barron had her locked up in his house all this time is even crazier. And the idea that I might not have killed Lila throws me so off balance that I don't know how to right myself.

I look in the mirror—staring at my face. Looking at the scraggly hair curling around my jaw and my ink-blot eyes, looking to see if I should be afraid. If I'm still a murderer. If I'm cracking up.

There's a dizzy sense of déjà vu as I glance at the reflection of the tub behind me. I stumble and barely catch myself.

I thrashed in the water and my hands turned to arms turned to starfish curling like snakes. Everything went wrong and I was coming apart and water closed over my head and—

More things I half-remember.

I turn and crouch on the floor, touching the tile near the tub faucet. I can almost recall my fingers reaching for the same handle, but then the memory goes surreal and dreamlike and my fingers become scrabbling black claws.

Animal fear, instinctual and horrible, overwhelms me. I have to get out of here—that's the only thing I can think. I head for the front door, barely smart enough to twist the knob so that the door locks behind me when it closes. I get into Grandad's car and sit for a moment, waiting to feel like a stupid kid running from some pretend ghost. I eat one of the candy bars while I wait. The chocolate tastes like dust, but I swallow it anyway.

I have to sort things out.

My memories are full of shadows, and no amount of chasing them around my head seems to make them any more substantial.

What I need is a worker. One that's going to give me answers without asking a lot of questions. One that can help me make these puzzle pieces fit together and show me the picture. I turn the ignition and head south.

The dirt mall on Route 9 is less a mall and more one big warehouse with aisles of individual shops separated by counters or curtains. Barron and I would get Philip or Grandad to drive us, and then we'd spend the day eating hog dogs and buying cheap knives to hide in our boots. Barron would complain about being stuck with me, but as soon as we got there, he'd disappear to chat up the girl who worked selling pickles out of vats.

The place doesn't look all that different from how it did then. Out front a woman stands by a barrel of pastel-colored baskets while a guy is trying to hawk a bunch of rabbit pelts. Three for five bucks.

Inside, the smells of fried food make my stomach growl. I head toward the back, past the eel-skin wallet stall and the place with the heavy silver rings and pewter dragons, toward the fortune-tellers with their velvet skirts and marked cards. They charge five dollars to say "You sometimes feel lonely, even in the company of others" or "You once experienced a tragic loss that has given you an unusual perceptiveness" or even "You are usually shy, but in the future you are going to find yourself the center of attention."

There are lots of little malls like these in Jersey, but this one's only twenty minutes from Carney. The fortune-tellers' real business is selling charms made by retired residents; a few workers even freelance their services out of the back. It's the best place to go for a little cheap curse work that's not directly related to the crime families. And the charms are a lot more reliable and varied than the kind you get from a regular mall or the gas station.

I walk up to a scarf-draped table. "Crooked Annie," I say, and the old woman smiles. One of her teeth is black with rot. She's wearing plastic and glass rings over her purple satin gloves, and she's got on several layers of dresses with tiny bells along the hem.

"I know you, Cassel Sharpe. How's your mother?"

Annie's been selling magic for longer than I've been alive. She's old school. Discreet. And with as little knowledge as I have, the one thing I'm sure of is that I can't afford to share it.

"Jail. Got caught working some rich guy."

Annie sighs. She's in the life, so she's not surprised or embarrassed for me, like people at school would be. She shifts her weight forward. "Out soon?"

I nod, although I'm not sure. Mom keeps saying she didn't do it (which I don't believe), that the evidence against her is prejudice and hand waving (which I sort of do believe), and that it will be overturned on the appeal that's been dragging on. "You miss your mother, don't you?"

I nod again, although I'm not sure about that, either. It's easier with her slightly removed, unable to upturn our lives at a moment's notice. From jail she's a benevolent, slightly crazy matriarch. At home she'd go back to being a despot.

"I need to buy a couple of charms. For memory. Good ones."

"What? You think I sell ones that are no good?"

I smile. "I know you do."

That turns her grin wicked. She pats my face with a satin-covered hand. I remember that I haven't shaved and that my cheeks are probably rough enough to catch the fabric, but she doesn't seem to mind. "Just like your brothers.

You know what they used to say about boys like you? Clever as the devil and twice as pretty."

It's kind of a ridiculous compliment, but it embarrasses me into looking at the floor. "I have some questions, too. About memory magic. Look, I know I'm not a worker, but I really need to know."

Annie pushes aside a worn pack of tarot cards. "Sit," she says, and rummages under the table, pulling out a large plastic toolbox. Inside it is an array of rocks. She pulls out a shining piece of onyx with a hole bored through the middle, and a chunk of cloudy pink crystal. "First things first. Here are the charms you're asking for."

Lots of really good amulets look like junk. These don't look so bad.

"I hate to ask," I say, sitting down backward on the hard metal folding chair. "But—"

"You want something fancier?"

I shake my head. "Just smaller."

She mutters under her breath and turns back to her stock. "Here, I've got this." She holds up a pebble, maybe a piece of driveway gravel.

"I'll take these," I say, pointing to the pebble and the onyx circle. "In fact, give me three of the little ones if you've got them. Plus the onyx."

Annie raises her eyebrows but says only, "Forty. Each."

Normally I would dicker with her, but I figure she's inflating the cost so she can justify giving me the information. I pull out the bills and slide them over.

She grins her black-toothed grin. "So, what do you want to know?"

"How can you tell if your memories have been changed? Is there just a black hole in your thoughts? Can memories be replaced with other memories?"

She lights a hand-rolled cigarette that stinks of green tea leaves. "I'm not admitting to knowing anybody when I answer this. I'm just speculating, you understand? All I do is I make some of these amulets and I sell a few that my friends make, and the government hasn't managed to make that illegal yet."

"Sure," I say, affronted. "Just because I'm not—"

"Don't get your nose in a twist. I'm not explaining for you. I'm explaining it for the edification of anyone who happens to be listening in on this conversation. And they do."

"Who does?"

She gives me a long look, like I'm slow, and sucks on her cigarette, blowing herbal smoke into the air. "The government."

"Oh," I say. Even though I'm pretty sure she's just paranoid, possibly with a touch of dementia, I feel an intense urge to look behind me.

"On to your questions. How it feels depends on who did the working. The best workers make it seamless. They'll remove a memory and replace it with a new one. The worst ones are slobs. They might be able to make you remember you owe them money, but if there's no money in your pocket and you don't remember spending any either, you're going to start asking questions.

"Most memory workers fall somewhere in the middle in terms of skill. They leave behind pieces, threads. A blue sky without the rest of a day. Aching sorrow with no cause."

"Clues," I say.

"Sure, if you want to call them that." She takes another long drag on her tea cigarette. "There's four different kinds of memory curses. A memory worker can rip memories right out of your head, leaving that big hole you're talking about, or they can give you new memories of things that never happened. They can sift through your memories and learn stuff, or they can simply block your access to your own memories."

"Why would they do that last one? The blocking access one?" I touch the smooth black circle of the memory stone. It glides against the pad of my gloved finger.

"Because it's easier to block access than to remove a memory entirely, which makes it cheaper. Just like changing a single piece of a memory is easier than creating a whole new one. And if you remove the block, then the memory comes back, which is nice if you want to be able to reverse the process."

I nod my head, although I'm not sure I'm following.

"A shady memory worker will charge for ripping a memory but just put a block in. Then he'll go and charge the victim to take the block back out again. That's bad business, but what do these kids know? They've got no respect anymore." She looks at me intently. "Your family never told you any of this?"

"I'm not a worker," I remind her, but shame heats my

face. I should know; my family should have trusted me enough. That they didn't speaks volumes about what they think of me.

"But your brother—," she says.

"Can it be reversed?" I ask, interrupting her. I really don't want to talk about my family right now.

She looks at me so intently that I drop my gaze. Then she clears her throat and starts talking like I wasn't just incredibly rude. "Memory magic's permanent. But that doesn't mean people can't change their minds. You can make someone remember that you're the hottest thing out there, but they can take a good look at you and decide otherwise."

I force a smile, but my stomach feels like I've swallowed lead. "What about transformation work?"

She shrugs her shoulders. The bells on her skirts jingle. "What about it?"

"Is it permanent too?"

"Another transformation worker can undo it, so long as the person was turned into a living thing. A changer can turn a boy into a boat and then back to a boy, but the kid won't live through the transformation. Once a living thing becomes a nonliving thing, that's that."

That's that. I want to ask her about a girl changed into a cat, but I can't risk being that specific. I've risked enough.

"Thanks," I say, standing. I'm not sure what I learned, except that the answers I need aren't going to be easy to get.

She winks. "You tell that grandfather of yours that Crooked Annie was asking after him."

"I will," I say, although I know I won't. If I told him I was down near Carney, he'd want to know why.

I start down the aisle when I remember something and turn back. "Hey, is Mrs. Z still living in town?"

Lila's mother. I think of how I hung up the pay phone at the sound of her voice, about the way she looked at me when she found me in the hotel room at Lila's birthday party.

How for years I thought she saw some secret darkness in me that even I hadn't seen.

"Sure is," Annie says. "Can't leave Carney, or that husband of hers is going to come after her."

"Come after her?"

"He thinks she knows where that daughter of theirs got to and won't tell him. I told her not to worry. She'll outlast him. Even the Resurrection Diamond can't work forever."

"That stone he got in Paris with Lila?" I remembered the diamond had something to do with Rasputin, but I didn't remember that it had a name.

"Supposed to hold a curse so that the wearer never dies. Sounds like a load of crap, right? That would mean a stone could do more than deflect curses. But it seems to work. No one's killed him yet, and plenty of people have tried. I'd love to have a look at it." She tilts her head to the side. "You were in love with his girl Lila, huh? Now that I think of it, I remember you mooning after her. You and that brother of yours."

"That was a long time ago."

She leans up to kiss my cheek, which startles me into flinching. "Two brothers in love with the same woman never goes well."

*   *   *

Barron dated lots of other girls while he dated Lila. Girls his age, girls that went to his school and had their own cars. Lila would call and ask for Barron, and I would tell some obvious sloppy lie that I hoped she saw through, but she always believed. Then we'd talk until either Barron came home in time to say good night to her or she fell asleep.

The worst times, though, were when he was home and he talked to her in a bored voice while he watched television.

"She's just a kid," he told me when I asked about her. "She's not my real girlfriend. Besides, she lives, like, two hours away."

"Why don't you dump her, then?" I thought about the sound of her breath on the phone, evening out into sleep. I didn't understand how he could want anyone more than her.

He grinned. "I don't want to hurt her feelings."

I slammed my hand down on the breakfast table. Stacks of plates and junk quivered. "You're just dating her because she's Zacharov's daughter."

His grin widened. "You don't know that. Maybe I'm dating her just to mess with you."

I wanted to tell her the truth about him, but then she'd have stopped calling.

The *yakuza* put pearls in their penises, one for every year they spend in jail. A guy makes a slit in the skin of his penis with a strip of bamboo and pushes the pearl inside. It must be spectacularly painful. I figured it couldn't be nearly as bad to shove three tiny pebbles under the skin of my leg.

In the backseat of Grandad's car I fold up the left leg of my jeans to my knee. I bought what I thought were the necessary supplies at the nearby mart, and now, in the parking lot, I dump them out of the plastic bag and onto the seat. First I shave a three-inch spot on my calf with a disposable razor and splash it clean with bottled water. It's slow going. The razor's cheap, and by the time I'm done, my skin is red and bleeding from tiny cuts.

I realize I don't have anything to mop up what's likely to be more blood than I expected. I take off my shirt and press it to the skin, ignoring the sting. I have a bottle of hydrogen peroxide to sterilize with, but I don't. Maybe I'll have the balls to use it at the end, but right now my leg is hurting enough.

Sliding a razor blade out of a box of them, I look guiltily out the window of the car. Families are walking through the lot, children pushed in the baskets of carts, men carrying trays of coffees. *Don't look*, I tell them silently, and slide the sharp edge over my leg.

It goes in so easily and with so little pain that it frightens me. I feel only a sharp sting and a cold strangeness move through my limbs. It even seems to trick my skin, because for a moment there's only a line on my leg where the flesh parts. Then blood blooms along the cut, first in spots, then welling up in a long strip of red.

Pushing in the pebbles is the agonizing part. It feels like I'm ripping off my own skin as I slide in the three pebbles, one for every year I thought I was a murderer. Each one hurts so much that I have to choke down nausea as I thread the needle, bend it, and give myself two terrible, sloppy, agonizing stitches.

I'm going to go home and get Lila and we're getting as far away as we can. Maybe we'll go to China and find someone to turn her back into a girl, maybe I'll take her to her father and try to explain. But we're going tonight.

I'm no further along in figuring out who the memory worker is than I was before the visit to Crooked Annie, but I'm more sure than ever that I've been worked. I'm guessing it's Anton, since obviously he and Philip and Barron are conspiring together. I thought Anton worked luck, but he might have messed up my head to think that. If he is the memory worker, he sure messed up Barron's.

And Philip just let it happen.

As I watch the hydrogen peroxide froth, I tell myself that it's okay to be light-headed now, okay for my hands to shake, because it's done. It's over. Nobody is going to be able to make me forget one single thing. Not ever again.

When I get out of the car in the driveway of the house, I notice the doors of the barn are open. I walk over and look inside. No traps. No cats. No eyes shining from the shadows.

I stand there, looking for a long moment, trying to understand what happened. Then I run to the house and yank open the door.

"Where are the cats?" I yell.

"Your brother called the animal shelter," Grandad says,

looking up from a pile of moth-eaten linens. "They came this afternoon."

"What about the white cat? My cat?"

"You know you couldn't keep her," he says. "Let her go to people that can take care of her."

"How could you do that? How could you let them take her?"

He reaches out his hand, but I step back.

"Which brother? Who called the shelter?" My voice is shaking with rage.

"You can't blame him," he says. "He was just trying to do right by this place. They were making a mess of the barn."

"Who was it?" I ask.

"Philip," he says with a defeated shrug of his shoulders. He's still talking, explaining something about how the cats being gone is a good thing, but I'm not listening.

I'm thinking about Barron and Maura and my stolen memories and the missing cat and how I'm going to make Philip pay for it. All of it. With interest.

CHAPTER NINE

I HATE WALKING INTO shelters. I hate the smell of urine, feces, food, and wet newsprint all tangled up together. I hate the desperate whining sound of animals, the endless crying from the cages, and the guilt at not being able to do anything for them. I'm already feeling a little crazy when I walk into the first shelter, and it takes me until the third to find her. The white cat.

She looks at me from the back of the cage. She's not howling or rubbing her face against the bars, like some of the other animals. She looks like a snake, ready to strike.

But she doesn't look like anything that was ever human.

"What are you?" I say. "Lila?"

That makes her stand up and come to the front of the bars. She meows once, plaintively. A shudder runs through me that's part terror and part revulsion.

A girl can't be a cat.

Unbidden the memory of the last time I saw Lila rises. I can smell the blood. I can feel the smile pulling at my mouth when I look down at her body. Even if that memory's false, it feels real. This—the idea that she's alive, that I can still save her—feels like playing pretend. Like lying to myself. Like losing my mind.

Her mismatched green and blue eyes are very like Lila's, though. And she's looking up at me. And even though I might be going crazy, even though it feels impossible, I'm certain it's her.

I turn, and she yowls again and again, but I make myself ignore her and walk out of the animal housing area. I go up to the desk, where a heavyset woman in a schnauzer-print sweatshirt is telling some guy where to hang flyers promising a reward for his missing ball python.

"I'd like to adopt the white cat," I tell her.

She slides me a form. It asks me for the name and address of my veterinarian, how long I've lived at my current address, and whether I approve of declawing. I put down the answers that I think they want to hear and I leave the vet part blank. My hands are shaking and I feel the way I did after my father's car accident, when time seemed to move differently for me than for other people. It's too fast and too slow, and all I can think is that if I walk out of here with the cat, then I'll be able to sit and wait for time to catch up with itself again.

"This is your birthday?" she asks me, tapping the paper. I nod.

"You're only seventeen." She points to where it says in bold print at the top of the page: *Must be 18 to adopt.* I just stare at the words. Normally I pay attention to things like that. I prepare. Map out the variables. But instead I'm sucking air like a fish.

"You don't understand," I say, and I watch a frown pinch her brows. "That didn't come out right. That's my cat—I mean, the one I wanted to adopt. Someone must have brought her here, but she's really mine."

"She didn't come in with a collar," she says. "Or tags."

I laugh uneasily, caught. "She's always catching it on something."

"Kid, that cat was a stray living in a barn. It came in only a couple of hours ago, and if someone was feeding it, they weren't feeding it much or for long."

"She was living in a barn," I say. "But now she lives with me."

The woman shakes her head. "I don't know what happened, but I can guess. You didn't get permission to bring that cat home and your parents sent it to a shelter. Irresponsible—"

"That's not what happened." I wonder what she'd do if I told her what I thought *had* happened. I almost laugh.

The bell in the front jingles as a couple with a kid walk in the door. The schnauzer-shirted woman turns toward them with a smile.

"We're here to get a puppy!" shouts the little girl. All around her mouth looks sticky. Her gloves are smeared with brown stains.

"Wait," I say desperately. "Please."

The woman gives me a quick, pitying look. "Come back when you convince one of your parents to give you permission. Like this kid."

I take a deep breath. "Are you working here tomorrow?" I ask her.

She puts a hand on her hip, annoyed now, probably more angry because she briefly felt sorry for me, but I don't care. "No, but the guy on tomorrow is gonna tell you the same thing. Get a parent."

I nod, but I'm not really listening anymore, because my head is full of the sound of Lila shrieking from behind bars. Crying and crying with no one coming.

My dad taught me this trick to calm down. Like, before I was going into a house to steal something or if the police were questioning me. He said to imagine that I was on a beach and concentrate on the sounds of clear blue water lapping at my feet. The feel of the sand beneath toes. Take deep breaths of sea air.

It doesn't work.

Sam picks up on the second ring. "I'm at play practice," he says in a near-whisper. "Stavrakis is giving me the stink eye. Talk fast."

I have very little to offer Sam. I'm trusting him despite

myself, and I know trust isn't worth much. I don't even know if he'll want it. "I really need your help."

"Are you okay? You sound serious."

I make myself laugh. "I have to spring a cat out of the Rumelt Animal Shelter. Think of it as a prison break."

It does the trick. He laughs. "Whose cat?"

"My cat. What do you think? That I break out the cats of strangers?"

"Let me guess, she was framed. She's innocent."

"Just like everybody else in prison." I think of Mom. The laugh bubbles up my throat all wrong: sarcastic, harsh. "Good, so tomorrow?" I say, once I've managed to stop.

"Yeah, it's him," I hear Sam say, but his voice is smothered, like maybe his hand is over the phone. "You want to come?" He says something else, too, but I can't hear it.

"Sam!" I say, hitting my hand on the dashboard.

"Hey, Cassel." It's Daneca, talking softly. Daneca with her hemp and her causes and her never noticing that I avoid her. "What's all this about a cat? Sam says you need some help."

"I just need one person," I tell her. The last thing I want is to have to pull this off with Daneca looking over my shoulder.

"Sam says he could use a ride."

"What's wrong with his car?" Sam drives a hearse, which apparently are gas guzzlers, so to be environmentally responsible, he's converted it to run on grease. The inside of it always smells pleasantly of fried food.

"Not sure," she says.

I guess I don't have a lot of choices. I bite the inside of

my cheek and grate out the words. "That would be great, then. You're a real pal, Daneca."

I hang up the phone before I can be more obnoxious, my mind occupied with imagining how I can possibly pay the debt I am going to owe them. If all friendships are negotiations of power, I've totally lost this negotiation.

Grandad is furious when I get home. He starts yelling at me when I walk through the door. Stupid crap about taking the car without permission and how this is my house and I should be the one taking care of it. He has a lot to say about how old and infirm he is, which just makes me laugh, and me laughing makes him yell louder.

"Just *shut up!*" I shout, and walk up to my room.

He doesn't say a thing.

Let's go with the cat being Lila. Just for another minute, even if you think I've lost it. Just to try and figure some things out.

Someone made her that way.

And that someone is working with my brothers.

And that someone must be a transformation worker, which makes him (or her) one of the most powerful workers in America.

Which means I'm screwed. I can't fight that.

The Magritte poster taped above me shows the back of a well-groomed nineteenth-century man looking into the mirror on his mantle, but the reflection in the mirror is the well-groomed back of his head. When I bought it, I liked that you could never see the man's face, but now when I look at it, I wonder if he has one.

My phone rings at around ten that night. It's Sam, and when I pick it up, I can hear he's drunk.

"Come out," he says, manic and slurring. "I'm at a party."

"I'm tired," I say. I have been staring at the same cracked patch of plaster for hours. I don't feel like getting up.

"Come on," he says. "I wouldn't even be here if it wasn't for you."

I roll onto my side. "What do you mean?"

"These guys love me now that I'm their bookie." He laughs. "Gavin Perry just offered me a beer! You did this for me, man, and I'm not going to forget it. Tomorrow we're going to get back your cat, and then—"

"Okay. Where are you?" It's kind of funny that he thinks he owes me anything when he's been doing stuff for me left and right. I push myself off the bed.

After all, there's no point in staying here. All I'm doing is thinking of Lila as a cat, stuck in a cage and crying until her throat is raw, or wearing my own memories thin with scrutinizing.

He gives me an address. It's Zoe Papadopoulos's place. I've been there before. Her parents travel for their jobs, meaning that she hosts a lot of parties.

Grandad is asleep in front of the television. On the news I see Governor Patton, who has been a big proponent of proposition two, the thing that's supposed to force every-body to get tested to ascertain who's a worker and who's not. Patton is going on and on about how he believes that workers should come forward in support of his proposition so that they can let the world know that they are the good, law-abiding citizens they claim to be. He says no one ever needs to know what's on the paper, except the individual. At this time he has no plans to propose any legislation that gives the government access to those private medical records. Right.

Grandad snores.

I pick up the keys and go.

Zoe's house is in one of the new developments in Neshanic Station, on a stretch of several acres with woods attached. It's huge, and when I get there, the driveway is clogged with cars. The massive double doors are flung wide open, and there's a girl I don't know laughing hysterically on the front porch, leaning against a fat Corinthian column with a bottle of red wine in her hand.

"What are you celebrating?" I ask her.

"Celebrating," she repeats, like she doesn't understand the word. Then a slow smile lifts the corners of her mouth. "Life!"

I can't even force a smile in return. My skin itches to be elsewhere. To be breaking into the animal shelter. To be *doing something*. The wait is the worst part of the con, the long stretch of hours before things start to happen. That's when nerves get the best of people.

I walk inside, willing my nerves not to get the best of me.

The living room is lit with candles that have burned down, so that melting wax pools on furniture. Only a few kids are there, sitting on the floor and drinking beer. A sophomore says something, and they all look over at me.

It took two and a half years to get people to forget what was different about me, and only fifteen minutes to get them to remember. My puny and pathetic social life is about to get worse.

I give them a nod and wonder if Sam's at least taking bets on the rumors about me. He'd better.

In the kitchen a bunch of seniors are gathered around Harvey Silverman, who's downing a pyramid of shots. Outside, by the pool, I see most of the rest of the partygoers. It's too cold to swim, but a couple of fully clothed people are anyway, their lips blue in the patio lights.

"Cassel Sharpe," Audrey says, looping her arm through mine. "Look what the cat dragged in."

Audrey's eyes are glassy, her smile vague. She still looks lovely. She glances toward Greg Harmsford leaning against a bookshelf, talking with two girls from the field hockey team. I wonder if they came to the party together.

"Just like always," she says, looking back at me. "Watching from the shadows. Observing everybody. Judging us."

"That's not what I'm doing," I say. I don't know how to explain how afraid I am of being judged.

"I liked when you were my boyfriend," she says, and leans her head against my shoulder, maybe out of habit, maybe because she's drunk. It's enough like tenderness for me to pretend. "I liked you watching me."

I resist the urge to promise her that if she tells me all the things I did right, I'll do them again.

"Didn't you like it when I was your girlfriend?" she asks, her voice gone so soft that it's mostly breath.

"You're the one who broke it off," I tell her, but my voice has dropped low, and the words come out like a caress. I don't care about what I'm saying. I only care about keeping her here, talking with me. She makes me feel like it's possible to slip out of my old life and into hers, where everything is easy and honest.

"I'm not over you," she says. "I don't think."

"Oh," I say, and then I lean in and kiss her. *I don't think. Don't think.* I just mash my mouth against hers. She tastes like tequila. It's an awful kiss, too full of grief and frustration and the knowledge that I am screwing everything up and don't know how to do anything but screw things up worse.

She reaches up her hands and touches my shoulders gently. She doesn't push me away. Her fingers curl against the nape of my neck, which tickles a little and makes me smile against her lips. I slow down. Better. She sighs into my mouth.

I let my fingers trace her collarbone, dip into the hollow of her neck. I want to kiss her there. I want to let my mouth and tongue follow the road map of freckles across her milky skin.

"Hey," Greg says. "Get off her."

Audrey stumbles back, nearly into Greg. I feel like I've come up out of such deep water that I have the bends. I forgot that we're at a party.

"You're drunk," Greg tells her, and grabs hold of her upper arm. Audrey sways a little unsteadily.

My fingers curl into fists. I want to shove him against the wall. I want to break open my knuckles on his face. I look at Audrey for a signal. I tell myself that if she looks scared or even angry, I am going to hurt him.

She's looking down, though, her face turned away from me. All that rage curdles into self-loathing.

"What are you even doing here?" Greg says. "I thought the dean finally figured out that you're a criminal and kicked you out."

"I didn't think this was an official school-sponsored event," I say.

"Nobody wants you around, working their girlfriends." His smile is smug. "You and I both know that's the only way you can get a date."

I think of Maura, and my sight narrows. It's like I'm looking at Greg through a tunnel of blackness. My fists clench so tightly that I can feel my nails through the leather of my gloves. I hit him, hard, sending him sprawling on the wooden floor. My foot is digging into his ribs before Rahul Pathak grabs me around the waist and pulls me away from him.

"Chill out, Sharpe," Rahul says, but I struggle against his hold. All I want to do is kick Greg again. Someone I can't see grabs my wrist and twists it behind me.

Audrey's gone.

Greg stands up, wiping his mouth. "I saw your mother's trial in the paper, Sharpe. I know you're just like her."

"If I was, I would make you beg to blow me," I sneer.

"Get him outside," someone says, and Rahul steers me

toward the door. The swimmers look up when we march through. Several people sitting on chaises rise, like they're hoping for a fight.

I try to pull my way out of the guys' grip, and when they let me go, I don't expect it. I drop onto the grass.

"What got into you?" Rahul says. He's breathing hard.

I look up at the stars. "Sorry," I say.

The other person holding me turned out to be Kevin Ford. He's short but built. A wrestler. He's watching me like he hopes I try something.

"Be chill," Rahul says. "This isn't like you, man."

"I guess I forgot myself," I say. I forgot that I didn't belong, that I would never belong. That I had charmed my way into being their bookie but that I was never their friend. I forgot the delicate foundation my excuse for a social life was built on.

Kevin and Rahul walk back to the house. Kevin says something, too low for me to hear, and Rahul snickers.

I look up at the stars again. No one ever taught me the constellations, so to me they are all just bright dots. Chaos. No pattern at all. When I was a kid, I made up a constellation, but I couldn't find it a second time.

Someone shuffles through the grass to loom over me, blotting out the chaotic stars. For a moment I think it might be Audrey. It's Sam. "There you are," he says.

I get up slowly as Sam turns, stumbles, and pukes in the hydrangea bush near the kitchen window. Some girls on lounge chairs start to laugh.

"I'm glad you're here," Sam says when he's done, "but I think you better drive me home."

*   *   *

I get him coffee at a drive-through fast-food place and mix in a lot of sugar. I figure it will help him sober up, but he vomits most of it onto the asphalt of the parking lot. He washes his mouth out with the rest.

I turn on the radio and we sit there listening to it as his stomach gurgles. Another song about being worked by love. Like it's romantic to be brainwashed.

"I used to pretend I was a worker when I was a kid," he says.

"Everyone does," I tell him.

"Even you?"

"Especially me." I offer him the other cup of coffee. It's mine and I've left it black, but there might be more packets of sugar somewhere. He shakes his head.

"How does anyone find out they're a worker? When did you know you weren't?"

"I'm sure it was the same with you. Our parents told us not to mess around with working. My mom went so far as to tell us that kids who did work before they were grown-up could die from the blowback."

"That's not true?"

I shrug. "Only way it kills you outright is if you're a very unlucky-with-blowback death worker, and even then it doesn't matter how old you are. But my brothers knew when they were pretty young. Barron won stuff by other people losing, you know? And Philip was always doing too well in a fight." I remember Mom getting called into the junior high when Philip had broken the legs of three guys much bigger than he was. The blowback made him sick for a month, but no one ever messed with him again. I don't know how she managed it, but no one reported him to the law, either. I try to think of an example with Barron in it, but nothing comes to mind. "Once you find out you're a worker, you learn secret stuff from other workers. I can't tell you that part because I don't know it."

"Are you supposed to tell me *any* of that?"

"Nope," I say, turning on the car. "But you're so drunk that I'm pretty sure you won't remember anyway."

Somewhere between apologizing to Mrs. Yu for bringing Sam home so late, dumping him onto his bed, and backing out of the driveway of his huge brick colonial, I realize something.

If Lila is a cat, then there's a transformation worker here in the United States. I knew that before, but I hadn't really thought about what it meant. The government would fall all over itself to hire him. The crime families would be desperate to recruit her. That's what they're conspiring about. If Philip knows who that person is, the memory work makes sense.

They've got a real transformation worker.

That's something worth making me forget.

CHAPTER TEN

SAM AND DANECA MEET
me outside the coffeehouse. They're sitting on the hood of
his 1978 vintage Cadillac Superior side-loading hearse in
the parking lot, and Sam looks awful, taking tons of tiny
sips from his cup like he's got the shakes. The car is perfectly polished; its waxed metallic black paint is marred
only by the sticker reading POWERED BY 100% VEGETABLE
OIL pasted just above the chrome bumper. Sam's wearing a
suit jacket over a white shirt with a tie, but the jacket is too
short in the arms, as if maybe it's been in the back of his
closet for a long time.

Daneca looks strange out of uniform. Her jeans are

worn along the bottom, above her thin flip-flops, but her white shirt is perfectly ironed.

"I see your car is out of the shop," I say to Sam.

He looks confused. "My car's—"

Daneca talks over him. "I thought I'd come along anyway, since I already said I would."

I take a deep breath and wipe my damp palms against my pants. I'm too nervous to care that they lied. "I really appreciate you guys giving up your Saturday to help me," I say, turning over a new leaf of gentlemanly behavior.

"So, what's the deal with this cat?" Daneca asks.

"It's a family friend," I say, hoping they'll laugh.

Sam looks up from his cup. I can see the shimmer of sweat on his face. He looks massively hungover. "I thought you said the cat was yours."

"Well, it is. It was. It was mine." I am confusing myself. I am forgetting the basics of lying. Keep it simple. The truth is complicated, which is why no one ever believes it over a halfway decent lie. "Here's what I need you to do—I guess you didn't get my text?"

"Am I not dressed rich enough?" Sam asks, leaning back so that we can appreciate the full glory of his suit. "Don't be drinking the Haterade."

"You look crazy," I say, shaking my head. "Like a crazy valet. Or a waiter."

He looks over at Daneca, and she bursts out laughing. "Is that why you're dressed like that?"

Sam flops back on the car. "This is so not good for my ego."

"Daneca can do it," I say. "Daneca looks the part."

"Humiliation on top of humiliation," Sam groans. "Daneca looks rich because she is rich."

"So are you," she tells him, which makes him put his sunglasses over his eyes and groan again. Sam's parents own a string of car dealerships, which makes it ironic that he both drives a hearse and opposes big oil.

"It won't be hard," I tell her, trying to push out of my head all the times I blew her off. "You're going to be a nice well-to-do girl who was supposed to be taking care of her grandmother's long-haired white cat. Its name is Coconut, but it has a longer show name that you don't know. The cat also had a Swarovski crystal collar worth thousands."

Sam sits up. "Your cat is a Persian? I love their little pushed-in faces. They always look so angry."

"No," I say as calmly as I can, even though I want to knock Sam in the head. "Not my cat. Her cat. Just let me finish."

"But she doesn't have a cat." He holds up his hands at my look. "Fine."

"First you go in looking for Coconut, but then you ask if they have *any* fluffy white cats. You're desperate. Your grandmother is going to be home on Monday and she's going to kill you. You'll pay the person behind the desk five hundred bucks for any all-white fluffy cat—no questions asked." They're staring at me strangely. "There aren't any monitors on the desk, I checked."

"So then they give me the cat and I give them the money?" Daneca asks.

I shake my head. "No. They don't have a fluffy white cat. Our cat is a shorthair."

"Dude, I think your plan has a flaw," Sam says slowly.

"Trust me," I tell them, and smile my biggest, charm-ingest smile.

Daneca goes over to the Rumelt Animal Shelter and comes back, looking a little shaken.

"How did it go?" I ask.

"I don't know," she says, and for a moment I'm furious that I couldn't have played her part too. I am furious that her parents haven't taught her how to lie and cheat prop-erly, so that now I am betrayed by her inexperience.

"Was there a woman there?" I ask, biting the inside of my mouth.

"No, it was a skinny guy. In his twenties, I'd guess."

"What did he say when you talked about the money? Or the collar?"

"Nothing," she said. "He didn't have any fluffy white cats. I don't know if I did it right. I was just so freaked out."

"It's okay." I take her hand. "Freaked out is good. You just lost Granny's Coconut. Anyone would be freaked out. Just tell me you gave him your number."

"That was the only time he seemed interested in what I was saying." She laughs. "Now what?"

I shrug my shoulders. "Now we wait. Next part can't happen for an hour—at least." I look over at Daneca, and she gives me the same look she gave me when I refused to sign up for any of her causes. The look that said I'd betrayed who she thought I should be. But she doesn't take her gloved hand out of mine.

"Is that when I get to do my part?" Sam asks. I'm sick with nerves. This part is delicate and if it doesn't work, my only backup plan is recruiting homeless guys to try and adopt the cat.

"I can handle it," I say.

He gives me a hurt look. "I want to come watch you work your magic."

I feel bad for dragging him out here on a Saturday for no reason. "Okay," I say finally. "Just follow my lead."

We wait an hour and a half, drinking coffee and hot chocolate until my skin feels jumpy. Finally I take a bracelet out of a Claire's bag, put it in my pocket, and pull out a bunch of flyers from my bag. Daneca's eating a package of chocolate-covered coffee beans and looking at me strangely. I wonder if I can ever go back to Wallingford or if I've already revealed too much of myself.

I wonder if I should tell her that her part's over and she can go home, but if I was going to tell her that, I should have told her more than an hour ago, so I decide that I better not do it now.

"What are those for?" Sam asks, pointing to the flyers.

"You'll see," I say. We cross the highway, which involves running across two lanes of traffic when the light changes, and then walk down a side street until we get to the shelter. There's a lot of people there on a Saturday, most of them in a cat room where giant carpet-covered trees are perched upon by dozens and dozens of hissing, dozing, and clawing felines. I feel my heart drop when I see that Lila is not in there. The possibility that she's been taken home with a family already stutters my heart.

Lila.

I'm not pretending or considering anymore when I think it.

The white cat is Lila.

Sam looks at me like he's just realized that I have no idea what I'm doing. I clear my throat. The guy at the desk looks up. His face is a mess of pimples.

"Hey, can I hang this here?" I say, and hold up a flyer.

It's on bright white paper, and there's a photograph I downloaded off the Internet of the cutest fluffy white Persian cat I could find without a collar. A dead ringer for our description of Coconut. Above it is the word "FOUND" and then a phone number. I put the flyer on the desk in front of the guy.

"Sure," he says.

He's a perfect mark. Young enough to want the money and the glory of helping out a pretty girl. I'm suddenly very glad Daneca decided to be part of the plan.

I start tacking another copy to the board, praying that in the chaos the desk guy looks at the flyer I left for him. An older woman starts asking him about a pit bull mix, distracting him. Sam is fidgeting next to me like he has no idea what's going on. I drop the copy as if it's an accident and pick it up again.

Finally the woman leaves.

"Thanks for letting me post this," I say to get the guy's attention, and he finally looks down at the flyer. I can see the gears move behind his eyes.

"Hey, you found this cat?" he says.

"Yeah," I say. "I'm hoping to keep her." People love to help. It makes them feel good. Greed is the icing on the cake. "My little sister is super excited. She's been wanting a cat for a while."

Sam gives me a look when I say "super." He's probably right; I need to tone it down.

I slip my hand into my pocket and take out the bracelet. It shines in the fluorescent lights. "Look at this gaudy collar." I laugh. "Who puts a cat in something like this?"

"I think I might know the owner," the guy says slowly. His eyes sparkle like the stones.

As convincers go, I've seen worse.

"Man, my sister's going to be disappointed." I take a breath, let it out again. "Well, tell your friend to call me."

This is the moment of truth, and when I look into the face of the mark at the counter, I can tell that I've got him. He's probably not a bad guy, but that five hundred dollars is quite a lure. Plus the collar.

Plus, he'd have an excuse to call Daneca.

"Wait," he says. "Maybe you could bring the cat here. I'm sure I know the owner. The cat's name is Coconut."

I turn toward the door and then back to him. "I was stupid to tell my sister, but now she's all excited and—well, I don't suppose you have a white cat here? All I told her about it was the color."

He looks eager. "We do. Sure."

I let out my breath. I'm not faking the relief that I know floods my face. "Oh, great. I'd love to have a white cat to take home to her."

He grins. Like I said, people love to help, especially when they can help themselves in doing so.

"Cool," I say. "Let me fill out the paperwork and we'll take the cat. Your friend's fluffy kitty is at this guy's house, so we'll go get her and bring her right to you." I gesture toward Sam.

"The thing's probably giving fleas to my mother's couch," Sam says, which is perfect. I wish I could tell him that, but all I can do is give him a grateful glance.

The mark hands me the form, and this time I know what to do. I write down my age as nineteen, specify a veterinarian, and make up a name that's not even close to my own.

"Do you have any ID?" he asks.

"Sure," I say, and reach into my back pocket for my wallet. I flip it open and touch the place where driver's licenses go. Mine's not there.

"Oh, *man*," I say. "This isn't my day."

"Where'd you leave it?" the guy asks.

I shake my head. "No idea. Look, I totally understand if that breaks the rules or whatever. I have one other place to hang up fliers, then I'll go look for my license. Maybe your friend can give me a call and I can just drop the cat with her. My sister will understand."

The guy gives me a long evaluating look.

"You have the adoption fee?" he asks.

I look down at the paper, but I already know what it says. "Fifty bucks, sure."

The door rings, and some people walk through it, but the man behind the desk keeps his eyes on me. He licks his lips.

I take out the cash and set it down on the counter in

front of him. I've blown through a chunk of my savings in the last few days, between bad bets and spending. I'm going to have to be careful if Lila and I wind up living on the rest.

"Okay, I'll hook you up," the mark says, taking the money.

"Oh," I say. "Cool. Thanks." I know better than to over-play it.

"So, this long-haired cat," Sam says, and I freeze, willing him not to stick his foot in it. He's looking at the guy behind the counter. "Do you need to call your friend or anything?"

"I will," he says, and I can see the red creeping up his neck. "I want to surprise her."

A woman walks up to the desk, a filled out form clutched in her hand. She looks impatient. I have to push.

"Can we take the cat now?" I ask. I put the bracelet down on the counter. "Oh, your friend will probably want her collar back too."

He looks at the woman and then at me. Then his hand closes over the bracelet and he heads into the back and comes back a few minutes later swinging a cardboard pet carrier.

My hand shakes when I take it. Sam grins at me in amazement, but all I can think of is that I have her. I did it. She's right here in my hands. I look through the air holes and I can see her, prowling back and forth. Lila. A cold jolt of terror runs through me at the wrongness of her impris-oned in that tiny body.

"Be back in an hour," I tell the guy, hoping I never see him again.

I hate this part.

I always hate the part where I know they are going to wait, their hope souring into shame at their own gullibility.

But I clench my jaw, take the cat carrier with Lila in it, and walk out the door.

When I open it up in the parking lot of the coffeehouse, the first thing she does is bite me hard on the heel of my hand. The next thing she does is purr.

Mom says that because she can make people feel what she wants them to, she knows how they think. She says that if I was like her, I'd have the instinct too. Maybe being a worker tempts you to be all mystical, but I think mom knows about people because she watches faces very closely. There're these looks people get that last less than a second—micro-expressions, they call them, fleeting clues that reveal a lot more than we wish. I think my mother sees those without even noticing. I see them too.

Like, walking back toward the coffee shop with the cat in my arms, I can tell that Sam is freaked out by the con, by his part in it, by my planning it. I can tell. No matter how much he smiles.

I'm not my mother, though. I'm no emotion worker. Knowing that he's freaked out doesn't help me. I can't make him feel any different.

I dump the cat onto one of the café tables and grab some napkins to wipe the blood off my wrist. My hand's throbbing. Daneca is smiling down at the cat like she's a full set of Gorham silver recently fallen off a truck.

Lila cries, and the barista looks over from behind the espresso machine. The cat cries again, then takes a lick of the foam on the edge of Daneca's paper cup.

I just stare at Lila the cat, utterly incapable of doing more than smothering the strange keening sound that's crawling up the back of my throat.

"Don't," Daneca says, waving the cat off. The cat hisses and then slumps down on the tabletop. She starts licking her leg.

"You won't believe how he did it," Sam tells Daneca, leaning forward eagerly.

I look at the barista, at the other customers, and then back at him. Everyone's already paying us too much attention. The cat starts chewing on the end of a claw.

"Sam," I say, cautioning.

"You know, Sharpe," he says, looking at me and then around. "You've got some interesting skills. And some interesting paranoia."

I smile in acknowledgment of his words, but it hurts. I've been so careful not to let anyone at school see the other side of me, to see what I am, and now I've blown that in a half hour.

Daneca tilts her head. "It's sweet. All this trouble for a kitty." She brushes the top of the cat's head, rubbing behind her ears.

My cell rings in my pocket, vibrating. I stand up, dropping the bloody napkins into the trash can, and answer the phone. "Hey."

"You better get over here with my car," Grandad says. "Before I call the cops and tell them you stole it."

"Sorry," I say contritely. Then the rest of what he said sinks in and I laugh. "Wait, did you just threaten me with calling the police? Because that I'd like to see."

Grandad grunts, and I think maybe he's laughing too. "Drive on over to Philip's—he wants to have some kind of dinner with us. He says Maura's going to cook. You think she's a good cook?"

"How about I pick up a pizza?" I say, looking at the cat. She's rubbing against Daneca's hand. "Let's just chill out at the house." I don't think I'm ready to see Philip and not spit in his face.

"Too late, you little slacker. He already picked me up and you're my ride home, so get your ass over to your brother's apartment."

I start to say something back, but the line goes dead.

"You in trouble?" Sam asks. The way he says it, I wonder if he's thinking about how to get out of here if I am.

I shake my head. "Family dinner. I'm late." I want to tell them how grateful I am, how sorry I feel that they had to get dragged into my mess, but none of it's true. I'm just sorry for myself. Sorry that now they know something I didn't want them to. I wish I could make them forget. For a moment I understand that memory working impulse right down to my bones.

"Uh," I say. "Can either one of you hold on to the cat for a few hours?"

Sam groans. "Come on, Sharpe. What's really going on here?"

"I'll take her," Daneca volunteers. "On one condition."

"Maybe I could keep her in the car," I say. Mostly I want to stare into her strange cat eyes and look at her tiny paws and ask her if she's Lila. Even though I've already decided. I want to decide again.

"You can't keep a *cat* in a *car*," she says. "She'll get too hot."

"Of course. You're right." I smile, but it feels like a rictus. Then I shake my head, like I'm trying to shake off my expression. I'm way off my stride. I'm rattled. "Could you hold on to her overnight?"

The cat growls deep in her throat.

"Trust me," I say to the cat. "I have a plan." Daneca and Sam look at me like I've lost my mind.

I don't want to be away from her, but I'm going to need a little time to get the rest of my money out of the library and get a hold of a car. Then we can leave town. That's the only way she's going to stay safe.

Daneca shrugs. "I guess, but I'm going to the dorm tonight. My parents have some conference, so they're driving up to Vermont after dinner. My roommate's not allergic or anything, though, and I'm pretty sure we'll be able to hide her. I think it will be okay."

Lila hisses, but I get up anyway, imagining them having a sleepover party together. I wonder what kind of dreams Daneca is going to have.

"Thanks," I say mechanically. My mind is racing with plans.

"Wait," she says. "I told you there was a condition."

"Oh," I say. "Sure."

"I want you to give me a ride home."

"I can—," Sam starts.

Daneca interrupts him. "No, I need Cassel to take me. And to agree to come in the house for a minute."

I sigh. I know her mother wants to talk to me, probably because she thinks that I'm a worker refusing to join the cause. "I don't have time. I have to get to my brother's place."

"You have time," Daneca says. "I said just a minute."

I sigh again. "Okay, fine."

Daneca's house is just off the main street in Princeton, an elegant old brick Colonial with green and amber hydrangeas framing the front walk. It stinks of old money, of the kind of education that allows the elite to stay that way, and of intimidating privilege. I have never even broken into a house like that.

Daneca, of course, goes inside like it's nothing. She drops her book bag in the entryway, sets down the cat carrier on the polished wood floor, and heads down a hallway filled with old etchings of the human brain.

The cat cries softly from her cage.

"Mom," Daneca calls. *"Mom."*

I stop in the dining room, where a blue and white vase filled with only slightly wilted flowers rests on a polished table, between silver candlesticks.

My fingers itch to shove those candlesticks in my bag.

I look back toward the hall, instinctively, and see a blond boy—he looks like he's around twelve—standing on the stairs. He's watching me like he knows I'm a thief.

"Uh, hi," I say. "You must be Daneca's brother."

"Screw you," the kid says, and walks back up the stairs.

"In here," Daneca's mom calls, and I head in that direction. Daneca's waiting for me near a half-open door to a room filled to its high ceilings with books. Mrs. Wasserman sits on a small sofa near a desk.

"Get lost?" Daneca asks me.

"It's a big house," I say.

"Well, bring him in," Mrs. Wasserman says, and Daneca ushers me inside. She flops down onto her mother's wooden desk chair and spins it a little with one of her toes.

I am left to perch on the edge of a brown leather ottoman.

"It's nice to meet you," I say.

"Really?" Mrs. Wasserman has a whole mess of light brown curly hair that she doesn't seem to bother corralling. Her bare feet are tucked up under a soft-looking oatmeal throw. "I'm glad. I heard that you were a little bit wary of us."

"I don't want to disappoint you, but I'm not a worker," I tell her. "I thought maybe there was some misunderstanding."

"Do you know where the term 'worker' comes from?" she asks, leaning forward, ignoring my floundering.

"*Working* magic?" I ask.

"It's much more modern than that," she says. "Long, long ago, we were called theurgists. But from about the seventeenth century until the 1930s, we were called dab hands. The term 'worker' comes from the work camps. When the ban was passed, no one knew how to actually enforce it, so people waited for prosecution in labor camps. It took the government a long time to figure out how to conduct a trial. Some people waited years. That's where the crime families started—in those camps. They started recruiting. The ban created organized crime as we know it.

"In Australia, for instance, where working has never been illegal, there is no real syndicate with the kind of power our crime families have. And in Europe the families are so entrenched that they are practically a second royalty."

"Some people think workers are royalty," I say, thinking of my mother. "And Australia never made curse work illegal because it was founded by curse workers—or dab hands or whatever—who'd been sent to a penal colony."

"You do know your history, but I want you to look at something." Mrs. Wasserman places a stack of large black-and-white photos in front of me. Men and women with their hands cut off, balancing bowls on their heads. "This is what used to happen to workers all over the world—and still does in some places. People talk about how workers abused their power, about how they were the real power behind thrones, kingmakers, but you have to understand that most workers were in small villages. Many still are. And violence against them isn't taken seriously."

She's right about that. Hard to take violence seriously when workers are the ones with all the advantages. I look at the pictures again. My eyes keep stopping on the brutal, jagged flesh, healed dark and probably burned.

She sees me staring.

"The surprising thing," she says, "is that some of them have learned to work with their feet."

"Really?" I look up at her.

She smiles. "If more people knew that, I don't know if gloves would be as popular. Wearing gloves goes back as far as the Byzantine Empire. Back then people wore them to protect themselves from what they called *the touch*. They believed that demons walked among people and their touch brought chaos and terror. Back then workers were thought to be demons who could be bargained with for great rewards. If you had a worker baby, it was because a demon had gotten inside of it. Justinian the first—the emperor—took all those babies and raised them in an enormous tower to be an unstoppable demon army."

"Why are you telling me this? I know workers have been thought of lots of different idiotic ways."

"Because Zacharov and those other heads of crime families are doing the same thing. Their people hang around bus stations in the big cities waiting for the runaways. They give them a place to stay and a few little jobs, and before they know it, they're like the Byzantine child-demons, in so much debt that they might as well be prisoners or prostitutes."

"We have a boy staying with us," Daneca says. "Chris. His parents threw him out."

I think of the blond boy on the stairs.

Mrs. Wasserman gives Daneca a stern look. "That's Chris's story to tell."

"I have to get going," I say, standing. I'm uncomfortable; I feel like my skin is too tight. I have to get out of this conversation.

"I want you to know that when you're ready, I can help you," she says. "You could save a lot of boys from towers."

"I'm not who you think I am," I say. "I'm not a worker."

"You don't have to be," Mrs. Wasserman says. "You know things, Cassel. Things that could help people like Chris."

"I'll walk you out," says Daneca.

I head toward the door quickly. I have to get away. I feel like I can't breathe. "That's okay. I'll see you tomorrow," I mumble.

CHAPTER ELEVEN

THE RICH ODOR OF garlicky lamb hits me when I open the door to Philip and Maura's apartment. Despite giving me all that crap about getting right over, Grandad is asleep in a recliner with a glass of red wine resting on his stomach, cradled in the loose grip of his left hand and tipping slightly toward his chest. On the television in front of him some fundie preacher is talking about workers coming forward and volunteering to get tested, so people can touch hands in friendship, ungloved. He says that all people are sinners and power is too tempting. Workers will give in eventually if they're not kept in check.

I'm not sure he's wrong, except about all that hand touching with strangers, which sounds gross.

I hear the clink of plates as Philip walks out of the kitchen. I flinch at the sight of him. It's like having some kind of surreal double vision. Philip my brother. Philip who's probably stealing Barron's and my memories.

"You're late," he says.

"What's the occasion?" I ask. "Maura's going all out."

Barron comes out behind Philip, holding two more glasses of wine. He looks thinner than the last time I saw him. His eyes are bloodshot and his lawyer-short hair looks grown out, shaggy, curling. "She's freaking. Keeps saying she's never thrown a dinner party before. You better get back in there, Philip."

I want to feel sorry for him, thinking of all those crazy notes to himself, but all I can see is the small steel cage on a floor made sticky with layers of piss. All I can imagine is him turning up his music to drown out Lila's crying.

Philip throws up his hands. "Maura always makes a big deal out of nothing." He heads back toward the kitchen.

"So why are we doing this?" I ask Barron.

He smiles. "Mom's appeal is almost over. We're just waiting for a verdict. It's happening."

"Mom's getting out?" I take the glass from his hand and drink the wine in a gulp. It's wrong that the first feeling I have is panic. Mom getting out of jail means her back in our lives, meddling. It means chaos.

Then I remember I'm not going to be here. On the drive over I gave up on the idea of getting a car. Tomorrow I'm going to use one of the school computers to book a train headed south.

Barron looks over at Grandad and then back at me. "Depends on the verdict, but I'm pretty optimistic. I asked a couple of my professors, and they thought there was no way she wouldn't win. They said she had one of the best cases they'd ever seen. I've been doing work on the case as an independent study, so my professors have been involved too."

"Great," I say, half-listening. I'm wondering if I can afford a sleeper car.

Grandad opens his eyes, and I realize he wasn't passed out after all. "Stop with all that crap, Barron. Cassel's too smart to believe you. Anyway, your mother's getting out and—God willing—should be happy to come home to someplace clean. Kid's been doing nice work."

Maura ducks her head out from the other room. "Oh, you're here," she says. She's got on a pink tracksuit. I can see her collarbones jutting out just above the zipper on her hoodie. "Good. Sit down. I think we're ready to eat."

Barron heads into the kitchen, and when I start to follow, Grandad grabs my arm. "What's going on?"

"What do you mean?" I ask.

"I know something's going on with you boys, and I want to know what it is." I can smell the wine on his breath, but he looks perfectly lucid.

I want to tell him, but I can't. He's a loyal guy, and it's hard for me to picture him having a hand in the kidnapping of his boss's daughter, but my lack of imagination isn't a good enough reason for trust.

"Nothing," I say, roll my eyes, and go sit down for dinner.

Maura spread a white tablecloth over the kitchen table and added a couple of folding chairs. On it are the silver candlesticks that a guy that goes by Uncle Monopoly gave Philip at his wedding, ones I'm pretty sure were stolen. The lit tapers make everything look better, mostly by throwing the rest of the kitchen into shadows. A lamb roast with slivers of garlic sticking out from the meat like bits of bone rests on a platter beside a bowl of roasted carrots and parsnips. Grandad drinks most of the wine out of a glass that Barron keeps refilling, but there's enough for me to feel pleasantly tipsy. Even the baby seems happy to bang a silver rattle against his tray and smear his face with mashed potatoes.

I recognize the plates we're eating off too. I helped Mom steal those.

Looking at the mirror in the hall, it's like I'm watching us all in a fun house glass, a parody of a family gathering. Look at us celebrating our criminal enterprises. Look at us laugh. Look at us lie.

Maura is just bringing out coffee when the phone rings. Philip gets up and comes back a few minutes later, holding it out to me.

"Mom," he says.

I take it from him and walk back into the living room. "Congratulations," I say into the receiver.

"You've been avoiding my calls." Mom sounds amused rather than annoyed. "Your grandfather said you were feeling better. He says that boys who feel better don't call their mothers. That true?"

"I'm tip top," I tell her. "The peak of health."

"Mmm-hmm. And you've been sleeping well?"

"In my own bed, even," I say cheerfully.

"Funny," she says. I can hear the long exhalation that tells me she's smoking. "That's good, I suppose, that you can still be funny."

"Sorry," I say again. "I've got a lot on my mind."

"Your grandfather said that, too. He said you were thinking a lot about a certain someone. Thinking leads to talking, Cassel. Other people were there for you back then. Be there for them and forget about her."

"What if I can't?" I ask. I don't know what she knows or whose side she's on, but some childish part of me wants to believe she'd help me if she could.

There is a moment's hesitation. "She's gone, baby. You've got to stop letting her have power over—"

"Mom," I say, interrupting her. I'm walking farther from the kitchen, until I stand near the picture window in the living room, close to the front door. "What kind of worker is Anton?"

Her voice drops low. "Anton is Zacharov's nephew, his heir. You stay away from him and let your brothers look out for you."

"Is he a memory worker? Just tell me that. Say yes or no."

"Put Philip back on the phone."

"Mom," I say again, "please. Tell me. I might not be a worker, but I'm still your son. Please."

"Put your brother back on the phone, Cassel. *Right now.*"

For a moment I consider hanging up. Then I consider

chucking the phone against the floor until it breaks. Neither option will give me anything but satisfaction.

I walk through the house and put the phone down next to Philip's plate of pie.

"In my day," Grandad says. He's in the middle of one of his speeches. "In my day workers were still respected. We kept the peace in neighborhoods. It was illegal, sure, but the cops looked the other way if they knew what was good for them."

He's clearly drunk.

Barron and Grandad go into the living room to watch television, while Philip talks to Mom on the extension in the loft. Maura stands at the sink, scraping food into the whirring garbage disposal. She scrubs a pot, and her lips draw back from her gums like a dog before it bites.

I want to tell her about the missing memories, but I don't know how to do it without pissing her off.

"Dinner was good," I say finally.

She spins around, relaxing her features into some pleasant and vague expression. "I burned the carrots."

I put my hands in my pockets, fidgeting. "Tasty."

She frowns. "Do you need something, Cassel?"

"I wanted to thank you. For helping me out the other day."

"And lying to your school?" she asks with a sly smile, drying the pot. "They haven't called yet."

"They will." I pick up another dish towel and start mopping the water off a knife. "Don't you have a dishwasher?"

"It dulls the blade," she says, taking it from me and sliding it into a drawer. "And the pot had too much gunk stuck on the bottom. Some things you still have to do by hand."

I set the rag down on the counter with sudden decision. "I have something for you." I walk out to where my jacket is hanging and reach into the inside pocket.

"Hey, come sit down," Barron calls.

"In a second," I say, walking quickly back to the kitchen.

"Look," I say to Maura, holding out my hand to show her the onyx charm. "I know what you said about a worker's wife and being—"

"Very thoughtful of you," she says. The stone shines under the recessed lights like a spilled droplet of tar. "Just like your brother. You don't understand favors, just exchanges."

"Get a needle and sew it into your bra," I tell her. "Promise?"

"Charming." She tilts her head. "You look like him, you know. My husband."

"I guess," I say. "We're brothers."

"You're handsome with all that messy black hair. And your crooked smile." They're compliments, but she doesn't sound complimentary. "Do you practice smiling like that?"

Sometimes in intense situations I can't help grinning a little. "My smile's naturally crooked."

"You're not as charming as you think you are," she says, walking up to me, so close that her breath is warm and sour on my face. I take a step back, and my legs bang against the edge of her counter. "You're not as charming as him."

"Okay," I say. "Just promise me that you'll wear it."

"Why?" she asks. "What kind of amulet is so important?"

I glance at the doorway. I can hear the television in the other room, some game show Grandad likes.

"A memory charm," I say softly. "It's better than it looks. Say that you'll wear it."

"Okay."

I try a smile, as non-crooked as I can make it. "We non-workers have got to stick together."

"What do you mean?" She narrows her eyes. "Do you think I'm stupid? You're one of them. I remember *that*."

I shake my head, but don't know what to say. Maybe it's better if I wait for the charm to show her the truth before I try to argue with her over things that don't matter anyway.

"Grandad's passed out," Barron says when I walk into the living room. "Looks like you're going to have to stay over. I don't think I'm going anywhere either." He yawns.

"I can drive him," I say. I feel suffocated by all the things I can't say, about all the things I suspect my brothers of doing. I want to get home and start packing.

"What did you tell Mom?" he asks. He's drinking black coffee from one of Maura's good cups, the kind with a saucer. "It's taking him a while to calm her down."

"Just that she knows something she's not telling me," I say.

"Come on, if we had a dollar for everything Mom never told us, we'd have a million bucks."

"I'd have a lot more money than you would." I sit down on the couch. I can't just leave without at least trying to warn him. "Can I ask you something?"

Barron turns toward me. "Sure. Shoot."

"Do you remember when we were kids and we went to the beach down by Carney? There were toads in the scrub brush. You caught a really tiny one that jumped out of your hands. I squeezed mine until it puked up its guts. I thought it was dead, but then when we left it alone for a moment, it disappeared. Like it sucked in its guts and hopped away. Do you remember that?"

"Yeah," Barron says, with a shrug of his shoulders. "Why?"

"How about when you and Philip got all those *Playboy* magazines out of the Dumpster and you cut out all the breasts and covered a lamp shade with them. And then it caught on fire and you gave me five dollars to lie to Mom and Dad about it?"

He laughs. "Who could forget that?"

"Okay. How about when you smoked all that weed that you thought was laced with something? You fell in the tub, but you refused to get out because you were convinced the back of your head was going to fall off. The only thing that would calm you down was reading out loud, so I read the only book in the bathroom—one of Mom's romances, called *The Windflower*, cover to cover."

"Why are you asking me about this?"

"Do you remember?"

"Sure, yeah, I remember. You read the whole book. It

was easy to clean up the blood once I got out. Now, what's with the interrogation?"

"None of those things happened," I tell him. "Not to you. You weren't there for the toad thing. My roommate told me the story about the boob lamp fire. *He* paid *his* little sister to lie. The third story happened to a guy Jace in my dorm. Sadly, no one had *The Windflower* on hand. Me and Sam and another guy on our hall took turns reading *Paradise Lost* through the locked door. I think it actually made him more paranoid, though."

"That's not true," he says.

"Well, he *seemed* more paranoid to me," I say. "And he still gets a little weird at the mention of angels."

"You think you're so funny." Barron sits up straighter. "I was just playing along, trying to figure out what your game was. You can't play me, Cassel."

"I did play you," I say. "You're losing your memories and you're trying to cover it up. I've lost memories too."

He gives me a strange look. "You mean about Lila."

"That's ancient history," I say.

He looks over at Grandad again. "I remember you were obviously jealous that I was dating her. You had a crush or something and you were always trying to get me to dump her. One day I walk into Grandad's basement and she's lying on the floor. You're standing over her with this stunned expression on your face." I suspect he's telling this story just to needle me, just to get me back for embarrassing him.

"And a knife," I say. It bothers me that the thing I most remember—my horrible smile—is absent from his telling.

"Right. A knife. You said you didn't remember anything, but it was obvious what happened." He shakes his head. "Philip was terrified that Zacharov would find out, but blood's thicker than water. We covered up for you—hid her body. Lied."

There's something wrong with the way he's describing the memory. It's like he's remembering a few lines from a textbook about a battle instead of actually remembering a battle. No one would really say blood's thicker than water when their memory should be full of smeared, clotted redness.

"You loved her, right?" I ask him.

He makes a gesture—a wave of his hands—that I can't interpret. "She was really special." A grin lifts a side of his mouth. "You certainly thought so."

He must have known what was in the cage in his spare room, what was crying and eating whatever he gave her and soiling his floor. "I guess it's true what they say—I have loved too much not to hate."

Barron tilts his head. "What do you mean?"

"It's a quote. From Racine. Also, you may have heard, there's a thin line between love and hate."

"So you killed her because you loved her too much? Or aren't we talking about you and her anymore?"

"I don't know," I say. "I'm just talking. I want you to be careful—"

I stop as Philip comes into the doorway.

"I just got off the phone with Mom," he says. "I need to talk to Cassel. Alone."

Barron glances at Philip and then back at me. "So, what is it you suspect is going on? You know, that I should be careful about."

I shrug my shoulders. "I'd be the last to know."

Philip leads me back to the kitchen and sits down at the table, folding his hands on the stained white cloth. Around him are a few remaining plates and several mostly empty wineglasses. He picks up a bottle of Maker's Mark and fills one of the used coffee cups with amber liquor. "Sit down."

I sit, and he regards me silently.

"What's with all the grimness?" I say, but my fingers reach down unconsciously to rub the spot where the pebbles rest under my skin. The soreness is reassuring and as addictive as touching the tip of my tongue to the raw socket of a recently lost tooth. "I must have really upset Mom."

"I have no idea what you think you know," Philip says. "But you have to understand that all I've been trying to do—all I've ever tried to do is protect you. I want you to be safe."

What a line. I shake my head, but don't contradict him. "Okay, then. What are you protecting me from?"

"Yourself," he says and now he looks me in the eye. For a moment I see the thug that people are afraid of—jaw clenched, hair shadowing his face. But after all these years, at least he's finally looking at me.

"Get over *yourself*," I say. "I'm a big kid."

"Things are tough without Dad," he says. "Law school

isn't cheap. Wallingford isn't cheap. Mom's legal bills alone are staggering. Grandad had some savings, but we burned through that. I've had to step up. And I'm doing the best I can. I want us to have things, Cassel. I want my son to have things." He takes another slug from the cup and then laughs to himself. His eyes shine when he looks over at me, and I wonder just how much liquor he's already had. Enough to get him pretty unwound.

"Okay," I say.

"That means taking some risks. What if I told you there was something I needed you for?" Philip says. "Something Barron and I both need your help with." I think of Lila in my dream, asking for help. The overlay of the memories is dizzying.

"Do you need my help?" I ask.

"I need you to trust us," Philip says, tilting his head to one side and giving me that superior older brother smile. He thinks he's teaching me a lesson.

"I should be able to trust my own brothers, right?" I ask. I think I manage to say it without sarcasm.

"Good," he says. There's something sad and tired in the sag of his shoulders, something that seems less like cruelty and more like resignation. It makes me unsure of my conclusions. I think of us being kids all together and how much I loved it when Philip paid me any attention—even the kind of attention that came in the form of an order. I loved to scramble to get a beer out of the fridge for him and pop the top like a bartender, then grin at him, waiting for the offhanded nod of acknowledgment.

And here I am, trying to find a way where he isn't the villain. Looking for the nod. All because he finally looked me in the eye.

"Things are going to be different for us real soon. Vastly different. We're not going to have to struggle." He makes a sweeping gesture that knocks over one of the wineglasses that Maura didn't clear. There's only a little bit of liquid in it, but it rushes over the white cloth in a tide of pink wetness. He doesn't seem to notice.

"What's going to be different?" I ask him.

"I can't tell you details," he says, and looks toward the living room. Then he stands up unsteadily. "For now, just don't rock the boat. And don't mess with Mom. Give me your word."

I sigh. The conversation is circular, pointless. He wants me to trust him, but he doesn't trust me. He wants me to obey him. "Yeah," I lie. "You've got my word. Family looks out for family. I get it."

As I stand up, I notice the wineglass he knocked over isn't as empty as I thought. Some kind of sediment remains at the bottom. I lean over and drag my finger through the sludge of sugar-like granules, trying to remember who was seated where.

Over Maura's protests and Barron's annoyed insistence, I half-carry Grandad out to the car. My heart beats like I'm in a fight as I turn down the offers to sleep in the study or on the sofa. I say I'm not tired. I invent an appointment Grandad has with a bingo playing widow in the morning.

Grandad is heavy and so drugged and drunk that he barely responds.

Philip drugged him. The reason eludes me, but I think of the sludge and I know Philip must have done it.

"You should just stay," Barron says for the millionth time.

"You're going to drop him," Philip says. "Careful."

"Then help me," I say, grunting.

Philip puts out his cigarette on the aluminum siding and slips his shoulder under Grandad's arm to lift him up.

"Just bring him back into the house," Barron says, and a look passes between them. Barron's frown deepens. "Cassel, how are you going to get him into the house on the other end if you need Philip's help getting him into the car?"

"He'll have sobered up some by then," I say.

"What if he doesn't?" Barron calls, but Philip walks toward the car door.

For a moment I think he's going to block my way, and I have no idea what I'll do if he does. He opens the door, though, and holds it while I heave Grandad inside and belt him in.

As I pull out of the driveway, I look back at Philip, Barron, and Maura. Relief floods me. I'm free. I'm nearly gone.

My phone rings, startling me. Grandad doesn't stir, even though it's loud; the sound is turned all the way up. I watch for the rise and fall of his chest to make sure he's still breathing.

"Hello?" I say, not even bothering to check who's calling. I wonder how far the hospital is and whether I should go.

Philip and Barron wouldn't kill Grandad. And if they were planning on killing him, Philip wouldn't poison him in his own kitchen. And if he did, he sure as hell wouldn't try and get me to put the body to bed in his guest room.

I repeat that thought to myself over and over.

"Can you hear me? It's Daneca," she says, whispering. "And Sam."

I don't know how long she's been speaking.

I look at the clock on the dashboard. "What's wrong? It's, like, three in the morning."

She tells me but I'm barely listening to her answer. My mind is going through all the possible things you can give someone to knock them out. Sleeping pills are the most obvious. They go great with booze too.

I realize the other end of the line is expectantly silent. "What?" I ask. "Can you say that again?"

"I said *your cat's disgusting*," she says slowly, clearly annoyed.

"Is she okay? Is the cat okay?"

Sam starts laughing. "The cat's fine, but there's a little brown mouse on Daneca's floor with its head ripped off. Your cat killed our mouse."

"Its tail looks like a piece of string," Daneca says.

"*The* mouse?" I ask. "The mouse of legend? The one everyone's been betting on for six months?"

"What happens if everybody loses a bet?" Sam asks. "Nobody got it right. Who the hell do we pay?"

"Who cares about that? What do *I* do?" Daneca says. "The cat is just staring at me, and I think there's blood on her mouth. I look at her and see the deaths of hundreds of mice and birds. I see them just lining up to march into her mouth along an unfurling carpet of tongue like in an old cartoon. I think she wants to eat me next."

"Pet the cat, dude," says Sam. "She brought you a present. She wants you to tell her how badass she is."

"You are a tiny, tiny killing machine," Daneca coos.

"What's she doing?" I ask.

"Purring!" says Daneca. She sounds delighted. "Good kitty. Who's an amazing killing machine? That's right! You are! You are a brutal, brutal tiny lion! Yes, you are."

Sam laughs so hard he chokes. "What is wrong with you? Seriously."

"She likes it," Daneca says.

"I hate to be the one to have to point this out to you," he says, "but she doesn't understand what you're saying."

"Maybe she does," I say. "Who can tell, right? She's purring."

"Whatever, dude. So, do we keep the money?"

"It's either that or release another mouse into the walls."

"Right, then," Sam says. "We keep the money."

I drive the rest of the way home, unbuckle Grandad, and shake him. When that doesn't work, I slap him in the face hard enough that he grunts and opens his eyes a little.

"Mary?" he says, which freaks me out because that's my grandmother's name and she's been gone a long time.

"Hold on to me," I say, but his legs are rubbery and he's not much help. We go slowly. I bring him right into the bathroom and let him slouch on the tiles while I mix up a cocktail of hydrogen peroxide and water.

When he starts puking, I figure that my Wallingford's AP chemistry class was good for something. I wonder if this would be a good argument to give Dean Wharton in favor of letting me back in.

CHAPTER TWELVE

"HEY, GET UP," SOMEONE is saying. I blink in confusion. I am lying on the downstairs couch and Philip's standing over me. "You sleep like the dead."

"If the dead snored," says Barron. "Hey, good job in here. The living room looks great. Cleaner than I've ever seen it."

Dread coils around my throat, choking me.

I look over at Grandad. He's still passed out in the reclining chair with a bucket next to him. Grandad was sick for hours, but he seemed fine by the time he fell asleep. Coherent. I would have thought all the noise would have woken him. "What did you give him?" I ask, throwing a leg out from under the afghan.

"He's fine," says Philip. "I promise. It will wear off by morning."

I am reassured by the rise and fall of Grandad's chest. As I watch him sleep for a moment I think I see his eyelids flicker.

"You always worry," Barron mumbles. "And we always tell you he's fine. They're always fine. Why do you worry so much?"

Philip shoots him a look. "Leave Cassel alone. Family looks out for family."

Barron laughs. "That's why he shouldn't worry. We're here to look after them both." He turns to me. "Better get ready fast, though, worrywart. You know how much Anton hates to wait."

I don't know what else to do, so I pull on my jeans and zip a hoodie over the T-shirt I slept in.

They seem totally comfortable waiting for me, so comfortable that, thinking over what Barron said, I come to the groggy conclusion that this has all happened before. They've gotten me out of this house—maybe my dorm—and I don't remember a thing. Have I ever panicked? I'm panicking now.

I grab my gloves and slide on a pair of work boots. My hands are trembling with adrenaline and fear—enough that I can barely get the gloves on.

"Let me see your pockets," Philip says.

"What?" I stop tying the laces to look up at him.

He sighs. "Turn them inside out."

I do, thinking of the stinging cut in my calf, the charms healing inside my skin. He rubs the pocket cloth, checking for something hidden in it, then pats down my clothes. My hands fist, and I want to take a swing at Philip so much that my arms ache from the strain of not hitting him. "Looking for a mint?"

"We need to know what you're bringing, is all," Philip says mildly.

Adrenaline has pushed back exhaustion. I'm wide awake and starting to get angry.

He looks at Barron, who reaches over for my arm. He's not wearing a glove.

I pull back. "Don't touch me!"

It's funny how instinct is; I keep my voice low when I say it. Because in some ridiculous part of my head this is still family business. It doesn't even occur to me to shout for help.

Barron holds up both his hands. "Hey, okay. But this is important. It takes a few minutes for the old memories to settle. Think back. We're in this together. We're on the same side."

That's when I realize they've already worked me. Before they woke me up. My skin crawls with horror and I have to take quick, shallow breaths to keep from running away from them, from the house. I nod, buying myself what time I can. I have no idea what memories they expect me to have.

I watch Barron pull his glove back on and flex his hand, stretching the leather.

I realize what a bare hand means.

Philip isn't the one behind the stolen memories. Anton's not the memory worker.

Barron is—he must be. He didn't lose his memories because he was worked; he's not absentminded. Every time he takes a memory from me or Maura or all the other people he must be stealing them from, he loses one of his own. Blowback. I search my memories for an occasion when he worked for luck, but there's nothing, just a dim sense that I know he's a luck worker. I can't even recall when I started "knowing" that.

Now that I focus on it, the memory doesn't even seem real. It slips away from me, like the blurred copy of a copy.

"You ready?" Philip asks.

I stand, but my legs are shaky. It's one thing to suspect my brother was working me, another to stand next to him once I know he's done it. *I'm the best con artist in this family*, I reassure myself. *I can lie. I can seem calm until I am calm.*

But another part of my mind is howling, rattling around and scraping for other false memories. I know it's impossible to look for what's not there, and yet I do, running through the last few days—weeks, years—in my mind, as though I will stumble in the gaps.

How much of my life has been reimagined by Barron? Panic chills my skin like a sickness.

We walk down the stairs of the house quietly, out to a Mercedes parked on the street with the headlights turned down and the engine humming. Anton's in the driver's seat. He looks older than the last time I saw him, and there's a scar that runs over the edge of his upper lip. It matches the keloid scar stretching across his neck.

"What took you so long?" Anton says, lighting a cigarette and throwing the match out the window.

Barron slides into the backseat next to me. "What's the rush? We've got all night. This one here doesn't have school in the morning." He musses my hair.

I shove away his gloved hand. The annoyance feels surreally familiar. It's like Barron thinks we're on a family car trip.

Philip gets into the passenger seat, looks back at us and grins.

I have to figure out what they think I know. I have to be smart. It sounds like they might believe some disorientation but not complete cluelessness. "What are we doing tonight?"

"We're going to rehearse for this Wednesday," Anton says. "For the assassination."

I'm sure I flinch. My heart hammers. Assassination?

"And then you're going to block the memory," I say, fighting to keep my voice steady. I remember what Crooked Annie said about blocking access to memories so that the block can be removed later and the memory loss reversed. I wonder if we've rehearsed before. If so, I'm screwed. "Why do you have to keep making me forget?"

"We're protecting you," Philip says automatically.

Right.

I lean forward in the seat. "So my job is the same?" I say, which seems vague enough not to show my ignorance, but encourages an answer.

Barron nods. "All you do is walk up to Zacharov and put your bare hand on his wrist. Then you change his heart to stone."

I swallow, concentrating on keeping my breathing even. They can't mean what they're saying. "Wouldn't shooting him be easier?" I ask, because the whole thing is ridiculous.

Anton looks at me with hard eyes. "You sure he can do this? All this memory magic—he's unstable. This is my future we're talking about."

My future. Right. He's Zacharov's nephew. Anything happens to the man in charge, the mantle slips onto his shoulders.

"Don't punk out on us," Philip says to me in his I'm-being-patient voice. "It's going to be a piece of cake. We've been planning this for a long time."

"What do you know about the Resurrection Diamond?" Barron asks.

"Gave Rasputin immortality or something," I say, deliberately vague. "Zacharov won it at an auction in Paris."

Barron frowns, like he didn't expect me to know even that much. "The Resurrection Diamond is thirty-seven carats—the size of a grown man's thumbnail," he says. "It's colored a faint red, as though a single bead of blood dropped into a pool of water."

I wonder if he's quoting someone. The Christie's catalog. Something. If I just concentrate on the details like it's a puzzle, then maybe I won't completely freak out.

"Not only did it protect Rasputin from multiple assassination attempts, but after him it went to other people. There have been reports of assassin's guns turning out not to be loaded at the critical moment, or poison somehow finding its way into the poisoner's cup. Zacharov was shot at on three separate occasions and the bullets didn't hit him. Whoever has the Resurrection Diamond can't be killed."

"I thought that thing was a myth or something?" I say. "A legend."

"Oh, so now he's an expert on working," Anton says.

But Barron's eyes are shining. "I've been researching the Resurrection Diamond a long time."

I wonder how much of that research he even remembers or if it has been winnowed down to just a few phrases. Maybe he wasn't quoting an auction catalog; maybe he was quoting one of his notebooks.

"How long have you been researching it?" I ask.

He's really angry now. "Seven years."

In the front seat Philip snorts.

"So you started *before* Zacharov got the diamond?"

"I'm the one who told him about it." Barron's expression is firm, certain, but I think I can see the fear in his face. He's lying, but he will never admit he's lying. There is no evidence in the world that will make him back off a claim once he's made it. If he did, he would have to admit how much of his memory is already gone.

Philip and Anton snicker to each other. They know he's lying too. It's like going to the movies with them in the summers when we all stayed in Carney with our grandparents. The familiarity makes me relax despite myself.

"So I actually agreed to do this?" I say.

They laugh more.

I have to proceed very carefully. "If the Resurrection

Diamond is supposed to prevent assassination, are you sure I'm going to be able to get around it?"

It seems to be within the bounds of believable ignorance or hesitation. Anton grins at me in the rearview mirror. "You're not doing death work. Whatever that stone is, it won't stop your kind of magic."

My kind of magic.

Heart to stone.

Me? I'm the transformation worker?

Who cursed you? I asked the cat in my dream.

You did.

I think that I'm going to be sick. No, I'm really going to be sick. I press my eyes shut, turn my head against the cold window, and concentrate on holding down my gorge.

He's lying. He's got to be lying.

"I'm—," I start.

I'm a worker. I'm a worker. I'm a worker.

The thought repeats in my head like one of those tiny ricocheting rubber balls that just won't stop banging into everything. I can't think past it.

I thought I'd give anything to be a worker, but somehow this feels like a hideous violation of my childhood fantasy.

What's the point of pretending to be anything less than the most talented practitioner of the very rarest curses? Except, I guess I'm not pretending anymore.

"You okay over there?" Barron asks.

"Sure," I say slowly. "I'm fine. Just tired. It's really late. And my head is killing me."

"We'll stop for coffee," says Anton.

We do. I manage to spill half of mine down my shirt, and the burn of the scalding liquid is the first thing that makes me feel halfway normal.

The entrance to the restaurant—Koshchey's—is so ornate that it looks like something out of another time. The front door is a brass so bright it looks like gold. Stone fire birds flank it, their feathers painted pale blue, orange, and red.

"Oh, tasteful," Barron says.

"Hey," says Anton, "it belongs to the family. Respect."

Barron shrugs. Philip shakes his head.

The sidewalk outside has the kind of stillness that comes only very early in the morning, and in that stillness I think the restaurant looks oddly majestic. Maybe I have bad taste.

Anton twists a key in the lock and opens the door. We walk into the dark room.

"You sure no one's here?" Philip asks.

"It's the middle of the night," says Anton. "Who's going to be here? This key wasn't easy to come by."

"Okay," Barron says, "so this place is going to be full of tables and political people. Rich bored folks that don't mind kicking it with gangsters. Maybe some workers from the Volpe and Nonomura families—we're currently allying ourselves with them." He walks across the room to point to a spot underneath a massive chandelier hung with a few huge blue crystals among the clear ones. It glitters, even in the dim light. "There will be a podium and loud, boring speeches."

I look around. "What is this?"

"Fund-raiser for 'Vote No on Proposition Two.' Zacharov is hosting it." Barron looks at me strangely. I wonder if I was supposed to know that.

"And I'm going to just walk up to him?" I ask. "In front of everyone?"

"Chill," Philip says. "For the millionth time, we've got a plan. We've been waiting too long for this to be idiots, okay?"

"My uncle has some very specific habits," says Anton. "He's not going to have his bodyguards close to him, because he can't have his society folks or the other families thinking he's afraid. So instead of guards he gets high-up laborers to take turns as his entourage. Philip and I are scheduled to be up his ass for two hours, starting at ten thirty."

I nod my head, but my gaze strays to the walls, to oil paintings of houses with chicken legs scampering beside women riding cauldrons through the skies, all reflected in massive mirrors. All our movements shimmer in them too, so that I keep thinking I see someone else moving when it's only myself.

"Your job is to keep an eye on us after that and wait for Zacharov to head to the bathroom. He wants it cleared when he uses it, so we'll be alone. That's where you're going to give him the touch."

"Where is it?" I ask.

"There are two men's bathrooms," Anton says, pointing. "One has a window. He'll pick the other one. I'll show it to you."

Barron and Philip head toward a glossy black door

stenciled in gold with the image of a man on horseback. I follow.

"We go in with Zacharov," Philip says. "You wait a few minutes and then go in yourself."

"I won't be in the room," Barron says. "I'll be outside—with you—to make sure everything goes smoothly."

I push the door and walk into a large bathroom. A mural of tiles takes up the whole far wall, an enormous bird of red and orange and gold flies in front of a tree covered in what look like cabbages but I assume are just really stylized leaves. The hand dryer is attached to that wall, but someone has painted it almost the same gold as the tiles. Stalls are along one side, urinals on the other, and a stretch of marble countertop filled with shining brass sinks.

"I'll play Zacharov," Anton says, and goes to stand at the sink. Then he looks at me, and I think he realizes he's about to be mock-assassinated. "No, wait. I'll play me. Barron, you be my uncle." They change places.

"Okay, go ahead," Anton says to me.

"What do I say?" I ask.

"Pretend you're drunk," says Barron. "Too drunk to notice you're not supposed to be there."

I stagger from near the doorway up to Barron.

"Get him out of here," Barron says in a fake accent that I think is supposed to be Russian.

I extend my gloved hand and try to slur my voice. "It's a real honor, sir."

Barron just looks at me. "I don't know if he'd shake."

"Sure he will," says Anton. "Philip here will say that Cassel's his little brother. Try again, Cassel."

"Sir, it's a real honor to be here. I really appreciate the way that you're doing your part to make workers safe so that we can exploit all the little people." I hold out my hand again.

"Stop being a comedian," Philip says, but not like he really means it. "Concentrate on the money and how you're going to get your fingers on his skin."

"I'm going to shove my hand under the cuff of his sleeve. Precut a hole in my glove. I just need my longest finger to touch skin."

Barron laughs. "Mom's old trick. The way she did that guy at the racetrack. You remembered."

I bite back a comment about remembering and just nod, looking down.

"Go ahead," Anton says. "Show me."

I extend my right hand, and when Barron takes it, I wrap my left hand around his wrist and shake. The left hand holds Barron's arm in place so that even if he struggles it'll take him a moment to get away. Anton's eyes widen a little. He's afraid. I can read his tells.

And just like that I'm sure he hates me. Hates being afraid and hates me for making him feel that way.

"A real honor, sir," I say.

Anton nods. "So, then you turn his heart to stone. That should look like—"

"Very poetic," I say.

"What?

"Very poetic, turning his heart to stone. Was that your idea?"

"It'll look like a heart attack—at least until the autopsy," Anton says, ignoring my question. "And that's what we're going to let them think it was. You're going to ride out the blowback in here, and then we're going to call for a doctor."

"You didn't seem drunk enough," says Barron.

"I'll seem drunker," I say.

Barron's looking at himself in the mirror. He smoothes out one of his eyebrows, then turns his head to admire his profile. His shave is so close that it might have come from a straight razor. Handsome. A real snake-oil salesman. "You should throw up."

"What? You want me to stick my finger down my throat?"

"Why not?

"Why?" I lean against the wall, studying Philip and Barron. Their faces are the two I know best in all the world, and right now they're unguarded. Philip shifts back and forth, grim-faced. He crosses and uncrosses his arms over his chest. He's a loyal laborer and he's got to be a little uncomfortable at the idea of taking out the head of the family, even if it means becoming rich and powerful overnight. Even if it means putting his childhood friend in charge and making himself indispensable.

Barron, however, appears to be having fun. I don't know what he's getting out of this, except that he loves to be in control. And it's obvious that he's managed to make Anton and Philip need him. He might be burning through his own memories to do it, but he's got power over all of us.

Of course, maybe he's in it for the money too. We're talking about a lot of money, being the head of a crime family.

"Afraid you won't be able to do it?" Barron asks, and I remember we're talking about vomiting. "But think— the hardest thing is getting in the door. This way you can burst in the door with your hand over your mouth, push into the stall, close it behind you, and toss your cookies. He'll be laughing at you when you come out. Easy mark."

"It's not a bad idea," Philip says, nodding.

"I've never made myself throw up before," I say. "I have no idea how long it will take."

"How about this," says Barron. "Go in the kitchen. Hurl in a bowl. We'll bottle up the puke and tape it behind the toilet in the first stall. If someone finds it, then you're on your own, but otherwise you can take whatever time you need now and not worry about it then."

"That's disgusting," I say.

"Just do it," says Anton.

"No," I say. "I can act drunk off my ass. I can pull it off." I don't intend to pull any of this off on Wednesday, although I don't quite know what I am going to do instead. But I can scheme in the morning; right now I need to observe.

"Throw up, or I am going to make you wish you did," Anton says.

I turn my neck to the side, so he can see the length of unmarked skin. "No scars," I say. "I'm not in your family, and you're not my boss."

"You better believe I'm your boss," Anton says, walking

up to me and grabbing the collar of my shirt, stretching it toward him.

"Enough." Philip gets between us, and Anton lets go of me. "You, get in the kitchen and stick your finger down your throat," he says to me. "Don't be so squeamish." He turns to Anton. "Lay off my brother. We're putting enough pressure on him."

It doesn't escape my notice that as Anton turns away and punches the door of a stall, Barron is smirking.

The more we fight, the more Barron is in control.

I push past Anton and keep going on through the big double doors to where I figure the kitchen is, pitch black and filled with the smells of paprika and cinnamon.

I reach around on the wall and flip the switch. Battered stainless and copper pots reflect the fluorescent lights. I could keep going out the back door, but there's no point. I need them to keep thinking that I'm clueless. I don't need them chasing me through the streets and then searching me until they find the amulets in my leg, even if staying here means the degrading and unpleasant duty of puking into a bowl. I open one of the industrial refrigerators and drink a few swallows of milk out of the carton. I hope it will coat my stomach.

The liners of my gloves are damp with sweat when I strip them off. My hands look pale in the lights.

I think of the hydrogen peroxide I fed to Grandad and wonder if this is some kind of karmic punishment. I put my finger on my tongue, testing how awful it's going to be. My skin takes like salt.

"Hey," someone says.

When I turn, I see that it isn't Anton or Philip or Barron. It's a guy I don't know with a long coat and a gun pointed right at me.

The milk slides out of my hands and falls to the floor, splashing out of the carton.

"What are you doing here?" the man says.

"Oh," I say, thinking fast. "My friend has a key. He works for one of the owners."

"Are you talking to someone?" comes a voice from the back, and another man with a shaved head walks into the room. His T-shirt has a deep V, revealing his necklace of scars. He looks over at me. "Who's that?"

"Hey, man," I say, holding up my hands. I'm making up a story in my head about who I am, falling into the role. I am a worker kid, just off the bus, looking for a job and a place to crash—someone told me about this place because of its connection to Zacharov. "I was just stealing food. I'm sorry. I'll wash the dishes or whatever to pay for it."

Then the door on the other side opens and Anton and Philip step through.

"What the hell?" the man with the shaved head says.

"Get away from him," says Philip.

The guy with the long coat swings his gun toward my brother.

I reach out my hand instinctively and touch the barrel, to push it away from Philip. The metal is warmer than I thought it would be. Then something in me reaches as instinctively as I reached out my hand and *changes* the gun.

It's like I can see the metal all the way down to the particles, but instead of being solid, it's liquid, flowing into endless shapes. All I have to do is choose one.

I look up, and the man is holding what I imagined, a snake coiling around his fingers, its green scales as bright as the wings of the phoenix out in front.

The man screams, shaking his arm like it's on fire.

The snake ripples, tightening its coils, its mouth opening and closing like it's choking. A moment later a bullet drops from its mouth, bouncing against the stainless steel counter and rolling.

Two shots ring out.

Something's wrong with me—with my body.

My chest constricts painfully and my shoulder jerks. For a moment I think that I'm the one that's shot, until I look down and see my fingers becoming gnarled roots. I take a step forward, and my legs buckle. One of them is covered in fur and bends backward. I blink, and I am seeing everything out of dozens of eyes. I can even see behind me, like I have eyes there, too, but all there is to see is cracked tile floor. I turn my head and see the two men lying on the ground. Blood is mixing with the milk, and the gun is slithering toward me, its tongue flicking out to taste the air.

I am hallucinating. I'm dying. Terror rises up in my throat, but I can't scream.

"What the hell were they doing here? Killing our people isn't part of the plan," Anton is shouting. "This wasn't supposed to happen!"

My arms are the trunk of a tree, the arms of a sofa, they are twisting into coils of rope.

Someone help me. Please help me. Help me.

Anton points at me. "All this is his fault!"

I try to stand, but my bottom half is like a fish's. My eyes are moving in my head. I try to speak, but gurgling sounds come from whatever I have in place of lips.

"We have to get rid of the bodies," Barron says.

There are other sounds then, snapping bone and a wet thunk. I try to roll my head so I can see, but I no longer know how.

"Keep him quiet," Anton shouts.

Was I making a sound? I can't even hear myself.

I feel hands clasp on me and lift me up, hauling me through the restaurant. My head falls back, and I notice that the ceiling is painted with a mural of an old naked man, his scimitar held high, riding a brown horse down a hill. The mane of the horse and the man's long hair are blowing in the wind. It makes me laugh, which comes out like a tea-kettle whistle.

"It's just blowback," Philip says softly. "You'll be okay soon."

He puts me down in the trunk of Anton's car and slams down the top. It stinks of oil and something else, but I'm so out of it I barely notice. I twist around in the dark as the engine starts, my body not my own.

We're on a highway when I come back to myself. Head-lights of following cars stream erratically through the out-line of the trunk. My head is banging uncomfortably against the carpeted tire well with each bump of the road, and I can feel the shaking of the frame underneath me. I push myself into a different position and touch plastic filled with something soft and still warm.

For a moment I think of laying my head against it, until I touch a patch of sticky wetness and realize what I'm touching.

Garbage bags.

I gag in the dark and try to crawl as far away from them as I can. I press myself against the far back of the car until I can't go any farther. The metal presses into my back and I can only support my neck awkwardly with my arm, but I stay like that for the whole ride.

When the car lurches to a stop, I am sore and light-headed. I hear the doors slam, gravel crunch, and then the trunk opens. Anton is standing over me. We're in the driveway of my house.

"What did you have to go and do that for?" he shouts.

I shake my head. I don't know why I changed the gun, or even how I did it. I look at my hand and see that it's smeared with a dull, dark red.

My bare hand.

"This is supposed to be a secret. *You* are supposed to be a secret." Then he notices my hands too. They must have left my gloves in the restaurant.

His jaw clenches.

"I'm sorry," I say, climbing woozily to my feet. I am sorry.

"How do you feel?" Barron asks me.

"Seasick," I tell him, but it isn't the recent car ride that is making me want to puke. I know I'm shaking, and there's nothing I can do to control it.

"I killed those men because of you," Anton says. "Their deaths are on your hands. All I want to do is bring back the old days when it meant something to be a worker. When it was good, not a thing to be ashamed about. When we owned all the politicians, all the cops. We were like princes in this city back then, and we can be again.

"Dab hands, they used to call us," he says. "Dab hands. Experts. *Skilled*. When I'm in charge, I'm going to bring back the old days and make this city tremble. That's a good goal, a worthy goal."

"And just how are you going to do that?" I ask. "You think the government is going to roll over because you've murdered your way to the top of a crime family? You think Zacharov could have the world by the balls, but he's all 'No, thanks'?"

Anton hits me square in the jaw. Pain explodes in my head and I stumble backward, barely keeping my balance.

"Hey," Philip says, pushing Anton back. "He's just a big-mouthed kid."

I take two steps toward Anton, and Barron grabs my arm.

"Don't be stupid," he says, and pulls my sleeves down over my hands.

"Hold him," Anton tells Barron. He looks at me. "I'm not done with you, kid."

Barron's grip on me tightens.

"What are you doing, Anton?" Philip asks, trying to sound reasonable. "We don't have time for this. Plus, he's going to wake up with those bruises. Think."

Anton shakes his head. "Get out of my way, Philip. I shouldn't have to remind you that I'm your boss."

Philip looks back and forth between me and Anton, weighing Anton's rage and my stupidity.

"Hey," I say, struggling against Barron's hold. I'm exhausted, and I don't struggle hard, but that doesn't stop my mouth. "What are you going to do? Murder me, too? Like those men? Like Lila. Come on, what did she really do? Did she get in your way? Insult you? Not grovel?"

Sometimes I am very stupid. I guess I deserve the punch that Barron holds me in place for. The one that catches me just under my cheekbone and makes my vision go white. I can feel the blow all the way to my teeth.

"Shut up!" Anton shouts.

My mouth floods with the taste of old pennies. My cheeks and tongue feel like they're made of raw hamburger, and blood dribbles over my lips.

"Enough," says Philip. "Enough already."

"I decide when it's enough," Anton says.

"Okay, I'm sorry," I say, spitting a mouthful of blood onto the ground. "Lesson learned. You can not beat the crap out of me now. I didn't mean it."

I look up in time to see Philip light a cigarette and turn away, blowing smoke into the air. And to see Anton bring his fist down on my gut.

I try to twist out of the way, but I'm already too hurt to be fast, and there's nowhere to go with Barron's hands clamped on me. Bright pain makes me sag forward, moaning. I'm grateful when I feel him drop my arms so I can slide to the ground and curl my body around itself. I don't want to move. I want to lie very still until everything stops hurting.

"Kick him," Anton says. His voice is shaking. "I want to know you're loyal to me. Do it or this whole thing is called off."

I force myself to sit up and try to push myself upright. The three of them are looking down at me like I'm something they found on the bottom of their shoes. The word "please" repeats in my mind. "Not in the face," I say instead.

Barron's foot knocks me to the ground. It only takes a few more kicks for me to lose consciousness.

CHAPTER THIRTEEN

I DON'T WANT TO MOVE because even breathing hurts my ribs. The bruises hurt more in the morning than they had the night before. Lying on the bed in my old room, I test my memory for blank spots. It reminds me of being a kid, sticking my tongue into my gums after a tooth fell out. But I remember last night very clearly: my brothers standing above me, Barron kicking my stomach over and over. I remember the gun changing, coiling around the man's wrist. The only thing I don't remember is how I got to bed, but I think that's because I blacked out.

"Oh, God," I say, rubbing my hand over my face, then looking at my hand to make sure it's still mine. Make sure it hasn't twisted into some other shape.

I reach my arm down slowly and carefully to touch the wound in my leg where the worked stones are. I feel the hardness of a whole one under my fingers and the outline of shards where two broke. My skin jumps, alight with pain, at the pressure. I wasn't crazy. A stone cracked last night, under my skin, each time Barron tried to work me.

Barron.

He's the memory worker. He's the one who changed Maura's memories. And mine.

My stomach clenches and I roll gingerly to one side, afraid that I'm going to throw up and then choke on it. Dizzily I see the white cat sitting on a pile of laundry, her eyes slitted.

"What are you doing here?" I whisper. My voice sounds like shards of glass are stuck in my throat.

She stands up, stretching her paws to knead the sweater she was lying on. Her nails sink into the fabric like little needles. Then her back arches.

"Did you see them bring me back here?" I croak.

Her pink tongue swipes her nose.

"Stop screwing with me," I say.

She hunkers down and then jumps onto the bed, startling me. I groan with fresh pain. "I know what you are," I say. "I know what I did to you."

Only you can undo the curse. Of course.

Her fur is soft against my arm, and I reach out a hand toward her. She lets me stroke down her back. I'm lying. I don't know what she is. I think I know who she was, but I'm not sure what she is anymore.

"I don't know how to turn you back," I say. "I figured out that it was me who changed you. I figured out that part. But I don't know how I do it."

She stiffens, and I turn to bury my face in her fur. I feel the rough pads of her paws. Her tiny claws are sharp against my skin.

"I don't have a dream amulet," I say. "I don't have anything to stop you from working me. You can make me dream, can't you? Like the rainstorm and the roof. Like before you were a cat."

Her purr is a rumble, like distant thunder.

I close my eyes.

I wake up still hurting. I am lying in a pool of blood, slipping as I try to rise. Leaning over me are Philip, Barron, Anton, and Lila.

"He doesn't remember anything," Lila the girl says. When she smiles, her canine teeth come to sharp points. She looks older than fourteen. She looks beautiful and terrible. I cower back from her.

She laughs.

"Who got hurt?" I ask.

"Me," she says. "Don't you remember? I died."

I push myself up onto my knees and find myself on the stage of the theater at Wallingford. Alone. The heavy blue curtain is closed in front of me, and I think that I can hear the sounds of a crowd beyond it. When I look down, the blood is no longer there, but a trapdoor is open. I scramble to my feet, slip, and nearly fall into the pit.

"You need makeup," someone says. I turn my head. It's Daneca, in shining plate mail, approaching me with a powder puff. She hits my face with it. There's a cloud of dust.

"I'm dreaming," I say out loud, which doesn't help nearly as much as it should. I open my eyes and find myself no longer on the Wallingford stage but in the aisle of a majestic theater. The wood-paneled walls are grooved with dust above a scarlet rug. Lights drip crystals, and the plaster ceilings are painted in frescoes of gold. In the rows of seats on the terraces in front of the stage, cats in clothes fan one another, wave programs, and mew. I turn around and around, and a few of them glance in my direction, their eyes shining with reflected light.

I stumble into one of the empty rows and take a seat as a dark red curtain opens.

Lila walks onto the stage, wearing a long white Victorian dress with pearl buttons. She's followed by Anton, then Philip and Barron. Each of the guys is in a costume from a different period. Anton's got on a purple zoot suit with an enormous feathered hat, Philip is dressed like an Elizabethan lord with a doublet and ruff, and Barron's wearing a long black robe. I can't decide if he's supposed to be a priest or a judge.

"Lo," Lila says, pressing the back of her wrist against her forehead. "I am a young girl and very much given to amusement."

Barron bows deeply. "It just so happens that I can be amusing."

"It just so happens," says Anton, "that Philip and I have

a little side thing going where I get rid of people for money. I can't have her father know. I'm going to take over the business someday."

"Alas, alack," says Lila. "Woe."

Barron smiles and rubs his hands together. "It just so happens that I like money."

Philip looks right at me, as though I was the one he was speaking to. "Anton's going to be our ticket out of being small time. And I think my girlfriend is pregnant. You understand, right? I'm doing this for all of us."

I shake my head. I don't understand.

On the stage Lila gives a small scream and starts shrinking, changing shape until she's the size of a mouse. Then the white cat springs down from one of the balconies, her dress tearing on the jagged splinters of the floorboards and pulling free from her furry body. Pouncing, she catches the Lila-mouse in her teeth and bites off the tiny head. Blood spatters across the stage.

"Lila," I say. "Stop it. Stop with all the games."

The cat gulps down the remains and looks out at me. And then the stage lights are turning toward me, the brightness making me blink in confusion. I stand up. The white cat stalks toward me. Her eyes—those blue and green eyes—are so clearly Lila's that I stumble back and into the aisle.

"You have to cut off my head," she says.

"No," I tell her.

"Do you love me?" she asks.

Her teeth are like ivory knives. "I don't know," I say.

"If you love me, you'll have to cut off my head."

Somehow I have a sword in my hand and am swinging it. The cat is changing like Lila did, but she's getting larger, growing into something monstrous. The audience's applause is deafening.

My ribs are throbbing, but I force myself to swing my legs off the bed. I walk into the bathroom, piss, and then chew up a handful of aspirin. Staring at myself in the mirror, taking in my bloodshot eyes and the mass of bruises near my ribs, I think over the dream, about the cat looming over me.

It's ridiculous, but I'm not laughing.

"Is that you?" Grandad's voice comes from down the stairs.

"Yeah," I call back.

"You slept late," he says, and I can hear him muttering, probably about how lazy I am.

"I'm not feeling good," I tell him from the stairwell. "I don't think I can clean today."

"I'm not that great myself," he says. "Rough night last night, huh? I drank so much I don't remember most of it."

I walk downstairs, cradling my ribs half-unconsciously. I stumble. Nothing feels right. My skin doesn't fit. I am Humpty Dumpty. All the king's horses and all the king's men have failed to put me back together again.

"Did anything happen you want to tell me about?" Grandad asks. I think of his eyes seeming to blink in the dark last night. I wonder what he heard. What he suspects.

"Nothing," I say, and pour myself a cup of coffee. I drink it black, and the warmth in my belly is the first comforting thing I remember feeling in a while.

Grandad tilts his head in my direction. "You look like crap."

"I told you I didn't feel good."

The phone rings in the other room, a shrill sound that jangles my nerves. "You tell me lots of things," Grandad says, and walks off to answer it.

I see the cat on the stairs, her white body ghostly in a beam of sunlight. She blurs in my vision. My brothers were uncomfortable, but not for the reasons I thought. Not because I was a murderer or an outsider. I was such an insider that I never even knew it. I was inside of the insiders. I was hidden inside my insides. For a moment I want to dash all the crockery to the floor. I want to scream and shout. I want to take this newfound power and change everything that I can touch.

Lead to gold.

Flesh to stone.

Sticks to snakes.

I hold up the coffee cup, and I think about the muzzle of the gun melting and shifting in my hand, but no matter how I try to summon that moment, the cup stays. The slogan keeps reading AMHERST TRUCKING: WE LIFT STUFF on a glossy maroon background.

"What are you doing?" Grandad asks me, and my hand jerks, sloshing coffee onto my shirt. He's holding out the phone. "Philip. For you. Says you left something over there."

I shake my head.

"Take it," Grandad says, sounding exasperated, and I can't think of an excuse not to, so I do.

"Yeah?" I say.

"What did you do to her?" His voice sounds thick with anger and something else. Panic.

"Who?" I ask.

"Maura. She's gone, and she took my son. You have to tell me where she is, Cassel."

"Me?" I ask him. Last night he watched Barron kick me in the stomach until I blacked out, and today he's accusing me of masterminding Maura's escape? Anger makes my vision blur. I grip the phone so tightly that I'm afraid the plastic case is going to crack.

He should be apologizing to me. He should be begging.

"I know you've been talking to her. What did you tell her? What did you do to her?"

"Oh, sorry," I say automatically, cold fury in every word. *"I don't remember."* I click the off button on the phone, feeling so vindictively pleased that it takes me a moment to realize how incredibly stupid I've just been.

Then I remember I'm not Cassel Sharpe, kid brother and general disappointment, anymore. I'm one of the most powerful practitioners of one of the rarest curses.

I'm not taking Lila and leaving town. I'm not going anywhere.

They should be afraid of me.

Grandad leaves about an hour later, asking me if I need anything from the store. I say I don't. He tells me to put some of my clothes in a bag.

"What's going on?" I ask.

"We're taking a road trip down to Carney," he says.

I nod my head, cradle my ribs, and watch him go.

Lila stares at me from the center of the mounds of papers, clothes and platters on the dining room table. She's eating something. I get closer and see a piece of bacon, the grease soaking into a scarf.

"Grandad give you that?" I ask.

She sits on her hind legs and licks her mouth.

My cell phone is ringing. The caller ID says Daneca.

"You gave her the slip," I say. "Did you really walk all the way here?"

Lila yawns, showing her fangs.

I know I have to change her, now before Grandad returns. Before my ribs start to hurt again and I can't concentrate.

If only I knew how.

Her eyes are shining as I walk toward her.

A curse was placed on me. A curse that only you can break.

I reach out my hand and touch her fur. Her bones feel light, fragile, like the bones of a bird. I think of the moment when the barrel of the gun began to turn to scales, try to summon the impulse that made it transform.

Nothing.

I imagine Lila, imagine the cat elongating, growing into a girl. As I picture it, I am aware that I don't know what Lila would look like now. I push that out of my head and let myself make up some combination of the girl I knew and the girl from my dream. Close enough is close enough.

I imagine her changing, imagine it until I'm shaking with concentration, but she still doesn't change.

The cat growls deep in her throat.

I push out one of the dining room chairs and flop down on it, resting my forehead against the wood of the back.

When I changed the gun, I wasn't thinking about it. Instinct took over. It was like some kind of muscle memory or a part of my brain that I could access only when someone I cared about was in danger.

I've been angry lots of times. I never accidentally turned my gloves to leaves or changed anyone into anything. So it isn't emotion.

I think about the ant Barron told me I never turned into a stick. I can't remember what I did do.

I look around the room. The sword I found when I was cleaning out the living room is right where I left it, leaning against the wall. I pick it up, feel the weight, as though I am distant from my body. I note the rust running down the blade. The sword feels heavy in my hands, not like the light fencing foils at school.

If you love me, cut off my head.

"Lila," I said. "I don't know how to change you."

She pads to the edge of the table and jumps onto the floor. Surreal. Everything is surreal. None of this is happening.

"I am thinking of doing something to force myself. Something crazy. To force the magic."

This is stupid. Someone has to stop me. She has to stop me.

She rubs her cheek against the blade, closing her eyes, and then rubs her whole body against it. Back and forth. Back and forth.

"You really think this is a good idea?"

She yowls and hops back up onto the table. Then she sits, waiting.

I reach out and place one hand on the fur of her back. "I'm going to swing this sword at your head, okay? But I'm not going to hit you."

Stop me.

"Stay still."

She's just watching me, just waiting. She doesn't move, except for her twitching tail.

I pull back the sword and swing it toward her tiny body. I swing it with all my weight behind it.

Oh, God, I'm going to kill her again.

And then I see it. Everything goes fluid. I know I can shift the sword in my hand into a coil of rope, a sheet of water, a dusting of dirt. And the cat is no longer a collection of fragile bird bones and fur. I can see the badly woven curse on her, obscuring the girl underneath. A simple mental tug and it pulls apart.

I'm suddenly bringing the sword down on the naked form of a crouching girl. I pull back, but my weight is way off balance.

I topple to the floor and the sword flies out of my hands. It crashes into a water-stained Venetian chest at the other end of the dining room.

She is a tangled mass of dredded curls the color of hay

and sunburned skin. She tries to stand up and can't. Maybe she's forgotten how.

This time when the blowback hits, it's like my body is trying to rip itself apart.

"Cassel," she says. She's bent over me, in a too big shirt. I can see almost the entire length of her bare legs when I turn my head. "Cassel, someone's coming. Wake up."

My ribs are hurting again. I don't know if that's a good thing or a bad thing. I just need to sleep. If I sleep long enough, when I wake up, I'll be back in Wallingford and Sam will be spraying himself with too much cologne and everything will go back to the way things are supposed to me.

She slaps me, hard.

I suck in a deep breath and open my eyes. My cheek is stinging. When I turn my head, I can see the hilt of the sword and a shattered vase that must have fallen off the chest. The whole floor is freshly strewn with books and papers.

"Someone's coming," she says. Her voice sounds different from how I remember. Scratchy. Hoarse.

"My grandfather," I say. "He went to the store."

"There are two people out there." Her face is both familiar and strange. Looking at her makes my stomach hurt. I reach out a hand.

She flinches back. Of course she doesn't want me to touch her. Look what I can do.

"Hurry," she says.

I stumble up. "Oh," I say out loud, because I remember the stupid thing I told Philip. I can't believe I ever thought that I was good at deception.

"The closet," I say.

The coat closet is choked with fur and moth-eaten wool. We kick out the boxes at the bottom and squeeze ourselves inside. The only way to fit without pressing against the door is to duck under the bar holding up the hangers and let that wedge me in. The rod bangs into my arm, and Lila comes in after me, closing the door. Then she's pressed against my sore ribs, breathing in short rapid gasps. Her breath smells like grass and something else, something richer and darker. It's warm against my throat.

I can't see her, just slivers of lights along the outline of the door. One of my mother's mink collars brushes my chin, and there's a faint trace of perfume.

I hear the front door open and then Philip's voice call, "Cassel? Grandad?"

Automatically I make a sudden movement. It's just a reflex, not much but it makes Lila grab my arms and dig her fingers into my biceps.

"Shhhhh," she says.

"*You* be quiet," I whisper back. I've grabbed hold of her shoulders without consciously deciding to, a mirror of her gesture. In the dark she's a phantom. Not real. Her shoulders are trembling slightly, vibrating under my hands.

Both our hands are bare. It's shocking.

She's leaning forward.

Then her mouth is sliding against mine. Her lips

open, soft and yielding. Our teeth click together, and she tastes like every dark thought I've ever had. This is the kiss I fantasized about when I was fourteen, and even later than that, even when I knew it was sick to think about her—the kiss I wanted and never got, and now that it's happening I can't stop it. My shoulders press against the wall. I reach out with one hand to steady myself, gripping the wool shoulder of a coat so hard I can feel the ancient cloth rip.

She bites my tongue.

"He's not here," Barron says. "The car's gone."

Lila turns away from me abruptly, tilting her neck so that her hair is in my face.

"What do you think he said to Grandad?" Philip asks.

"Nothing," Barron says. "You're overreacting."

"You didn't hear him on the phone," says Philip. "He remembered—I don't know what. Enough to know someone had been working him."

Something crunches under one of their feet. Considering all the stuff scattered on the floor, it could be anything. "He's a smart-ass. You're just being paranoid."

Lila's breath is hot on my neck.

Footfalls on the stairs tell me they're going to look for me up there.

We're so close that it's impossible not to touch her. And that makes me recall that she must have been touching me to make me dream.

"That night, at Wallingford—were you in the room with me?" I whisper.

"They needed me to get you," she says. "To make you sleepwalk out to them. I made lots of people sleepwalk right into their hands."

I picture a white shape on the steps, the hall master's dog starting to bark before she made the dog dream too.

"Why did you kiss me?" I ask her, keeping my voice low.

"To shut you up," she says. "Why do you think?"

We're silent for a moment. Above us I can hear my brothers walking across the creaking boards. I wonder if they're in their old bedrooms. I wonder if they're in my bedroom, going through my things like I went through Barron's.

"Thanks," I say, finally, sarcastically. My heart is beating like a rattle.

"You don't remember any of it, do you? I figured that part out. Barron told me that you laughed when he told you I was in a cage, but you didn't laugh, did you?"

"Of course I didn't," I say. "No one told me you were alive."

She gives a weird short, gurgling laugh. "How did you think I died?" I think of the cage and of her being there for the last three years. How that could drive anyone crazy. Not that she seems crazier than anyone else. Me, for instance.

"I stabbed you." My voice breaks on the words, even though I know the memory's not true.

She's quiet. All I can hear is the hammering of my own heart.

"I *remember* it," I say. "The blood. Slipping on the blood. And feeling gleeful, like I'd gotten away with it. Looking down at your body and feeling the way I did—the memory still seems so real. Like something that no one could make up, because it was so awful. And how I was—It's worse than feeling nothing, like you're just psycho. It's much worse to think you enjoyed it." I'm glad we're in the dark. It is impossible to imagine saying all this to her face.

"They were supposed to kill me," Lila says. "Barron and I were in your grandfather's house in the basement, and he grabbed my arms. At first I thought he was kidding around, that he wanted to wrestle, until you and Philip walked in. Philip was saying something to you, and you just kept shaking your head."

I want to say that it isn't true, that it didn't happen, but of course I really have no idea.

"I kept asking Barron to let me get up, but he wouldn't even look at me. Philip took out a knife, and that's when you seemed to change your mind. You walked over to me and looked down, but it was like you weren't really looking at me. Like you didn't even know who I was. Barron started to get up, and I was relieved, until you took my wrists and pressed them down on the shag rug. You pressed them down harder than he did."

I swallow hard and close my eyes, dreading what she'll say next.

Steps on the stairs make her clam up.

"Tell me," I whisper. My voice comes out louder than I planned. Probably not loud enough to get their attention. "Tell me the rest."

She presses her bare hand against my mouth. "Shut up." She's whispering, but she sounds fierce.

If I struggle, I really am going to make noise.

"I don't want you to tell Anton," Philip says. He sounds close, and Lila's body jolts. I try to slide my hand against her upper arms to gentle her, but that only seems to make her shake worse.

"Tell him what?" asks Barron. "That you think Cassel's going to flake? Do you want this whole thing to come apart?"

"I don't want it to blow up in our faces. And Anton's acting more unstable."

"We can take care of Anton when this is over. Cassel's fine. You baby him too much."

"I just think that this is risky. It's a risky plan and Cassel needs to be on board. I think you forgot to make him forget."

"You know what I think?" Barron says. "I think that bitch wife of yours is the problem. I told you to cut her loose."

"Shut up." I hear the growl under Philip's seeming calm.

"Fine, but he was hanging around her last night after dinner. She obviously figured out enough to leave."

"But Cassel—"

"Cassel nothing. She told him what she suspected. And he did a little fishing to find out if it was true. See how you'd react. He doesn't know anything yet, unless you freak out. Simple. Case closed. Now let's go."

"What about Lila?"

"We'll find her," he says. "She's a cat. What can she do?"

I hear the front door slam. We wait what feels like ten minutes and then slide under the pole to open the closet door. I look around the room. It's trashed, but no more than it was before.

Lila steps out behind me, and when I look back at her, her mouth curves up at one corner. She turns toward the bathroom.

I catch her wrist. "Why are you doing this? Tell me. How you got away from Barron. Why you lured me up to the roof of Smythe Hall with that crazy dream."

"I wanted to kill you," she says, that slight smile widening.

I drop her wrist like it's burning me. "You what?"

"I couldn't do it," she says. "I hated you even more than I hated them, but I still couldn't do it. That's something, right?"

I feel like she knocked the air out of my lungs.

"No," I say. "It's nothing. Less than nothing."

The kitchen door opens with a creak. Lila presses herself against the wall, shooting me a warning glance. There's no time to dash for the closet, so I step into the kitchen to take whatever's coming. To give Lila a few minutes to hide.

Philip smiles from the doorway. "I knew you were here."

"I just walked in," I say, even though he knows I'm lying.

He takes a step toward me, and I take a step back. I wonder if he's going to try to kill me. I hold up my hands, still bare. He doesn't seem to even notice.

"I need you to tell her," Philip says, and for a moment I don't know who he's talking about. "Tell Maura I was weak. Tell her I'm sorry. Tell her I didn't know how to stop."

"I told you I don't know where Maura is."

"Fine," he says tightly. "See you Wednesday night. And, Cassel, maybe you're pissed off or you have questions, but it's going to be worth it in the end. Trust us just a little bit longer and you're going to have everything you ever wanted."

He walks out and down the hill to Barron's idling car. Lila walks into the room and puts her hand on my shoulder. I shrug it off.

"We have to get out of here," she says. "You need to rest."

I turn to agree, but she's already pulling out gloves and a coat from the closet.

CHAPTER FOURTEEN

LATE AFTERNOON SUN-
light streams through the window, and I wake up with my
head pillowed against blond curls and warm skin. At first
I'm so disoriented that I can't understand who could be
next to me and why she doesn't have many clothes on.

Sam's closing the door to the room. "Hey, dude," he says
in a whisper.

Lila makes a small gesture of complaint and rolls
against the wall, her body sliding against mine, her shirt
rucking up. She mashes the pillow over her head.

I dimly recall walking to the convenience store three
blocks from my house, calling a cab, and then sitting on
the sidewalk to wait, Lila leaning against me. I figured my

dorm room was going to be empty for a couple of hours. There was no other place I could think of to go.

"Don't worry," Sam says. "I haven't seen Valerio. But next time put a sock on the door."

"A sock?"

"My brother says that's the universal signal for getting some—the nice way to alert your roommate so that he can make other plans for the evening. As opposed to letting your roommate walk in on you."

"Uh, yeah," I say, yawning. "Sorry. Sock. I'll remember."

"Who is she?" he whispers, indicating her with his chin. "Does she even go to school here?" He drops his voice even lower. "And are you crazy?"

Lila rolls over again and smiles sleepily at Sam. "The uniform's cute," she says in her new, rough voice.

Sam flushes.

"I'm Lila, and yes, he's crazy. But you must have noticed that before now. He was crazy back when I knew him, and he's obviously gotten crazier over time." Her gloved fingers tousle my hair.

I grimace. "She's an old friend. A family friend."

"Everyone's coming back," Sam says, raising his eyebrows. "You and your buddy better get out."

Lila pushes herself up on her elbow. "You feeling better?" It doesn't seem to bother her to be half dressed with one leg pressed against me. Maybe she got used to being naked when she was a cat, but I am completely unused to it.

"Yeah," I say. My ribs are sore, but the pain is duller.

She yawns and stretches up her arms, canting her body to one side and making her spine crack audibly.

It feels like the whole world has turned upside down. There aren't any more rules.

"Hey," I say to Sam, because if the world's gone crazy, then I guess I can do whatever I want. "Guess what? I'm a worker."

He stares at me, openmouthed. Lila jerks to her feet.

"You can't tell him that," she says.

"Why not?" I ask, then turn to him. "I didn't have any idea until yesterday. Wacky, right?"

"What kind?" he manages to squeak out.

"If you tell him *that*," Lila says, "I'm going to kill you, but first I'm going to kill him."

"Consider the question retracted," Sam says, holding his hands out in a peace offering.

Some of my clothes are still in the drawers and in the closet. I grab what I need, then head for the library to take out a loan from my business.

We walk down to the corner store where all the Wallingford students go to shoplift gum. Lila picks out a bottle of shampoo, some soap, an enormous cup of coffee, and three bars of chocolate. I pay.

The owner, Mr. Gazonas, smiles at me. "He's a good kid," he tells Lila. "Polite. No stealing. Not like the other kids who come in here. Hang on to this one."

That makes me laugh.

I lean against the wall outside. "Do you want to call your mom?"

Lila shakes her head. "With all the gossip down in Carney? No way. I don't want anyone but my father to know I'm back."

I nod slowly. "So we call him, then."

"I need to take a shower first," Lila says, winding the plastic handle of the bag around her wrist. She has rolled up a pair of my dress slacks and looks homeless in them, the baggy shirt and some lace-up boots she found in the back of my closet.

I dial the same cab company that gave us a lift over here. "We don't have any place to clean up," I say.

"Hotel room," she tells me.

There's a hotel not too far a walk from where we're standing, a nice basic place that parents stay at sometimes, but it's not going to work. "Believe me, they are not going to let the two of us get a room. Kids try all the time."

She shrugs.

I hang up on the dispatcher. "Fine," I say. I'm thinking of how when the rooms get cleaned, the doors are open. We're never going to be able to get a room, but we might be able to steal one for a shower if we get lucky.

As we start across the parking lot, I see Audrey with two of her friends, Stacey and Jenna. Stacey gives me the finger. Jenna nudges Audrey with her elbow. I know I should look away, but I don't. Audrey lifts her head. Her eyes are shadowed.

"Do you know her?" Lila asks.

"Yeah," I say, and finally turn toward the hotel.

"She's pretty," says Lila.

"Yeah," I say again, and jam my hands in my pockets, deep—gloved fingers against the crease.

Lila keeps looking back. "I bet she's got a shower."

Here's another thing Mom told me over and over about scams. The first thing you have to get is the mark's confidence, but it's always more convincing when someone other than you suggests the score to the mark. That's why most confidence schemes demand a partner.

"Cassel told me all about you," Lila tells Audrey. Her smile changes her from homeless vagabond to regular girl, even with her matted hair.

Audrey looks from me to Lila and then back at me, as if she's trying to decide whether this is part of some game.

"What did he say?" asks Jenna, taking a long swig of her Diet Coke.

"My cousin just got back from India," I say, and nod in Lila's direction. "Her parents were living in some ashram. I was telling her about Wallingford."

Audrey's hands go to her hips. "She's your cousin?"

Lila scrunches her eyebrows for a moment, then a wide grin splits her face. "Oh! Because I'm so pale, right?"

Stacey flinches. Audrey looks at me like she's trying to see if I'm offended. Wallingford's idea of political correctness is never to mention anything about race. Ever. Tan skin and dark hair are supposed to be as invisible as red hair or blond hair or skin so white its marbled with blue veins.

"No, it's all good," says Lila. "We're stepcousins. My mother married his mother's brother."

My mother doesn't even have a brother.

I don't lift an eyebrow.

I don't smile.

I don't admit to myself that scamming the girl I might still be in love with is making my pulse race.

"Audrey," I say, because I know this script pretty well, "can we talk for a minute?"

"*Cassel,*" says Lila. "I have to cut my hair. I have to take a shower. Come on." She grins at Audrey and grabs my arm. "It was nice meeting you."

I keep my gaze on Audrey, waiting for her to answer.

"I guess you can talk when you get back to school," says Jenna.

"She could use the shower at the dorm," Audrey says hesitantly.

I am a very bad person.

"So we can talk?" I ask her. "That would be great."

"Sure," she says, not looking at me.

As we all walk back to Wallingford, Lila flashes me a grin. "Smooth," she mouths.

Audrey and I sit on the cement steps in front of the arts building. Her neck is blotchy, the way it gets when she's nervous. She keeps pushing her red hair out of her face, hooking it over one ear, but it tumbles loose with every breeze.

"I'm sorry about what happened at the party," I say. I want to touch her hair, smooth it back, but I don't.

"I'm an independent woman. I make my own decisions," she says. Her gloved hands pull at the weave of her gray tights.

"I just meant that I—"

"I know what you mean," she says. "I was drunk, and you shouldn't kiss drunk girls, certainly not in front of their boyfriends. It's not chivalrous."

"Greg's your boyfriend?" That certainly explains his reaction.

She bites her lower lip and shrugs.

"And then I hit him!" I say quickly, to make her laugh. "No pistols at dawn. You must be so disappointed. Chivalry is truly dead."

She grins, clearly relieved I'm not going to interrogate her. "I *am* disappointed."

"I'm funnier than Greg," I say. It's easy to talk to her today, knowing I didn't kill the last girl I was in love with. I had no idea how heavy a burden that was until I set it down.

"But he likes me better than you ever did," she says.

"He must like you a whole lot, then." I look into her eyes as I say it, and am rewarded by the blotchy blush spreading across her cheeks.

She punches me in the arm. "Oooh. You are funny."

"Does that mean you're not quite over me?"

She leans back and stretches. "I'm not sure. Are you coming back to school?"

I nod. "I'll be back."

"Tick tock," she says. "I might forget all about you."

I grin. "Absence diminishes little passions and increases great ones."

"You've got a good memory," she says, but her gaze is focused somewhere behind me.

"Did I mention that I was smarter than Greg too?" When she doesn't react, I turn to see what she's staring at.

Lila is heading across the quad toward us in a long skirt and a sweater that she obviously talked someone out of. She cut off so much of her hair that it's shorter than mine: a pale silvery cap on her head. She's still wearing my boots, and her lips are shining with pink gloss. For a moment I don't breathe.

"Big difference," Audrey says.

Lila's smile widens. She walks up and links her arm with mine. "Thank you so much for letting me use the shower."

"No problem," says Audrey. She's watching us, like she suddenly thinks that there's something off about what occurred. Maybe it's just how different Lila looks.

"We have to catch a train, Cassel," says Lila.

"Yeah," I say. "I'll call you."

Audrey nods her head, still looking bewildered.

Lila and I head toward the sidewalk, and I know what this is. The blow-off and the getaway. High stakes or low stakes, the steps are the same.

Turns out I'm not like my dad at all. I really am just like my mother.

The train station is practically empty without the weekday commuter traffic. A guy about my age sits on one of the painted wooden benches, arguing with a girl whose eyes look red and puffy. An old woman leans over a pull cart of groceries. Standing in the far corner two girls with slender mohawks dyed a deep pink giggle together over a Game Boy.

"We should call your dad." I fish my cell phone out of my pocket. "Make sure he's going to be in his office when we get there."

Lila stares into the glass of a vending machine, her expression unreadable. Her reflection wavers a little, like maybe she's trembling. "We're not going to New York. We have to get him to meet me somewhere else."

"Why?"

"Because I don't want anyone but him to know I'm back. Anyone. We have no idea who's working with Anton."

"Okay," I say, nodding. After all she's been through, a little paranoia is probably not misplaced.

"I overheard a lot," she says. "I know their plan."

"Okay," I say again. I never thought she didn't.

"Promise me you won't tell him what happened to me," she says and lowers her voice. "I don't want him to know I was a cat."

"Okay," I say again. "I'm not going to say anything you don't want, but he's going to expect me to say *something*." I'm ashamed at my own relief. I wasn't sure what would happen next. As angry as I am at Barron and Philip, as much as I hate them right now, if Zacharov knew what they did, he'd kill them. I'm not sure I want them dead.

Lila reaches out her hand for my phone. "You won't be there. I'll go by myself."

I open my mouth, and she gives me a warning look that lets me know I better think carefully before I talk. "Look, just let me come with you on the train. I'll take off once you're wherever. Safe."

"I can take care of myself," she says, and there is a burr in her voice that sounds like a growl.

"I know that." I hand her the phone.

"Good," she says, flipping it open.

I frown as she punches in the numbers. Not telling Zacharov, even if it delays my need to make decisions, isn't a solution. His life is in danger. We need a strategy. "You can't think your dad is going to blame you? That's crazy."

"I think my father is going to feel sorry for me," she says. I can hear the ringing on the other end.

"He's going to think you were brave."

"Maybe," she says, "but he's not going to think I can take care of myself."

I hear a woman's voice, and Lila puts the phone to her ear. "I'd like to talk with Mr. Ivan Zacharov."

There is a long pause. Her lips press together into a thin line. "No, this is not a joke. He'll want to talk to me."

She kicks the wall with one too large boot. "Put him on the line!"

I raise my eyebrows. She covers the receiver with her hand. "They're getting him," she mouths.

"Hello, Daddy," she says, closing her eyes.

A few moments later she says, "No, I can't prove I'm me. How could I prove that?" I can hear his voice like a distant buzz, growing louder.

"I don't know. I don't remember," she says tightly. "Don't call me a liar. I *am* Lillian!"

She bites her lip and, after a few more moments, thrusts the phone in my direction. "Talk to him."

"What do you want me to say?" I keep my voice low, but the prospect of talking to Mr. Zacharov makes my palms sweat.

She reaches over to a tray of brochures and shoves one at me. "Tell him to meet us there."

I look down at it.

"He's got a room at the Taj Mahal," Lila hisses.

I take the phone. "Um, hello, sir," I say into the receiver, but he's still yelling. Finally it seems to register that she's no longer on the line.

His voice is that of someone used to his commands being obeyed. "Where is she? Where are you now? Just tell me that."

"She wants us to meet you in Atlantic City. She says you have a place there. At the Taj Mahal."

The phone goes so silent that for a moment I think he hung up on me.

"What kind of setup am I walking into?" he says finally, slowly.

"She just wants you to meet her. Alone. Be there at nine tonight. And don't tell anyone." I don't know how else to keep him from arguing, so I close the phone.

I look at Lila. "Can we actually get there by nine?"

She spreads open the schedule. "Yeah, plenty of time. That was perfect."

I carefully feed a twenty into the machine out by the steps and punch in our destination. The change comes in coins, silver dollars ringing against the tray like bells.

You can't take a train from the middle of Jersey directly to Atlantic City. You have to ride all the way to Philadelphia and change trains at Thirtieth Street Station for the Atlantic City line. As soon as we settle into our seats, Lila rips open the bag and eats the three chocolate bars in quick greedy bites. Then she wipes her face with a fist, knuckles down over her cheek to her nose. It isn't a human gesture, or at least it isn't how humans make the same gesture.

Uncomfortable, I look out the cracked grimy glass at the sea of houses blurring past. Each one, full of secrets.

"Tell me what happened that night," I say. "The rest of it. When I changed you."

"Okay," she says. "But first I need you to understand why my father can't know what happened to me. I'm his only child and I'm a girl. Families like mine—they're really traditional. Women might be powerful workers, but they're seldom leaders. Get it?"

I nod my head.

"If Dad found out what happened, he'd bring down vengeance on Anton and your brothers—maybe even on you. But afterward I'd be the daughter who needed to be protected. I could never be the head of the family.

"I'm going to get my own vengeance and I'm going to save my father from Anton. Then he's going to see that I deserve to be his heir." She crosses her legs, propping her feet next to me. My boots are huge on her, and one of the laces has come undone.

It's hard to picture her as the head of the Zacharov family.

I nod again. I think of Barron kicking me in the ribs. I think of Philip looking down at me as I writhed. Anger rises up in me, white hot and dangerous. "You're going to need me to do that."

Her eyes narrow. "Is that a problem?"

I loathe them, but they're my family. "I want you to leave my brothers out of your plans."

I can see her jaw clench as she brings her teeth together abruptly. "I deserve revenge," she says.

"You want to deal with your family your way. Fine. Let me deal with *my* family."

"You don't even know what they did to you."

I flinch from the surge of dread I feel. Swallow it down. "Okay, tell me."

She licks her lips. "You want to know what happened that night? I told you that they were arguing. Anton told Barron to get rid of me. You were supposed to turn me into . . . into something. Something glass so he could smash me. Something dead so I'd be dead. That's what they kept saying while you were pinning me to the floor.

"Philip said that if you didn't do it, they were going to have to hurt me and it would make a mess. Barron kept saying something about remembering what I did to you and I kept shouting that I didn't do anything." Her gaze drops for a moment.

Tells. Everyone has them. "Why did Anton want you dead?"

"He wants to take over my family. He was afraid Dad would never tap him as his heir with me around. So he always wanted me dead. He just needed a way to make it happen that wouldn't implicate him.

"The excuse for getting rid of me was that Barron had asked me to make some people sleepwalk out of their houses. I would brush against them during the day, and then that night they'd have a dream and they'd get up and go stand on their lawns. Sometimes they woke up on the way out and the curse faded, sometimes not. I didn't know what it was for. Barron said they were people who owed my father money and that Barron would be able to talk to them, keep them from getting hurt. Anton found out that Barron had used me to help and told him that I had to be killed or else."

"Or else what? What's the big deal about making people sleepwalk?" I lean back. The vinyl seat squeaks.

"Um, your brothers? They make people disappear. That's what they do."

"They kill people?" My voice comes out too loud. I don't know why I'm shocked. I know criminals do bad things, and I get that my brothers are criminals. I had just assumed that whatever Philip did for Anton was small time. Leg-breaking stuff.

Lila frowns at me and looks around the train, but even after my outburst no one seems interested in us. Her voice goes low, to practically a whisper, like she can make up for my mistake through overcompensation. "*They* don't kill anyone. They get their little brother to do it for them. He turns people into objects. Then they dump the objects."

"What?" I heard her; I just can't believe I heard her right.

"They've been using you as a human garbage disposal." She makes a frame with her hands and looks at me through it. "Portrait of a teenage assassin."

I stand up, even though we're on a train and there's nowhere for me to go.

"Cassel?" She reaches out for me, and I step back.

There's a roaring in my ears. I'm grateful. I don't think I can listen to much more.

"I'm sorry. But you had to suspect—"

I think I'm going to throw up.

I push my way through the heavy doors and onto the platform between the cars. The joining between the two cars swings back and forth beneath my feet. I am standing right above the hooks and chains that connect the train into its snaking shape. Cold air blows back my hair, then hot air from the engine hits my face.

I stand there, hands against the sliding metal, until I start to calm down.

I think I understand why all those workers got rounded up and shot. I think I understand that kind of fear now.

We are, largely, who we remember ourselves to be. That's why habits are so hard to break. If we know ourselves to be liars, we expect not to tell the truth. If we think of ourselves as honest, we try harder.

For three whole days I wasn't a killer. Lila had come back from the dead, and with her, the abatement of my self-loathing. But now the pile of corpses teeters above me, threatening to crash down and suffocate me with guilt.

All my life I wanted my brothers to trust me. To let me in on their secrets. I wanted them, Philip especially, to think of me as a worthy accomplice.

Even after they kicked the crap out of me, my instinct was to try and save them.

Now I just want revenge.

After all, I'm already a murderer. No one really expects a murderer to stop killing. I grip the metal bar on the rolling train, my fingers clenching around it like it's Philip's throat. I don't want to be a monster, but maybe it's too late to be anything else.

The door swings open and the conductor steps onto the platform and past me. "You can't ride out here," he says, looking back.

"Okay," I say, and he opens the door to the next car, ready to collect more tickets. He doesn't really care. I could probably stay where I am for a long while before he comes back through again.

I suck in another couple breaths of fetid air and then go back to Lila.

"Very dramatic," she says when I sit down. "Storming off and all." Her eyes look bruised around the edges. She'd found a pen somewhere and started doodling in ink on her leg, below the knee.

I feel awful, but I don't apologize.

"Yeah," I say, "I'm a dramatic guy. High strung."

That makes her smile, but it fades fast. "I hated you, lying in your comfortable bed at your school, caring about grades and girls and not about what you did to me."

I grit my teeth. "You slept in my bed. You really think it's that comfortable?"

She laughs, but it sounds more like a sob.

I look out the window. We're in woods now. "I shouldn't have said that. You were sleeping in a cage. I'm not a good person, Lila." I hesitate. "But I did—I do care what I've done to you. I thought about you every single day. And I am sorry. I'm grovelingly, pathetically sorry."

"I don't want your pity," she says, but her voice sounds gentler.

"Too bad," I say.

She gives me a wry lopsided grin and kicks me with my own boot.

"I'd like it if you'd tell me the rest of what happened. How I transformed you. How you got away. I'm not going to freak out anymore. I'll listen to whatever you want to tell me."

She nods and goes back to drawing on her leg. Swirls that spiral out from an ink blue center. "Right. So. There you are, pressing me down to the carpet.

"You look crazy, angry. But then you get this weird smile on your face. I'm scared, really scared, because I think you're going to do it. You lean down and whisper in my ear. '*Run.*' That's what you say."

"Run?" I ask.

"I know. Crazy, right? You're still on top of me—how

am I supposed to do anything? But then I start to change."
The pen presses against her skin, hard now. It's scratching her leg. "It felt like my skin was getting tight and itchy.
My bones twisted and I grew hunched, small. My vision
blurred, and then I could crawl away from you. I didn't
know how to run on four legs, but I ran anyway.

"I heard you scream, but I didn't look back. There was a
lot of shouting.

"They caught me under some bushes. I made it out of
the house, but I just couldn't run fast enough."

She stops drawing lines and starts punching the point
of the pen against her leg.

"Hey," I say, putting my gloved hand on top of hers.

She blinks quickly, like she forgot where she was. "Barron put me in a cage and he put a shock collar around my
neck—the kind they use on little dogs. He said that it was
better than if I was dead. I was out of the way, but he could
still use me. I made people sleepwalk right out to you guys;
it's easy for a cat to slip into a house and to touch someone.
I even made you sleepwalk out of the dorms to where your
brothers were waiting.

"You looked at me like I was nothing. An animal." Her
nostrils flare. "I thought you'd been trying to save me. But
you never tried to save me again."

I don't know what to say. I feel a deep, aching sorrow
that hurts more than I know how to express. I don't have
the words. I want to touch her, but I don't deserve it.

She shakes her head. "I know Barron worked you. I'm
here now because of you. I shouldn't say that."

"It's okay." I take a deep breath. "I have a lot to be sorry for."

"I should have guessed that they'd changed your memories. Barron's so busy trying to make people remember what he wants them to and make them forget everything else that he doesn't notice that he's strip-mining his own brain. He can't pull the strings because he's forgotten where they are.

"It's just that you go so crazy being alone like that. Sometimes he'd forget my water or food and I'd cry and cry and cry." She stops talking and looks out the window. "I would try to tell myself stories to pass the time. Fairy tales. Parts of books. But they got used up.

"In the beginning I tried to escape, but I guess after a while I just used up all my hope like I used up the stories." Lila lowers her voice and leans into me, so close that the hairs on the back of my neck rise with her breath. "When I found out you were going to hurt my dad, when I overheard them, I realized escaping didn't matter. I knew I had to kill you."

"I'm glad you didn't," I say. I think of my bare feet sliding on slate.

She smiles. "It turned out Barron wasn't watching me as closely as he had before. I wore down the nylon part of the collar enough. It was still hard to get it the rest of the way off, but I did it."

I think of the blood crusted on her fur when I saw her that first time.

"Do you still hate me?" I ask.

"I don't know," she says. "A little."

My ribs ache. I want to close my eyes. Somewhere on the train a baby starts to cry. The businessman two seats in front of us is on the phone. "I don't want sorbet," he says. "I don't like sorbet. Just give me some damn ice cream."

I think maybe I deserve for my ribs to hurt more.

CHAPTER FIFTEEN

THE LIGHTS OF ATLANTIC

City glitter along the boardwalk, as bright as day. We finally get out of the taxi in front of the Taj Mahal hotel, both of us sleepy and stretching from the long trip.

I look at my watch. It's about fifteen minutes after nine. She's late.

"I guess I can take it from here," Lila says.

Yawning, I take out a pen, her pen. The one she was writing on her leg with. I write my number on her arm, right above the top of her glove.

She's watching with half-lidded eyes as ink marks stretch across her skin. I wonder what it would be like to kiss her now, under the streetlight, with my eyes open.

"Let me know when you're okay," I say softly instead.

She looks at the number. "Are you going back?"

I shake my head. "I'll stretch my legs and get something to eat. I'm not going anywhere until you call."

She nods. "Wish me luck."

"Luck," I say.

I watch her walk off, a swagger in her stride, toward the hotel entrance. I wait a couple of minutes, then I start through the doors into the casino.

Inside I inhale the familiar smell of stale cigarillos and whisky. The machines sing and clank. Coins clatter in the distance. People hunker over the slots, big plastic cups in one hand and tokens in the other. Some of them look like they've been there a long time.

Two security guys peel away from the wall and start in my direction.

"Hey, kid," one of them calls. "Wait a sec." They probably figure I'm underage.

"Just leaving," I say, and push through the back door. The sea air stings my face.

I stalk down the worn gray planks, hands in my pockets, thinking of Lila upstairs with her father. When I was a kid, Zacharov was a shadowy figure, a legend, the boogeyman. I met him maybe three times, and one of those times was while I was being thrown out of his daughter's birthday party.

He laughed, I remember that.

At the back of the Taj Mahal a few old women lean over a railing, throwing something onto the sand. Some guys in tracksuits smoke near the entrance, calling to women as they pass. And a man in a long cashmere coat and silvery white hair looks out at the sea.

I touch my pocket with my phone in it. I should call Grandad, but I'm not ready to make excuses.

The white-haired man turns toward me. Glancing around, I notice two huge guys trying to look inconspicuous near a taffy shop window.

"Cassel Sharpe," Mr. Zacharov says, slight accent making my name sound exotic. Even though it's already dark, sunglasses cover his eyes. A fat, pale red stone glitters in the pin on his tie. "I believe a phone call was made to me from your cell phone."

Turns out Mom was right about landlines after all.

"Okay," I say, trying to act casual.

He looks around as if he'll be able to pick her out of the crowd. "Where is she?"

"Up in the room," I tell him. "Where she said she was going to be."

There's a deep-throated yowl, and I turn suddenly, my body jerking. My muscles hurt. I forgot how sore they already were.

Mr. Zacharov laughs. "Cats," he says. "Dozens of feral cats under the boardwalk. Lila always loved cats. You remember."

I don't say anything.

"If she was in the room, my people would have called." He tilts his head and slips a gloved hand into his pocket. "I think you are playing a game. Who did you get to pretend to be my daughter on the phone? Were you going to ask me for money? This seems like a very stupid game."

"She said to meet her alone." I lean toward him, and he holds out a gloved hand to stop me from getting too close. One of his goons heads toward us. I lower my voice. "She probably saw one of *your people* and split."

He laughs. "You are a pathetic villain, Cassel Sharpe. A real disappointment."

"No," I say. "She really is—" The big guy jerks my arms back and up, hard.

"Please," I gasp. "My ribs."

"Thanks for telling me where to hit," the guy says. His nose is permanently bent to one side. He's a living stereotype.

Mr. Zacharov pats my cheek. I can smell the leather of his glove. "I thought you might turn out more like your grandfather, but your mother spoiled all you boys."

That makes me laugh.

The guy jerks my arms up again. They make a sound like they're popping out of their sockets, and I make a different kind of sound.

"Daddy." Lila's voice, pitched low and oddly menacing, cuts through the noise of the boardwalk. "Leave Cassel alone."

Lila steps up from the beach. For a moment I see her as he must, half ghost and half stranger. She's a woman, not the child that he lost, but her cruel mouth is identical to his own.

Besides, there can't be that many people with a single blue eye and a single green one.

He blinks. Then he takes off his sunglasses slowly. "Lila?" He sounds as brittle as glass.

The guy relaxes his grip, and I jerk away from him. I try to rub some feeling back into my arms.

"I hope you trust your men," she says. Her voice breaks. "Because this is secret. I am a secret."

"I'm sorry," says Mr. Zacharov. "I didn't think you were real—" He reaches out gloved hands toward her.

She just stands there, bristling, like she's fighting something wild inside her. She doesn't go to him.

"Let's get out of here," I say, touching her arm. "We'll get this sorted out in private."

Zacharov looks at me like he can't quite remember who I am.

"Inside," I say.

The two big guys in long coats seem relieved to have something to do.

"People are looking," one of them says, putting his hand on Mr. Zacharov's back and steering him into the casino.

The other glances at me warily. Lila takes my gloved hand and gives him a cold look that I'm grateful for. He backs off, hanging behind us as we head into Taj Mahal.

I raise my eyebrows at Lila.

"You have a real talent for getting your ass kicked," she says.

No one questions us as we walk across the casino floor and get into the elevator.

The raw emotion on Zacharov's face is something private—something I know he wouldn't want me to see. I wonder if I should try to leave, but Lila's gloved hand is clutching mine hard enough to hurt. I try to keep my gaze trained above the elevator doors, watching the numbers go up and up and up.

In the suite there's a wood-paneled wall with a single flat screen, a leather divan, and a bowl of fresh hydrangeas on a low table. The place is enormous, cavernous, with massive windows open to show the expanse of ink black ocean beyond. One of the big guys throws his coat over a chair and lets me see the guns strapped underneath his arms and across his back. More guns than he's got hands.

Zacharov pours pale liquid into cut glass and throws it back. "You two want a drink?" he says to us. "Minibar is full of Cokes."

I get up.

"No," he says. "I am your host." He nods to one of his men. The man grunts and moves to the refrigerator.

"Just water," Lila says.

"Some aspirin," I say.

"Oh, come on," the guy says as he hands over the glasses and the pills. "I didn't hurt you that bad."

"Nope," I say. "You didn't." I chew three aspirins and try to lean back against the pillows in a way that doesn't make me want to scream.

"You go down to the casino," Zacharov tells the guys. "Win some money."

"Sure thing," one says. He gets his coat again and they head slowly for the door. Zacharov looks at me like he wants to ask me to join them.

"Cassel," he says, "how long have you known the location of my daughter?"

"About three days," I say.

Lila narrows her eyes, but I figure there's no point in hiding that.

He pours himself another drink. "Why didn't you call me sooner?"

"Lila just showed up out of nowhere," I say, which is basically true. "I thought she was dead. I haven't seen her since we were both fourteen. I was just following her lead."

Zacharov takes a sip from his glass and winces. "Lila, are you going to tell me where you've been?"

She shrugs slim shoulders and avoids his gaze.

"You're protecting someone. Your mother? I always thought she'd taken you away from me. Tell me you got fed up with the old—"

"No!" Lila says.

He's still lost in the thought. "She practically accused me of having you murdered. She told the FBI that I said you were better off dead than with her. The FBI!"

"I wasn't with Mom," Lila says. "Dad, Mom had nothing to do with this."

He stops and stares at her. "Then what? Did someone do . . ." He leaves the sentence unfinished and turns toward me. "Did you? Did you hurt my daughter?"

I hesitate.

"He didn't do anything to me," Lila says.

Zacharov touches a gloved hand to my shoulder. "Your mother's appeal is coming up, isn't it, Cassel?"

"Yes, sir," I say.

"I'd hate to see anything go wrong with that. If I find out—"

"Leave him alone," says Lila. "Listen to me, Dad. Just listen for a minute. I'm not ready to talk about what happened. Stop trying to find someone to blame. Stop with the interrogation. I'm home now. Aren't you glad I'm home?"

"Of course I'm glad," he says, clearly stricken.

I touch my sore ribs without thinking. I want another aspirin, but I don't know where the guy put the bottle.

"I'm trusting you for her sake," he says to me, and then his voice softens. "My daughter and I need to talk. We need to be alone—you understand that, right?"

I nod my head. Lila is looking out at the black water. She doesn't turn.

Zacharov takes his wallet from inside his jacket and counts out five hundred dollars. "Here," he says.

"I can't take that," I say.

"I'd feel better if you did," he says.

I stand up and try not to wince while doing it. I shake my head. "I hope you didn't have your heart set on feeling better."

He snorts. "One of the boys will see you home."

"I can go? Really?"

"Don't kid yourself. I can pick you up like a dime off the sidewalk anytime I want."

I want to say something to Lila, but her back is still to me. I can't guess her thoughts.

"I'm having a little party on Wednesday at a place called Koshchey's. A fund-raiser. You should come," Zacharov says. "Do you know why I like Koshchey's?

I shake my head.

"Do you know who Koshchey the Deathless is?"

"No," I say, thinking of the strange mural on the ceiling of the restaurant.

"In Russian folklore Koshchey is a sorcerer who can become a whirlwind and destroy his enemies." Zacharov touches the glittering pin on his chest. "He hides away his soul in a duck's egg so he can't be killed. Don't cross me, Cassel. I am not a safe man to make your enemy."

"I understand," I say, and open the door. What I understand is that Lila and I are on our own and we don't even have a plan.

"And, Cassel?"

I turn.

"Thank you for bringing my daughter back."

I walk out the door. As I wait for the elevator to come, my phone rings. I am so tired that it seems a huge effort to take it out of my pocket.

"Hello?" I say.

"Cassel?" says Dean Wharton. He doesn't sound happy. "I'm sorry to be calling so late, but we just got the final call from one of our board members on the West Coast. Welcome back to Wallingford. We got the report from your doctor and the whole board voted. We'd like you to remain a day student on a probationary basis, but so long as you don't get into any more trouble, we may consider letting you return to the dorms for your senior year."

I smother the ironic laughter that threatens to crawl up my throat. My con worked. I can go back to school. But I can't go back to being the person I thought I was. "Thank you, sir," I manage to say.

"We'll expect to see you tomorrow morning, Mr. Sharpe. Since you've paid through the end of the year, please feel free to eat breakfast and dinner in the cafeteria."

"Monday morning?" I echo.

"Yes, tomorrow, in the morning. Unless you have other plans," he says dryly.

"No," I say. "Of course not. See you tomorrow, Dean. Thank you, Dean."

One of Zacharov's guys drives me home. His name turns out to be Stanley. He's from Iowa and doesn't know practically any Russian. He's not good with languages, he says.

He tells me all that when he lets me out in front of my house. Even though he made me sit in the back of the town car with the tinted privacy divider up, I guess he could see more than I thought. I guess he watched me unbutton my shirt and brush my fingers over the bruises purpling the skin over my ribs, testing each bone for give. I'm not guessing that just because he was so friendly when we got to the house—he also gave me his entire bottle of aspirin.

CHAPTER SIXTEEN

MY GRANDFATHER'S NOT at home when I get there, but there's a note scratched in pen on the back of a receipt and stuck to the fridge with an I ♥ CHIHUAHUAS magnet.

Gone to Carney for a few days.
Call me when you get in.

I stare at the note, trying to decipher what it means, but I can't quite think beyond the fact that there won't be a car for me to borrow tomorrow. I stumble upstairs, set the alarm on my phone, push a chair up against the door, and chew up another handful of aspirin. I don't even bother kicking off my shoes or getting under the covers; I just smother my face in the pillow and drop down into sleep like a dead man finally returning to his grave.

For a moment after my alarm goes off and I'm jolted awake, I don't know where I am. I look around the bedroom that I slept in when I was a kid and it seems that it must have belonged to someone else.

I lean over and switch off my phone, blink a few times. My head feels clearer than it has in days.

The pain has abated some—maybe because I finally got some sleep—but the reality of what's happened and what's about to happen seems to finally be sinking in. I don't have a lot of time—three days—to plan.

And I need to stay away from my brothers long enough to do it. Wallingford will be good for that. They don't know I've been let back in, and even if they figure it out, at least being at school isn't obviously hiding. At least I can continue to act like I'm a killer robot waiting for them to utter a command word.

I fumble in my closet for my scratchy shirt and uniform pants. I didn't bring my jacket or shoes with me when I packed up the stuff in my dorm, but I have a bigger problem than that. I don't have a ride to school.

I put on sneakers and call Sam.

"Do you have any idea what time it is?" he says groggily.

"I need you to pick me up," I tell him.

"Dude, where are you?"

I give him the address and he hangs up. I hope he doesn't just roll over and go back to sleep.

In the bathroom, as I brush my teeth, I see that my cheek is purpled with bruising above the thin beard that's grown in. My hair was getting too long before and it's even shaggier now, but I wet it down and try to comb it into shape.

I don't shave, even though it's against the rules to be anything but as smooth as a baby's bottom, because I can just guess how bad that bruise would look if they could see the rest of it.

Downstairs, as I brew the coffee and watch the black liquid drip down, I think of Lila looking out at the sea. I think of her with her back to me as I'm walking out the door.

Mom says that when you're scamming someone, there needs to be something at stake, something so big that they're not going to walk away, even if things get sketchy. They have to go all in. Once they're all in, you win.

Lila's at stake. She's not walking away, which means I can't walk away either.

I'm all in.

They're winning.

All the teachers are really nice to me. They mostly—with the exception of Dr. Stewart, who gives me a whole bunch of zeros, enunciating the numbers carefully as he puts each one in the grade book—understand that I failed to keep up with the homework, even though they emailed me assignments daily. They tell me they're happy I'm back. Ms. Noyes even hugs me.

My fellow students look at me like I'm a dangerous lunatic with two heads and a nasty communicable disease. I keep my head down, eat my Tater Tots at lunch, and try to look interested in my classes.

All the while I'm daydreaming schemes.

Daneca sits down next to me in the lunchroom and pushes her civics notebook in my direction. "You want to copy my notes?"

"Copy your notes?" I say slowly, looking at the book.

She rolls her eyes. Her hair is in two braids, each one tied with rough string. "You don't have to if you don't want to."

"No," I say. "I do. I definitely do." I look at the notebook in front of me, flipping the pages, seeing her looping handwriting. I outline the marks with my gloved finger, an idea starting to form in my mind.

I start to grin.

Sam sets down a tray on the other side. It's piled with a gooey lump of delicious-smelling mac-n-cheese.

"Hey," he says. "Prepare to be very happy."

That's the last thing I expect him to say. "What?" I ask. My fingers are tracing new words in the margin of Daneca's notebook. Plans. I'm writing in a familiar style, but not my own.

"Nobody thought you were coming back. Nobody. Nooooooobody."

"Thanks. Yeah, I can see how you'd think I'd find that thrilling."

"Dude," he says. "A lot of people just lost a lot of money. We made up for that bad bet. We're kings of finance!"

I shake my head in amazement. "I always said you were a genius."

We punch each other in the shoulder and punch fists and just keep smiling like morons.

Daneca wrinkles her brow, and Sam stops. "Uh," Sam says. "There were some other things we wanted to talk to you about."

"Less fun things, I'm guessing," I say.

"I'm sorry about losing your cat," she says to me after a few moments.

"Oh," I say, looking up. "No. The cat's fine. The cat's back where she belongs."

"What do you mean?"

I shake my head. "Too complicated."

"Are you in some kind of trouble?" Sam asks. "Because if you were in some kind of trouble, maybe you could tell us. Dude, no offense, but you seem like you're losing it."

Daneca clears her throat. "He told me what you told him when he found you in bed with that girl. About being a—"

I look around the cafeteria, but no one seems close enough to hear. "You told her I was a worker?"

Sam looks down quickly. "We've been hanging out a lot, what with the play and all. I'm sorry. Sorry. I know that wasn't cool."

Of course. Normal people gossip. Normal people tell each other things, especially when they're trying to impress each other. I guess I should feel betrayed, but all I feel is relief.

I'm tired of pretending.

"Are you guys a thing?" I ask. "A boyfriendly-girlfriendly thing?"

"Yeah," Daneca says, her expression some combination of pleasure and embarrassment.

Sam looks like he's going to pass out.

"That's great," I say. "I didn't mean to lie to your mother, Daneca. I didn't know." But I know I wouldn't have told her. I would have lied; I just didn't get a chance.

"Are you going out with that girl?" she asks. "The one you were sleeping with?"

That startles a laugh out of me. "No."

"So, what, you were just—"

"We weren't," I say quickly. "Believe me, we weren't. For one thing, she's probably insane. And for another, she hates me."

"Okay, so who is she?" Daneca asks.

"I thought you'd want to know what I am."

"I want you to believe you can trust me. And Sam. You can trust us." She pauses. "You have to trust somebody."

I bow my head. She's right that if I want any plan to succeed, I'll need help. "Her name is Lila Zacharov."

Daneca gapes at me. "The girl that disappeared back, like, when we were in middle school?"

"You heard of her?"

"Sure," Daneca says, picking up one of my Tater Tots. Oil soaks her glove. "Everyone heard about it. A crime family princess. Her case was on the news a lot. My mom got weird about letting me go anywhere by myself after it happened." She puts the tot into her mouth. "So, what really happened to her?"

I hesitate, but it's all or nothing now. "She was turned into a cat," I say. I can feel my face twisting into an awkward grimace. It feels so unnatural to tell the truth.

Daneca chokes, spitting the food into her hand.

"A transformation worker?" Daneca says. Then, after a moment, she whispers. "*The* cat?"

"That's *crazy*," says Sam.

"I know you think that I'm making this up," I say, rubbing my face.

"We don't," she says, and she shifts a little.

Sam winces. I think she kicked him under the table. "I didn't mean crazy like 'You're crazy,'" he says. "I meant it like 'Whoa.'"

"Sure. Okay." I'm not sure if they believe me, but I feel a dizzy sense of hope.

It occurs to me that I've done exactly what I need to in order to set up Daneca and Sam for a con job. They're already invested. They trust me. They've seen me pull a scam before. This is bigger stakes; I just have to promise them a bigger score.

My phone buzzes and I look down. It's a number I don't know. I flip it open and bring it to my ear.

"Hello?"

"This is what I want you to do," says Lila. "You're going to go to the party on Wednesday and pretend to work my dad—the same way you were supposed to. I'm trusting you to fake it. I think Dad's smart enough to go along with you."

"That's the plan?"

"That's your part. I can't talk for long, so you have to listen.

A few minutes later I'm going to come through the door with a gun, shoot Anton and save Dad. My part. Simple."

There is so much that can go wrong with that plan that I don't even know where to start. "Lila—"

"I even got your brother Philip out of it—just like you wanted," she says.

"How?" I ask, startled.

"I told my bodyguard he was poking around the penthouse and saw me. They let me lock him up here. That means we just have Barron and Anton to worry about."

Just Barron and Anton. I rub the bridge of my nose. "You said you were going to keep *both* my brothers out of it."

"Our arrangement has changed," she says. "There's just one problem."

"What's that?"

"No one here is supposed to carry a gun at the party. They won't let me have one."

"I don't have a—" I stop myself. Really not a good idea to talk about me and guns in school—especially not in the same sentence. "I don't have one."

"There's going to be a metal detector," she says. "Get one and think of a way to get it in."

"That's impossible," I say.

"You owe me," says Lila. Her voice is as soft as ash.

"I know," I say, defeated. "I know that."

The line goes dead.

I am left staring at the cafeteria wall, trying to convince myself that she isn't setting me up.

"Did something happen?" Sam asks.

"I've got to go," I say. "Class is going to start."

"We'll skip class," says Daneca.

I shake my head. "Not on my first day back."

"We'll meet up at activities period," Sam says. "Outside the theater. And then you're going to tell us what's going on."

On the way to class, I call back the number Lila called from.

A man answers; not Zacharov. "Is she there?" I ask.

"I don't know who you're talking about," he says gruffly.

"Just tell her I need two more tickets for Wednesday."

"There's no one here—"

"Just tell her," I say.

I have to believe he does.

Leaning against the brick wall of the building, I start talking. Telling Sam and Daneca feels like peeling off my own skin to expose everything underneath. It hurts.

I don't play them. I don't even try. I just start at the beginning and tell them about being the only nonworker in a family of workers. I tell them about Lila and thinking that I'd killed her, about finding myself on the roof.

"How could all of you be curse workers?" Sam asks.

"Working is like green eyes," Daneca says. "Sometimes it just shows up in families, but if the parents are both workers, worker kids are more likely. Like, look at how almost one percent of Australians are workers, because the country was founded as a worker penal colony, but only, like, one one-hundredth of a percent of people in the U.S. are workers."

"Oh," says Sam. I don't think that he was expecting such a comprehensive answer. I know I wasn't.

Daneca shrugs.

He turns to me. "So, what kind of worker are you?"

"He's probably a luck worker," says Daneca. "Everyone's a luck worker."

"He's not," Sam says. "He'd tell us that."

"What I am . . . doesn't matter. The point is that my brothers want me to kill this guy and I don't want to do it."

"So you're a death worker," Sam says.

Daneca punches him in the arm, and despite being huge, he flinches. "Ow."

I groan. "Look, it really doesn't matter because I'm not going to work anyone, okay?"

"Can you just bail?" Sam asks. "Skip town?"

I nod for a moment, then shake my head. "Not going to."

"Let me try to understand," Sam says. "You believe your brothers can potentially make you kill someone, but you're going to stick around and let them try. What the hell?"

"I *believe*," I say, "that I am a very clever young man with two fantastically clever friends. And I further believe that one of those friends has been looking for an opportunity to display his expertise in fake firearms."

At that, Sam's eyes take on an acquisitive gleam. "Really? The guy who's getting shot has to put the wires through his pants, put the trigger in his pocket or something. And it would have to be timed so it happens at the exact moment as the gunshot. Unless you're talking about faking death work. That's a whole lot easier, really."

"Gunshots only," I say.

"Wait," Daneca says. "What is it—exactly—that you're planning on doing?"

"I have a couple of ideas," I say, as innocently as possible. "Mostly bad ones."

We talk through the plan a dozen times at least. We refine it down from the ridiculous to the unlikely to something that might work. Then, instead of going to dinner in the cafeteria, they drive me over to Barron's house and I show them how to pick a lock.

Without Grandad the house feels empty and enormous. I miss the teetering piles as I brew a pot of coffee. This house feels unfamiliar and disturbingly full of possibilities. I spread out the new notebooks in a fan in front of me, crack my knuckles, and get ready for a long night.

When I wake up Tuesday morning with drool darkening the cuff of my shirt and Sam hitting the horn in the driveway, I barely manage to brush my teeth before I stumble out the door.

He hands me a cup of coffee. "Did you sleep in those clothes?" he asks.

I almost can't stand the thought of drinking more coffee, but I do. "Sleep?" I ask.

"You have blue ink on your cheek," he says.

I flip down the visor and look in the tiny mirror. My face scruff is looking scruffier and my eyes are bloodshot. I look terrible. The smear of ink across my jawline is the least of my problems.

At school I am so out of it that Ms. Noyes takes me aside and asks if everything is okay at home. Then she checks to see if my pupils are dilated. Dr. Stewart tells me to shave.

I fall asleep in the back of the debate team meeting. I wake up in the middle of a debate about whether or not to wake me. Then I drag myself over to the drama department for a tutorial from Sam on weapons.

I wolf down dinner and then head out to the parking lot with Sam.

"Mr. Sharpe," Valerio calls, walking toward us. "Mr. Yu. I hope you weren't thinking of going off campus."

"I'm just going to drive Cassel home," Sam says.

"You have a half hour to get back before study hall starts," he says, pointing to his watch.

I go back to the table and the notebooks and wind up sleeping on the downstairs couch with all the lights on. There's so much work to do. I don't remember half of what I write and when I look at the words in the morning, they don't look like I wrote them at all.

Sam arrives right on time.

"Can I borrow your car?" I say. "I don't think I'm going to school today. I've got a big night."

He hands over the keys. "You'll want a hearse of your own when you feel how this thing hugs the road."

I drive him to school, then I break back into Barron's house. I'm the best kind of thief, the kind that leaves behind items equal in value to those he's stolen.

Then I go home and shave until my skin is as slick as any slickster's.

*   *   *

I'm so exhausted that I fall asleep at four and don't wake up until Barron shakes my arm.

"Hey, sleepyhead," says Barron, sitting in the chair I've never liked, with his arms folded. He rocks back, pushing the front legs off the floor with his weight.

Anton leans against the door frame leading into the dining room. A toothpick rests on the swell of his bottom lip. "Better get dressed, kid."

"What are you doing here?" I ask, trying to sound sincere. I walk past them into the kitchen and pour myself some of the day-old coffee. It tastes a little bit like battery acid, but in a good way.

"We're going to a party," Barron says making a face when he sees what I'm doing. "In the city. It's going to be pretty swank. Lots of hoodlums."

"Philip's stuck," says Anton. "Zacharov sent him on an errand at the last minute." I know that's not true, but I can't tell if Anton is worried. I can imagine Lila sending him a message with Philip's phone.

I rub my hand over my eyes. "You want me to come?"

Anton and Barron exchange glances. "Yeah," Barron says. "I thought we told you about it."

"No—look, you guys go ahead. I've got a lot of homework."

Anton takes the cup out of my hand and spits his toothpick into it. "Don't be stupid. No kid your age wants to sit home doing homework instead of partying. Now get upstairs and get in the shower."

I go. The shower feels like hot needles on my back,

relaxing my muscles. There's a spider—one I missed—hunched in a corner of the ceiling, tending a knot of eggs. I shampoo my hair and watch the beads of water catch in her web.

When I step out into the foggy bathroom, the door is open and Barron's there to hand me a towel. He gives me a quick glance before I wrap it around me. I try to turn to one side, but I'm not fast enough.

"What's that on your leg?"

I realize that naked means easy to check for amulets.

"Hey," I say, "there's this thing called privacy. You might have heard of it."

He grabs my shoulder. "Let me see your leg."

I clutch the towel tighter. "It's just a cut."

He lets me push past him into the hall, but Anton's waiting in my bedroom.

"Grab him," Barron says, and Anton kicks my leg, knocking me off balance. I fall onto the bed, which isn't bad except that Barron locks his arm under my jaw and pulls me up on the mattress.

"Get off me!" I yell. The towel is gone and I struggle, embarrassed and scared, while Anton reaches into his back pocket.

A knife blade springs up out of the ebonized hilt in his hands. "What have we here?" Anton says, poking my calf where the stones are sewn up in my skin. The whole area throbs when he presses on it. Infected.

When he cuts me, I can't help it. I scream.

CHAPTER SEVENTEEN

"SLICK," BARRON SAYS, looking at my bloody leg. He places the remains of three wet, red pebbles into his pocket. "How long have you been using that trick?"

Even the best plans go wrong. The universe doesn't like anyone thinking it can be controlled. All plans require some degree of improvisation, but they usually don't go wrong *right away*.

"Shove it up your ass," I say, which is pretty juvenile, but he's my brother and he brings that out of me. "Come on, hit me so hard that you knock a couple of my teeth out. That will be a great party look."

"He remembers," says Anton, shaking his head.

"We're screwed to the wall, Barron. Nice work."

Barron curses under his breath. "Who did you tell?"

I turn to him. "I know I'm a worker. A *transformation worker*. Let's start with *you* telling *me* why you made me think I wasn't one."

They exchange a maddening glance, like somehow they're going to be able to call a time out, go into the other room, and discuss what to tell me.

Barron sits on the end of my bed and composes himself. "Mom wanted us to lie to you. What you are—it's dangerous. She thought you'd be better off if you didn't know until you were older. When you figured it out as a little kid, she asked me to make you forget. That's how it started."

I look down at the gory sheets and the sluggishly bleeding hole in my leg. "So she knows? About all of this?"

Barron shakes his head, ignoring the dark look Anton sends in his direction. "No. We didn't want her to worry. Jail's been tough on her and the blowback from her work makes her emotions unstable. But money's been tight, even before she went inside. You know that."

I nod slowly.

"Philip came up with a plan. Assassination is the biggest, quickest money there is. And the crazy money goes to killers who are reliable—who can get rid of bodies permanently. With you, we could do that." He says all this like I'm going to be thrilled with my brother's cleverness. "Anton made sure that no one knew who was really responsible for the murders."

"And I don't get a say? In being a killer?"

He shrugs his shoulders. "You were just a kid. It didn't seem fair for you to go through a bunch of trauma. So we made you forget everything you did. We were trying to protect—"

"How about kicking me in the stomach? Was that the right amount of trauma? Or how about that?" I point to my leg. "You still protecting me, Barron?"

Barron opens his mouth, but no clever lie comes out.

"Philip tried to protect you," Anton says. "You wouldn't shut your mouth. You've had it easy. Time to toughen up." He hesitates, his tone becoming less sure. "When I was your age, I knew enough not to talk back to worker royalty. My mother cut these marks in my throat when I turned thirteen and reopened them to pack them with ash every year until I turned twenty. To remind me who I was." He touches the scars pearling his neck. "To remind me pain is the best teacher."

"Just tell us if you talked to anyone," Barron says.

You can't con an honest man. Only the greedy or the desperate are willing to put aside their reservations to get something they don't deserve. I've heard lots of people— my dad included—use that to justify grifting.

"Cut me in on the money," I say to Anton. "If I'm earning it, I decide how to spend it."

"Done," Anton says.

"I told my roommate Sam that I was a worker. Not what kind, just that I was one."

Anton lets out a long breath. "That's it? That's all you did?" He starts to laugh.

Barron joins in. Soon we're laughing like I told the best joke anyone ever heard.

A joke they're greedy and desperate enough to believe.

"Good, good," Anton says. "Put on a nice suit, okay? This isn't some school dance we're going to."

I limp to my closet. Leaning down, I sort through my rucksack as if for something appropriate. Pushing aside my uniform and a few pairs of jeans, I find a dress shirt and straighten up.

"So Philip had an idea and you went along with it? That doesn't sound like you," I say, walking awkwardly back to the doorway. Something catches my foot accidentally-on-purpose and I fake-stumble into Barron. My fingers are quick and nimble. "Whoa, sorry."

"Careful," he says.

I lean against the door frame and then yawn, covering my mouth with my hand. "Come on. Tell me why you really didn't say anything."

A weird half smile grows on Barron's face. "It's so unfair. You, of all people, get the holy grail of curse work. And me stuck with changing memories like I'm some kind of cleanup crew. Sure, it's useful when you want to make some mundane thing easier. I could cheat at school or I could keep someone from remembering what I did to them, but what does that mean? Not much. Do you know how many transformation workers are even born in the world in a given decade? Maybe one. Maybe. You were born with real power and you didn't even appreciate it."

"I didn't *know* it," I say.

"It's wasted on you," he says, placing his ungloved hand on my shoulder. The hair on the back of my neck rises.

I try to react like I haven't palmed the last unbroken stone charm he cut out of me and then swallowed it. Maybe transformation work is wasted on me, but sleight of hand isn't.

I end up taking one of Dad's old suits out of my parents' room. Mom, predictably, didn't throw out any of Dad's belongings, so all the suits still hang in the back of his closet, slightly out of date and smelling of mothballs, as though they're waiting for him to return from a long vacation. A double-breasted jacket fits me surprisingly well, and when I stick my hands in the pockets of the pin-striped pants, I find a crumpled tissue that still smells like his cologne.

I make a fist around it as I follow Anton and my brother out to Anton's Mercedes.

In the car Anton smokes cigarette after nervous cigarette, watching me in the rearview mirror. "You remember what you're supposed to do?" he asks as we head into the tunnel to Manhattan.

"Yeah," I say.

"You're going to be okay. After this, if you want, we'll cut you a necklace. Barron, too."

"Yeah," I say again. In Dad's suit I feel strangely dangerous.

The brass front door of Koshchey's is wide open when we pull up in front, and there are two enormous men in sunglasses and long wool coats checking a list. A woman in a glittering gold dress pouts on the arm of a white-haired man as they wait behind a trio of men smoking cigars. Two valets come and open the doors of the Mercedes. One of them looks about my age, and I grin at him, but he doesn't smile back.

We're waved right through. No list for us. Just a quick check for guns.

The inside is packed with people. Lots of them crowding the bar, passing drinks back for people to carry to tables. A bunch of young guys are pouring shots of vodka.

"To Zacharov!" one toasts.

"To open hearts and open bars!" calls another.

"And open legs," says Anton.

"Anton!" A slim young man leans over with a grin, holding out a shot glass. "You're late. Better catch up."

Anton gives me a long look, and he and the other man move away from Barron and me. I push on into the large ballroom, past laughing laborers from who knows how many families. I wonder how many of them are runaways, how many of them slipped out of some normal life in Kansas or one of the Carolinas to come to the big city and be recruited by Zacharov. Barron follows me, his hand pressing against my shoulder blades. It feels like a threat.

Up on the little stage on the other side of the ballroom, a woman in a pale pink suit is speaking into the podium microphone. "You might ask yourselves why we here in New York need to give funds to stop a proposition that's going to affect New Jersey. Shouldn't we save our money in case we need to fight that same fight here, in our own state? Let me tell you, ladies and gentlemen, if proposition two passes in one place, especially in a place where so many of us have relatives and family, then it will spread. We need to defend the rights of our neighbors to privacy, so that there will be someone left to defend ours."

A girl in a black dress, her brown curls pulled back with rhinestone clips and her smile a little too wide, brushes against me. She looks great, and I have to stop myself from telling her so.

"Hi," Daneca says languorously. "Remember me?"

I somehow manage not to roll my eyes at her over-the-top performance. "This is my brother Barron. Barron, this is Dani."

Barron looks between us. "Hey, Dani."

"I beat him at chess when his school came up to play my school," she says, embellishing on the simpler cover story we came up with yesterday.

"Oh, yeah?" He relaxes a little and grins. "So you're a very smart girl."

She blanches. Barron looks sharp in his suit, with his cold eyes and angelic curls. I don't think that Daneca's used to slick sociopaths like him flirting with her; she stumbles over her words. "Smart enough to—smart enough."

"Can I talk to her for a minute?" I ask him. "Alone."

He nods. "I'll get some food. Just watch the time, player."

"Right," I say.

He grips my shoulder. His fingers dig into the knotted muscles in a way that feels good. Brotherly. "You're ready, right?"

"I will be," I say, but I have to look away. I don't want him to know how much it hurts for him to act kind now, when none of it's true.

"Tough guy," he says, and walks off toward the samovars of tea, and the trays heaped with dilled herring, with fish glistening in the ruby glaze of pomegranate sauce, and with about a million different kinds of piroshki.

Daneca leans into me, presses a blood packet wrapped with wires under my jacket, and whispers, "We got the stuff to Lila."

I look up involuntarily. The knots in my stomach pull tighter. "Did you talk to her?"

Daneca shakes her head. "Sam's with her now. She's really not happy that all we could get in is a pretend gun that Sam is still gluing together."

I picture Lila's sharp-edged smile. "She knows what she's got to do?"

Daneca nods. "Knowing Sam, he's overexplaining it. He wanted me to make sure you were okay with reattaching your wires to the trigger mechanism."

"I think so. I—"

"Cassel Sharpe," someone says, and I turn. Grandad is wearing a brown suit and a hat turned at a rakish angle, feather pin through the band. "The hell are you doing here? You better have some peach of an explanation."

Yesterday when we went over the plan again and again, I never thought about Grandad showing up. Because I'm an idiot, basically—an idiot with poor planning skills. Of course he's here. Where else would he be?

Seriously, what else could go wrong?

"Barron brought me," I say. "Aren't I allowed out on a school night? Come on, this is practically a family event."

He looks around the room, like he's looking for his own shadow. "You should go on home. Right now."

"Okay," I say, placatingly, holding up my hands. "Just let me get something to eat and I'll go."

Daneca backs away from us, heading in the direction of the bar. She gives me a wink that seems to indicate the outrageous assumption that I have things under control.

"No," he says. "You are going to get your ass out on the sidewalk, and I am going to drive you home."

"What's wrong? I'm not getting in any trouble."

"You should have called me after I left you a message, that's what's wrong. This isn't a good place for you, understand?"

A man in a dark suit with a gold tooth looks over in our direction with a laugh at the familiar story we're playing out. Bratty kid. Old man. Except that Grandad's acting crazy.

"Okay," I say, looking up at the clock. Ten after ten. "Just tell me what's going on."

"I'll tell you on the way," he says, wrapping his hand around my upper arm. I want to pull away from him, but my arm's been wrenched out of its socket too many times in the last few days. I let him lead me toward the door until I come close enough to the bar to be able to get Anton's attention.

"Look who I found," I say. "You know my grandfather."

From the way Anton's eyes narrow I'm guessing Grandad isn't his favorite person. The zinc bar top is littered with shot glasses and at least one empty bottle of Pshenichnaya.

"I just stopped in to see some old friends," Grandad says. "We're going."

"Not Cassel," Anton says. "He hasn't had a drink yet." He

pours one for me, which gets the attention of some of the other young laborers. They turn their evaluating gazes in my direction.

There is a burning intensity in Anton's face, belied by his half smile and the languid way he's leaning against the bar. If he wants to lead the family, he's going to have to lead guys like Grandad. He can't afford to be shown up by an old man. He's got something to prove, and he's happy to use me to prove it.

"Take the drink," Anton says.

"He's underage," says Grandad.

That makes the guys at the bar laugh. I throw back the vodka in a single swallow. Warmth floods my stomach and sears my throat. I cough. Everyone laughs harder.

"It's like everything," one of the guys says. "The first one's the worst."

Anton pours me another shot. "You're wrong," he says. "The second one's the worst because you know what's coming."

"Go ahead," Grandad says to me. "Take your drink, and then we're going."

I look up at the clock. Ten twenty.

The second shot burns all the way down.

One of the guys claps me on the back. "Come on," he says to my grandfather. "Let the kid stay. We'll take good care of him."

"Cassel," Grandad says firmly, making my name into a reprimand. "You don't want to be tired for that fancy school of yours."

"I came with Barron," I say. I reach across the bar and pour myself a third shot. The guys love that.

"You're leaving with me," Grandad says under his breath.

This time the vodka goes down my throat like water. I step away from the bar and make myself stumble a little. I feel heady with confidence. *I'm Cassel Sharpe.* My mouth wants to shape the words. *I'm smarter than everybody else and I've thought of everything.*

"You okay?" Anton asks, looking at me like he's trying to figure if I'm drunk. His plans depend on me. I look as blank as possible and hope that it freaks him out. No point in my being the only miserable one.

Grandad tugs me toward the double doors, against the tide of people. "He'll sleep it off in the car."

"Let me just run to the bathroom," I tell Grandad. "I'll be right back."

He looks furious.

"Come on," I say. "It's a long ride." On the wall the clock reads ten thirty. Anton's going to be heading into position, guarding Zacharov. Barron's probably already looking for me. But how long before Zacharov will show is anyone's guess. His bladder could be made of iron.

"I'll go with you," Grandad says.

"I think you can trust me to piss without getting in any trouble."

"Yeah," he says, "but I don't."

We head toward the bathrooms, which are near enough to the kitchen that we have to head into the shadowy, windowless area behind the bar. I look over and see Zacharov and a beautiful woman with long honey-colored hair hanging on his arm. The pale red gem on his tie is overmatched by the rubies hanging from her ears. People are declaring their support and shaking his hand, leather glove against leather glove.

There in the crowd I think I see her. Lila. Her hair white under the lights. Her mouth painted blood bright.

She's not supposed to be here yet. She's going to ruin everything.

I veer off toward the buffet. Toward her. By the time I get there, she's gone.

"What now?" Grandad asks.

I pop a rose-flavored *syrniki* in my mouth.

"I'm trying to sneak food," I say, "since you're so crazy that you won't let me eat."

"I know what you're trying to do," he says. "I see you looking at the clock. No more bull, Cassel. Piss or don't."

"Okay," I say, and walk into the bathroom. Ten forty. I don't know how much longer I can drag my feet.

There are a few other guys in here, combing their hair in the mirrors. A skinny puffy-eyed blond is doing a line of coke off the counter. He doesn't even look up when the door opens.

I go into the first stall and sit down on the lid of the toilet seat, trying to calm myself.

My watch reads ten forty-three.

I wonder if Lila wants everything ruined. I wonder if I really saw her in the crowd or if I just conjured her out of my fears.

I take off my suit jacket, unbutton my shirt, and tape the packet of fake blood directly onto my skin, resigning myself to the gluey hair removal I am going to get later when I rip it off. I tug the wire through the inside of my pants pocket, ripping the seam and adding more tape so the trigger's easy to grab.

Ten forty-seven.

I check for the bottle of puke taped behind the toilet bowl. It's there, but I have no idea which one of them finally gave in and threw up. I smile at the thought.

Ten forty-eight. I attach the wire to the trigger.

"You okay in there?" Grandad calls. Someone snickers.

"Just a second," I say.

I make a choking noise and pour out half the contents of the puke bottle. The room fills with the vinegary three-day-old smell of sick. I gag again, this time for real.

I pour out the other half and carefully return the empty bottle to the tape. Leaning down is the worst. I gag again.

"You okay?" Grandad doesn't sound impatient anymore. "Cassel?"

"Fine," I say, and spit.

I flush the toilet and button up my shirt carefully, then pull on the suit jacket but don't button that.

The door opens and I hear Anton's voice. "Everyone out. We need the bathroom clear."

My legs feel unsteady with relief. I open the door of the stall and lean against the frame. Almost everyone has already been chased out by my fake vomiting, but the stragglers and the cokehead are filing past Anton. Zacharov stands at the sinks.

"Desi Singer," he says, rubbing the side of his mouth. "It's been a long time."

"This is a very nice party," my grandfather says gravely, nodding toward Zacharov, his nod almost a bow. "I hadn't figured you for politics."

"We who break laws should care the most about them. We deal with them more than other people, after all."

"They say that all really great crooks eventually go into politics," Grandad says.

Zacharov smiles at that, but when he sees me, his smile fades. "No one's supposed to be in here," he tells Anton.

"Sorry," I say, sticking out my hand. "I'm a little drunk. This is a great party, sir."

Grandad grabs for my arm to pull it away, but Anton stops him.

"This is Philip's little brother." Anton's grinning, like this is all a hilarious joke. "Give the kid a thrill."

Zacharov extends his hand slowly, looking me in the eye. "Cassel, right?"

Our eyes meet. "It's okay, sir. If you don't want to shake."

He holds my gaze. "Go ahead."

I take his hand in mine and cover his wrist with my other hand, pushing my gloved fingers up his sleeve, worming my finger through the small opening in the leather so I can brush the skin of his wrist. His eyes open wide when I touch him, like I've given him an electric shock. He jerks back.

I pull him sharply toward me. "You have to pretend to die," I whisper against his ear. "Your heart just turned to stone."

Zacharov staggers away from me, stricken. He looks toward Anton, and for a moment I think he's going to ask something that will doom me. Then he lurches abruptly against the hinge of one of the stalls and, stumbling back, bangs his head against the hand dryer. He gasps soundlessly and slides down the wall, hand knotting in his shirt like he is trying to grasp his chest.

We watch him as his eyes close. His mouth gapes once more, like he's trying for a last gasp of air.

Zacharov's not a bad con man himself.

"What did you do?" Grandad shouts. "Undo it, Cassel. Whatever you've done—" My grandfather looks at me like he doesn't know me.

"Shut up, old man," Anton says, punching the stall behind Grandad's head.

I want to snap at Anton, but there's no time. Lack of blowback's going to give me away.

I concentrate on transforming myself. I picture a blade coming toward my own head, try to feel the impulse to work the work that danger feeds.

I have to freak myself out. I think of Lila, and me with a knife standing over her. I imagine raising the blade and feel the full weight of horror and self-loathing. The false memory still has the power to terrify me.

I actually jerk my hand a tiny bit in response, and then I feel my flesh go malleable. I imagine my father's hand in place of my own. I picture his blunt fingers and rough calluses.

My father's hand to go with his suit.

A small transformation. A little change. One that I hope will have minimal blowback.

A ripple runs through my flesh. I concentrate on taking a step toward the wall, but my foot feels like it's spreading out, melting.

Anton reaches into his coat and flips open a butterfly knife. It twirls in his fingers, as bright as the scales of a fish. He leans over Zacharov and carefully cuts the pin from his tie. "Everything's going to be different now," he says, slipping the Resurrection diamond into his pocket.

Anton turns toward me, still holding the knife, and suddenly this seems like a terrible, terrible plan.

"I'm sure you don't remember," Anton says, his voice low. "But you made me an amulet. Don't even think about trying to work *me*."

As if I could do anything but fall to my knees as my body twists and contorts.

Through blurry, changing vision, I see my grandfather crouching near Zacharov.

My limbs change, fins rising on my skin, and fifth and sixth arms banging into the wall. My head thrashes back and forth. My tongue forks. Everything cramps as the bones wrench themselves out of their sockets. My eyes become a thousand eyes, blinking together at the painted ceiling. I tell myself it will be over soon, but it goes on and on and on.

Anton walks toward Grandad. "You're a loyal worker, so it makes me sad to have to do this."

"Stop right there," Grandad says.

Anton shakes his head. "I'm glad Philip doesn't have

to watch. He wouldn't understand, but I think you do, old man. A leader's got to be careful who gets to tell stories about him."

I try to turn over, but my legs are hooves and they clatter against the tiles. I don't know how to work them. I try to shout, but my voice isn't my own—there's a birdlike whistle in it, probably from the beak hardening on my face.

"Good-bye," Anton says to my grandfather. "I'm about to become a legend."

Someone bangs on the door. The knife stops, hovering in front of Grandad's throat.

"It's me," Barron says from the other side. "Open up."

"Let me open the door," says Grandad. "Put away the knife. If I'm loyal to anyone, it's this boy here. And if you want him loyal to you, you'll be careful."

"Anton," I say from the floor. It's hard to form the words with my curling tongue. "Door!"

Anton looks at me, slings the knife back into its sheath, and opens the door.

I concentrate on moving my transformed hand into the pocket of my pants.

Barron takes a few stiff steps into the room, then staggers forward, like he was pushed from behind.

"Keep your hands where I can see them," a girl's voice calls. Lila is wearing a red dress as tight as it is short. Her only accessory is the huge silver gun gleaming in the fluorescent lights. The door swings shut behind her. The gun sure looks real. And she's pointing it straight at Anton.

Anton's lips part, like he's going to say her name, but no words come out.

"You heard me," she says.

"He killed your father," Anton says, pointing the closed knife at me. "It wasn't me. It was him."

Her gaze shifts to where Zacharov's body is resting, and the barrel of the gun wavers.

I reach under my jacket, hoping that my fingers stay fingerlike long enough to be usable. My tongue is working again. "You don't understand. I never meant—"

"I'm tired of your excuses," she says, leveling the gun at me. Her hand is shaking. "You didn't know what you were doing. You don't remember. You didn't mean to hurt anyone."

She doesn't sound like she's pretending.

I try to stand. "Lila—"

"Shut up, Cassel," she says, and shoots me.

Blood spatters cover my shirt.

I gasp like a fish.

As my eyes close, I hear Grandad choke out my name.

There's nothing like a gunshot to make you the life of the party.

CHAPTER EIGHTEEN

IT HURTS. I EXPECTED THAT, but it still knocks the breath out of me. Wetness seeps through my shirt, making it stick to my skin.

I try to still my breathing as much as possible. My body's shifting has slowed; the blowback's wearing off. I want to keep my eyes open, but I need Anton to really believe I was shot, so I listen instead of looking.

"Both of you, against the sinks," Lila says. "Put your hands where I can see them."

People are moving around me. I hear a grunt from my grandfather's direction, but I can't afford to look.

"How can you be here?" Anton asks her.

"Oh, come now," Lila says, low and dangerous. "You

know how I got here. I walked. From Wallingford. On my little paws."

I try to shift, just a little, so it will be easier to stand later.

Like a stage magician, the con artist misdirects suspicion. While everyone's watching for him to pull a rabbit out of a hat, he's actually sawing a girl in half. You think he's doing one trick when he's actually doing another.

You think that I'm dying, but I'm laughing at you.

I hate that I love this. I hate that the adrenaline pumping through the roots of my body is filling me with giddy glee. I'm not a good person.

But deceiving Anton and Barron feels fantastic.

I can hear footsteps echoing around me, moving toward her. "I'm sorry, Lila," says Anton. "I know that—"

"You should have killed me when you had the chance," she says.

Someone touches my shoulder, and I almost flinch. Rough bare fingers on my neck, looking for a pulse. The one thing I can't fake. He pulls open my jacket. If he unbuttons my shirt, he's going to see wires.

"You're a little devil, Cassel Sharpe," Grandad says under his breath.

Clever as the devil and twice as pretty. I force myself not to smile.

"Give me the gun," Anton says, and this time I do open my eyes a sliver. He's got the knife in one hand. "You know you don't want to do this."

"Get against the sinks!" she says.

He drops his knife and swipes his hand toward her, knocking the gun out of her grip. It skitters across the floor.

She lunges for it at the same time he does, but he gets to it first. I try to get up, but Grandad presses me back down.

Lifting the gun, Anton fires three times into her chest.

She staggers back, but she isn't wired up so there's no bang, no blood. The pellets hit her harmlessly, bouncing to the floor.

We're made.

Anton stares at her, then at the gun in his hand. Then he looks at me. My eyes are wide open.

"I'll kill you," he growls, throwing aside the fake gun. It hits the tiles so hard a piece of it chips off.

This is bad.

My grandfather gets between us, and I try to shove him out of the way, as a voice comes from the other side of the room.

"Enough," Zacharov says, into a sudden pocket of silence. He climbs unsteadily to his feet and stretches his neck, as though it's stiff.

Anton stumbles back, like Zacharov's a ghost. We all freeze.

Barron points an accusing finger in my direction. "You played me." He sounds unsteady.

"You're all playing," Zacharov says in his accented voice. "You were like this with water pistols when you were children. Waving them around and soaking everything."

"Why did— What did you know?" Anton asks. "Why did you pretend—"

Zacharov grimaces. "I would never have believed that you, Anton, would betray our family. I would never have believed that you would plot to kill me. You, of all people, who I would have made my heir." Zacharov looks at my grandfather. "Family means nothing anymore, does it?"

Grandad looks from Barron to me, like he's not sure how to answer.

Anton takes two steps toward Zacharov, his mouth twisting in an ugly way. Barron picks up the knife that Anton dropped and flips it around in his hand. Flips it closed, then open again.

I roll over and push myself up, skittering across the floor on fake blood. I manage to get up onto my knees.

"You're never going to leave here alive," Anton tells Zacharov, gesturing to Barron and the knife.

I have only one card left to play, but it's a good one. I stand. This is like being on the roof of Smythe Hall all over again; if I slip, I die.

"I'm not afraid," Zacharov says, still looking at Anton. "It takes guts to kill a man with your hands. You don't have the balls."

"Shut up," says Anton. He turns to Barron. "Give me the knife. I'll show him scared."

Lila rushes Anton, but her father grabs hold of her arms and pulls her back against him.

Her lip curls. Her eyes smolder with banked fire as she stares at her cousin. "I'll kill you," she says.

Barron doesn't hand over the knife, but he does start to smile. He raises the tip to Anton's throat.

"Don't point that thing at me," Anton says, shoving at Barron's hand. "What are you waiting for? Give it here."

"I'm pointing the right way," Barron says. "Sorry."

I take a deep breath and spring my trap. "We've been meeting with Zacharov for months, Barron and me. Right, sir?"

Zacharov gives me a hard look. I imagine he's fed up with my shenanigans, but he's got to realize that keeping the knife at Anton's neck is the most important thing. Zacharov's fingers tighten on Lila's arms. "That's right."

Barron nods.

"No, you haven't," Anton says to Barron. "Why? Even if you'd screw me over, there's no way you'd screw Philip."

"He's in this too," says Barron. He twists the knife in his hand, letting the fluorescent lights reflect off the blade.

"Philip would never turn on me. That's impossible. We planned this together. We planned it for years."

Barron shrugs his shoulders. "If that's true, then where is he? If he was so loyal, wouldn't he be here?"

Then Anton looks at me. "This doesn't make any sense."

"What doesn't make sense?" Lila asks. She cuts her eyes toward me for a moment. "You think you're the only one who can betray people, Anton? You think you're the only liar?"

I can see the conflict in Anton's face. He's still trying to figure out his next move.

"We had to be sure you were serious about killing the head of our family," Barron says. He doesn't look confused; he doesn't even flinch.

"But he's going to kill you, idiot," Anton says. He sounds lost. "You threw everything away for nothing. You kidnapped his daughter. You're dead men. He's going to execute us all."

"He forgave us," Barron says. "He made a deal with Philip and me to let that slide. It was more important to prove that you planned to kill him. We're nobodies. You're his nephew."

Zacharov snorts softly, shaking his head. Then he extends his hand toward Barron, who gently drops the knife into Zacharov's hand.

I let out a breath I didn't know I was holding.

"Anton," Zacharov says, letting go of Lila as though he suddenly realizes that he should. "You're outnumbered. Time to pack it in. Get down on the floor. Lila, you go get Stanley. Tell him there's something in here we've got to deal with."

Lila wipes her hands on her dress and doesn't look any of us in the face. I try to catch her eye, but it's impossible. She heads toward the door.

Zacharov is the one who meets my gaze. He knows that I played him, even if he doesn't know how. He gives me a slight nod of his head.

I guess I proved myself after all.

"Thank you, Barron. And Cassel, of course." I can hear the grind of his teeth as he thanks my brother and me for a lie. "Why don't you both go with Lila and wait for me in the kitchen? We're not done here. Desi, you make sure they don't wander off."

"You," Anton says, looking at me. "You did this. You made this happen."

"I didn't make you into a moron," I say, which maybe isn't the smartest thing, but I'm dumb and giddy with relief.

Plus, you know I'm terrible at keeping my mouth shut.

Anton lunges at me, closing the distance before I can react. We crash backward into one of the stalls, and my head slams into the tile beside one of the toilets. I see Grandad grabbing for Anton's neck like he's going to pull him off me, but Anton is way too huge and hardened for that.

His knuckles slam against my cheekbone. I lean up, cracking my forehead against his skull hard enough to make me dizzy with pain. He arches up, like he's going to punch me again, when his eyes lose focus. He falls heavily on top of me and just lies there, heavy as a blanket.

I scrabble backward, not caring about the filthy floor, just trying to get out from under his weight. He looks pale, his lips already going blue.

He's dead.

Anton is dead.

I'm still staring at him when Lila leans down and touches a wad of toilet paper to my mouth. I didn't even realize I was bleeding.

"Lila," Zacharov says. "Come on. I need you out of here."

"You ever think you're too clever for your own good?" she asks me softly, before going back over to her father.

Grandad is holding his own wrist, hunched over it protectively.

"Are you okay?" I ask him, pushing myself up and leaning heavily against the wall.

"I'll be okay when we get out of this bathroom," Grandad says. Then I notice that his right hand is bare and his ring finger is darkening, blackness spreading down from the nail.

"Oh," I say. He saved my life.

He laughs. "What? You didn't think I still had it in me?"

I'm embarrassed to admit that I forgot he's *still* a death worker. I've always thought of his being a worker in the past tense, but he killed Anton with a single touch, a press of fingers against a vulnerable neck.

"You should have let me help you," Grandad says. "I overheard them talking after dinner that night when they dosed me."

"Lila, Barron," Zacharov says, "you two come with me. We'll leave Cassel and Desi alone for a moment to clean themselves up." He looks at us. "Don't go anywhere."

I nod as they go.

"You've got a lot of explaining to do," Grandad says.

I'm still pressing the wad of paper to my cheek. Real blood drooling from my mouth drops onto my shirt next to the fake blood. I look down at Anton's body. "You thought I was still memory worked—that's why you were trying to drag me out of here."

"What was I supposed to think?" Grandad says. "That you three had some ridiculously complicated plan? That Zacharov was in on it too?"

I grin in the mirror. "We're not in on anything. I forged

Barron's notebooks. Barron believes everything in those books. He has to, what with his memory loss."

That's what I did that last day and a half. What I stayed up all night doing. Rewriting pages and pages of notes in handwriting easy to forge because I already knew it so well. I constructed an entirely different life for Barron; the kind of life where he'd want to save the head of a crime family because Zacharov is Lila's dad. The kind of life where my brothers and I worked together for noble purposes.

The easiest lies to tell are the ones you want to be true.

Grandad frowns, and then understanding smoothes his features out into shock. "You mean he never met with Zacharov?"

I shake my head. "Nope. He just thinks he did."

"Did *you* meet with Zacharov?"

"Lila wanted us to take care of things ourselves," I say. "So, also no."

He groans. "This is trouble heaped on top of trouble."

I give Anton's body a last look. Something glitters in the light. Zacharov's diamond tie tack near Anton's left hand. He must have taken it from his pocket.

I lean down and pick up the pin.

Zacharov is leaning against the doorway when I stand. I didn't hear him come in. "Cassel Sharpe." He sounds tired. "My daughter tells me that this was her idea."

I nod my head. "It would have worked better with a real gun."

He snorts. "Since it was her idea, I am not going to

cut off your hand for touching my skin. Just tell me one thing—how long have you known you are a transformation worker?"

For a moment I open my mouth to protest. I didn't work him; how can he be sure that I wasn't faking? Then I remember the blowback, and me twisting on the tile floor. "Not long," I say.

"And you knew?" Zacharov turns to Grandad.

"His mother wanted to keep it a secret until he was old enough. She was going to tell him after her release." Grandad looks over at me. "Cassel, what you can do is very valuable to some people. I'm not saying your mother was right, but she's a smart lady and—"

I cut him off. "I know, Grandad."

Zacharov is watching us, like he's weighing something in his mind. "I want to make this clear: I never agreed to let your brothers live. Either of them."

I nod, because I can hear that he's not done talking.

"Your grandfather's right. You're valuable. And now you're mine. So long as you keep working for me, your brothers stay alive. Understand?"

I nod again.

I should tell him I don't care. That it doesn't matter to me if they're dead. But I don't. I guess it's true; no one will ever love you like your family.

"We're settled here," he says. "For now. Go into the kitchen and see if someone can scare you up a clean shirt."

Grandad pulls back on his right-hand glove. Now one of its fingers hangs as floppily as those on his left hand.

"Oh. I found—," I say to Zacharov, holding out the Resurrection Diamond before I notice something strange. A corner of the huge rock is chipped.

Zacharov takes it from me with a tight smile. "Thank you once more, Cassel."

I nod, trying not to let it show that I know the Resurrection Diamond can't protect anyone. It's worthless. It's made of glass.

Outside the bathroom the party is still going full swing. The noise crashes over me like a surreal wave, music and laughing and speeches loud enough to cover gunshots. None of what's happened—definitely not Anton being dead—seems real in the dancing light of the chandeliers or reflected in thousands of champagne bubbles.

"Cassel!" Daneca yells, running up to me. "Are you all right?"

"We were worried," Sam says. "You were in there for too long."

"I'm fine," I say. "Don't I seem fine?"

"You're covered in blood standing in the middle of a party," Sam says. "No, you don't seem fine."

"This way," Zacharov says, pointing toward the kitchens.

"We're coming with you," says Daneca.

I feel drained, and my cheek is throbbing. My ribs still hurt. And I don't see Lila anywhere.

"Yeah," I say. "Okay."

People nearly trip over themselves getting out of my way as I walk. I guess I really do look bad.

The kitchen looks smaller with people running around in it, carrying out trays of blini slathered in caviar, golden pastries leaking garlic butter, and tiny cakes topped with crystallized lemon.

My stomach growls, surprising me. I shouldn't be hungry after watching another person be killed, but I'm starving.

Philip is standing in the back flanked by two burly men who appear to be restraining him. I don't know if Lila brought him to the party or if Zacharov sent to have him escorted over from wherever she was keeping him.

When he sees me, his eyes narrow.

"You took everything from me," he shouts. "Maura. My son. My future. My friend. You took *everything*."

I guess I did.

I could tell him that I didn't mean for it to happen.

"Sucks, doesn't it?" I say.

He struggles against the bodyguards holding him. I'm not worried. I let Daneca steer me to the area by the pantry and sinks.

"I'm going to make you regret the day you were born," Philip shouts to my back. I ignore him.

Lila is waiting with a bottle of vodka in one hand and a rag in the other. "Get up on the counter," she says.

I do, pushing aside a bowl of flour and a spatula. Philip's still yelling, but his voice seems to come from far away. I smile. "Lila, this is Daneca. I think you met Sam. They're my friends from school."

"Did he actually admit we're his friends?" Sam asks, and Daneca laughs.

Lila pours some vodka onto the napkin.

"I'm sorry I didn't tell you about the rest of my plan," I say to Lila. "About Barron."

"The notebooks, right? You fixed them somehow."

When I look surprised, she smiles. "I lived with him for years, remember? I saw the notebooks. Clever." She presses the cloth against my cheek, and I hiss. It stings like crazy.

"Ow," I say. "You ever think you're kind of a bully?"

Her smile goes wide. If it could, I think it would curl up at the corners. She leans close to me. "Oh, I know I am. And I know you like it."

Sam snickers. I don't care.

I do like it.

CHAPTER NINETEEN

I SPEND THE NEXT TWO weeks slammed, making up all the homework I missed. Daneca and Sam help me, sitting with me in the library until in-room curfew, when I have to head home and they have to go back to the dorms. I spend so much time at school that Grandad gets me my own car. He takes me to some friend of his who hooks me up with a 1980 Mercedes-Benz Turbo for two grand.

It runs like crap, but Sam promises to help convert it to grease. He won some kind of state science fair with the conversion of his hearse, and he thinks we can make it all the way to an international science fair with the tinkering he's got planned for my ride. Until then, I keep my fingers crossed that the engine keeps turning over.

When I go out to my car to drive myself home that Tuesday, I find Barron leaning against it, twirling keys around one black-gloved finger. His motorcycle is parked next to my car in the lot.

"What do you want?" I ask.

"Pizza night," he says.

I look at him like he's lost his mind.

He returns the look. "It's Tuesday."

The problem with forging an entire year of someone's life very quickly is that your fantasies creep in. Maybe you meant to just get in the stuff that you needed, but that leaves a lot of space to fill. I filled the space with the relationship I wished we had.

It's a little embarrassing now that Barron is standing here, really believing we go out for pizza every other Tuesday and talk about our feelings.

"I'll drive," I say finally.

We order a pizza heaped with cheese and sauce and sausage and pepperoni at a little place with booths, and miniature jukeboxes above each linoleum tabletop. I cover my slice with hot pepper flakes.

"I'm going back to Princeton to finish school," he says, biting into a chunk of garlic bread. "Now that Mom's getting out. Something tells me she's going to need a lawyer again soon." I wonder if he can go back, if he can fill the holes in his brain with law books and remember them as long as he doesn't work anymore. That's a big "as long as."

"Do you know when her actual release happens?"

"They say Friday," he says. "But they've already changed the date twice, so I don't know how seriously to take it. But I guess we should get a cake or something, in case. Worst case scenario: We eat the cake anyway."

Memory is funny. Barron seems relaxed, like he really likes me, because he doesn't remember hating me. Or maybe he remembers the feeling of dislike but he assumes that he liked me more than he hated me. But I'm not relaxed. I can't stop remembering. I want to leap up out of the chair and choke him.

"What do you think is the first thing she's going to do when she gets out?" I ask.

"Meddle," he says, and laughs. "What do you think? She's going to start trying to get everything to go the way she wants it to go. And we all better pray that's the way we want it to go too."

I suck soda through my straw, lick grease off my glove, and contemplate transforming Barron into a slice of pizza and then feeding him to the kids at the next table.

Still, it's nice to have a brother I can talk to.

Keep your friends close and your enemies closer.

That's what Zacharov says when he explains that he's keeping Philip working for the family, where he can keep an eye on him. People don't usually leave crime families alive, so I guess I shouldn't be surprised.

I ask Grandad if he's seen Philip, but all he does is grunt.

*   *   *

Lila calls me on Wednesday.

"Hey," I say, not recognizing the number.

"Hey, yourself." She sounds happy. "You want to hang out?"

"I do," I say, my heart slamming. I switch my messenger bag over to the other shoulder with suddenly clumsy hands.

"Come up to the city. We can get hot chocolate, and maybe I'll let you beat me at a video game. I'm four years out of practice. I might be a little rusty."

"I'll beat you so bad your own avatar will laugh at you."

"Jerk. Come up on Saturday," she says, and hangs up.

I smile all the way through dinner.

On Friday at lunch I head out onto the quad. It's warm out and lots of kids have brought their food to eat on the grass. Sam and Daneca are sitting with Johan Schwartz, Jill Pearson-White, and Chaiyawat Terweil. They wave me over.

I hold up my hand and turn toward a small copse of trees. I've been thinking through everything that happened, and there's one thing still bothering me.

I take out my phone and punch in a number. I don't expect anyone to pick up, but she does.

"Dr. Churchill's office," says Maura.

"It's Cassel."

"Cassel!" she says. "I was wondering when you'd call. You know what the best feeling in the world is? Just driving down the road with the music blasting, the wind in your hair, and your baby gurgling happily in his car seat."

I smile. "You know where you are headed?"

"Not yet," she says. "I guess I'll know when we get there."

"I'm glad for you," I say. "I just wanted to call and tell you that."

"You know what I miss most?" she says.

I shake my head, and then realize she can't see me. "No."

"The music." Her voice drops, low and soft. "It was just so beautiful. I wish I could hear it again, but it's gone. Philip took the music with him."

I can't help shuddering.

Daneca is walking toward me when I hang up the phone. She looks annoyed.

"Hey," she says. "Come on. We're going to be late."

I must look shell-shocked or something, because she hesitates. "You don't have to do this if you don't want to."

"It's not that. I want to," I say. I'm not sure I mean it, but I am sure that Daneca and Sam were there for me when I really needed them. Maybe the point of real friendship isn't that you have to repay kindness, but whatever. At least I should try.

As Daneca, Sam, and I cross the quad, I see Audrey eating an apple near the entrance to the arts center.

She's smiling at me the way she used to. "Where are you guys going?"

I take a deep breath. "HEX meeting. Learning about worker rights."

"For real?" She looks toward Daneca.

"What can I say?" I shrug. "I'm trying new things."

"Can I come?" She doesn't stand up, like she's expecting me to say no.

"Of course you can," Daneca says, before I can get past the idea that she *wants* to come. "HEX meetings are for us all to better understand one another."

"They have free coffee," Sam says.

Audrey chucks her apple toward the shrubs by the entrance. "Count me in."

The meeting is being held in Ms. Ramirez's music room; she's the adviser. A piano sits in one corner, and a few drum toms rest near the back wall, against a bookshelf filled with thin folders of sheet music. A cymbal balances on the low shelf near a wall of windows, near a gurgling coffeemaker.

Ms. Ramirez is sitting the opposite way on the piano bench in a circle of students. I come in and pull up four more chairs. Everyone scoots politely aside, but the girl who's standing doesn't stop talking.

"The thing is that it's really hard to stop discrimination when something's illegal," the girl says. "I mean, everybody thinks of workers as being criminals. Like, people use the word 'worker' to mean criminals. And, well, if we work a work, even once, we are criminals. So most of us are, because we had to figure it out somehow and that was usually by making something happen."

I don't know her name, just that she's a freshman. She doesn't look at anyone when she speaks, and her voice is affectless. I am a little awed by her bravery.

"And there are lots of workers who never do anything bad. They go to weddings and hospitals and give people good luck. Or there's people who work at shelters and they give people hope and make them feel confident and positive. And that word—'cursing.' Like all we can do is bad magic. I mean, why would you even want to do the bad stuff? The blowback's awful. Like, if all a luck worker ever does is make people have good luck, then all he has is good luck too. It doesn't have to be bad."

She pauses and raises her gaze to look at us. At me.

"Magic," the girl says. "It's just all magic."

When I get home that night, Grandad is making a cup of tea in the kitchen. We've cleaned up a lot. The counters are mostly clear and the stove is no longer crusted with old food. There's a bottle of bourbon on the table, but the cap's still on it.

"Your mother called," he says. "She's out."

"Out?" I repeat dumbly. "Out of prison? Is she here?"

"No. But you do have a guest," he says, turning back to wipe the faucet. "That Zacharov girl is in your room."

I look up, like I can see through the ceiling, surprised and happy. I wonder what she thinks of the house, and then I remember she's been here before, lots of times. She's even been in my room before—just as a cat. Then the rest of what Grandad said hits me. "Why are you calling Lila 'that Zacharov girl'? And where's Mom? She can't have gotten far. Jail has to slow you down a little."

"Shandra rented a hotel room. She says she doesn't want us to see her the way she is. Last I heard, she was ordering champagne and french fries drenched in ranch dressing up to her bubble bath."

"Really?"

He laughs, but it sounds hollow. "You know your mother."

I walk past him and the remaining boxes of unsorted stuff in the dining room, up the stairs, taking them two at a time. I don't understand his mood, but my need to see Lila overwhelms other concerns.

"Cassel," he calls, and I turn, leaning over the banister. "Go up there and bring her down. Lila. There's something I need to tell you both."

"Okay," I say automatically, but I don't really want to hear whatever it is. Two quick steps down the hall and I open the door to my bedroom.

Lila is sitting on the bed, reading one of the old collections of ghost stories I never returned to the library. She turns to give me a sly smile. "I really missed you," she says, reaching out a hand.

"Yeah?" I can't stop looking at her, at the way the sunlight from the dirty window catches on her lashes, making them gleam like gold, the way her mouth parts slightly. She looks like the girl I remember climbing trees with, the one who pierced my ear and licked my blood, but she looks unlike that girl too. Time has hollowed her cheeks and made her eyes feverishly bright.

I've thought of her so many times in this room that it seems like those thoughts conjured her, a fantasy Lila, spread out on my bed. The unreality makes it easier to walk over to her, although my heart is beating like a hammer in my chest.

"Did you miss me?" she asks, stretching her body like a cat might. She drops the book without marking her place.

"For years," I say, helplessly honest for once. I want to press bare fingers against the line of her cheek and trace the dusting of freckles on her pale skin, but she still doesn't seem real enough to touch.

She leans in close, and everything about her is dizzyingly warm and soft.

"I missed you, too," she says, voice low and breathless.

I laugh, which helps me clear my head a little. "You wanted to kill me."

She shakes her head. "I always liked you. I always wanted you. Always."

"Oh," I say stupidly. And then I kiss her.

Her mouth opens under mine and she lies back, drawing me down onto the bed with her. Her arms twine around my neck and she sighs against my mouth. My skin feels pricklingly hot. My muscles tense, like I'm ready for a fight, everything clenched so hard that I'm shaking.

I take a single shuddering breath.

I am full of happiness. So much happiness that I can barely contain it.

Now that I've started touching her, I can't seem to stop. Like somehow the language of my hands will tell her all the things I don't know how to say out loud. My gloved fingers slide under the waistband of her jeans, over her skin. She shimmies a little, to shove her pants down, and reaches for mine. I am breathing her breath, my thoughts spiraling into incoherence.

Someone bangs on the door to the room.

For a moment I don't care. I don't stop.

"Cassel," Grandad calls from the other side of the door.

I roll off the bed and onto my feet. Lila is flushed, breathing hard. Her lips are red and wet, her eyes dark. I am still reeling.

"What?" I yell.

The door opens and my grandfather is there, holding the phone. "I need you to come and talk to your mother," he says.

I look over at Lila apologetically. Her cheeks are stained pink and she's fumbling with her jeans, trying to get them buttoned.

"I'll call her back." I'm glaring at him, but he barely seems to notice.

"No," he says. "You take this phone and you listen to what she has to say."

"Grandad," I say.

"Talk to your mother, Cassel." His voice is harder than I've ever heard it.

"Fine!" I grab the phone and walk into the hall, ushering Grandad out with me.

"Congrats on getting out of jail, Mom," I say.

"Cassel!" She sounds ecstatic to talk to me, like I'm the prince of some foreign country. "I'm sorry about not coming right home. I want to see my babies, but you don't know what it's like to live with a bunch of women for all these years and never have a moment alone. And none of my clothes fit. I lost so much weight from that awful food. I need a lot of new things."

"Great," I say. "So you're at a hotel?"

"In New York. I know we have a lot to talk about, baby. I'm sorry I didn't tell you about being a worker sooner, but I knew people would try to take advantage of you. And look at what they did. Of course, if the judge had just listened to me and realized that a mother needs to be with her children, none of this would have happened. You boys needed me."

"It happened before you went to jail," I say.

"What?"

"Lila. They tried to get me to kill her before you went to jail. They locked her in a cage before you went to jail. It had nothing to do with you."

She falters a little. "Oh, honey, I'm sure that's not true. You're just not remembering right."

"Don't—talk—to me—about—memories." I practically spit out the words. Each one falls from my tongue like a drop of poison.

She goes silent, which is so unusual that I can't remember it ever happening before. "Baby—," she says finally.

"What's this call about? What's so important that Grandad made me talk to you right this second?"

"Oh, it's nothing really. Your grandfather is just upset. You see, I got you a present. Something you always wanted. Oh, honey, you don't understand how happy I am that you managed to get your brothers out of a bad situation. Your *older* brothers too—and you, the baby, taking care of them. You deserve something just for you."

Cold dread uncoils in my stomach. "What?"

"Just a little—"

"What did you do?"

"Well, I went to see Zacharov yesterday. Did I ever tell you that we know each other? We do. Anyway, I ran into that adorable daughter of his on the way out. You always liked her, didn't you?"

"No," I say. I'm shaking my head.

"You didn't like her? I thought—"

"No. No. Mom, please tell me that you didn't touch her. Say you didn't work her."

She sounds uncertain, but also unrepentant, like she's trying to cajole me into liking a sweater she bought on sale. "I thought you'd be happy. And she grew up very pretty, don't you think? Not as handsome as you, of course, but prettier than that redhead you were spending all your time with."

I step back against the wall, slamming my shoulders against it like I no longer remember how to move my legs. "Mom," I moan.

"Baby, what's wrong?"

"Just tell me what you did. Just say it." It is a terrible desperate thing to plead with someone to crush your hope.

"This really isn't the kind of thing you just say over the phone," she says reprovingly.

"Say it!" I shout.

"Okay, okay. I worked her so that she loves you," Mom

says. "She'll do absolutely anything for you. Anything you want. Isn't that nice?"

"Fix it," I say. "You have to undo it. Put her back the way she was. I'll take her to you and you can work her again so she's back to normal."

"Cassel," she says, "you know I can't do that. I can make her hate you. I can even make her feel nothing at all for you, but I can't take away what I've already done. If it bothers you so much, just wait it out. The way she feels will fade eventually. I mean, she won't be exactly the same as she was before—"

I hang up the phone. It rings over and over again. I watch it light up, watch the hotel's name scroll across the caller ID.

Lila finds me sitting in the hall, in the dark, holding a still-ringing phone when she comes out to see what's taking so long. "Cassel?" she whispers.

I can barely look at her.

The most important thing for any con artist is never to think like a mark. Marks figure they're going to get a deal on a stolen handbag, then they get upset when the lining falls out. They think they're going to get front row tickets for next to nothing off a guy standing out in the rain, then they're surprised when the tickets are just pieces of wet paper.

Marks think they can get something for nothing.

Marks think they can get what they don't deserve and could never deserve.

Marks are stupid and pathetic and sad.

Marks think they're going to go home one night and have the girl they've loved since they were a kid suddenly love them back.

Marks forget that whenever something's too good to be true, that's because it's a con.